Harper

His Life and Trials

E. S. Freeman

Cover illustration by Olivia Iris Wilson

Harper
***His* Life and Trials**

First published in the UK by ESF Publishing.

A CIP record for this book is available from the
British Library
ISBN 978-1-999696603

Laughter is a medicine that we can all use. It's the only medicine that carries no risk of side effects or overdose and no one outgrows the need of it. Therefore, Curious One, allow me to prescribe **Harper - His Life and Trials.**

Product information
245 pages; 1000 mg of laughter per chapter

Dosage
As many pages as you like to be read daily or as directed by own curiosity and humour.

Recommendations
Read the blurb before use (if you wish)

Safety information
Keep in the sight and reach of children.

Storage instructions
Keep it about your person; do not allow it to gather dust.
Can also be kept in hand luggage, hand bags and man bags.

Possible side effects

Diverse manifestations of irritation and jealousy from others, provoked by your soul-deep laughter.

Contents

Chapter one

Harper Hepplesthwaite: Charity begins at home

"Ob-knock-shus. Ob-knock-shus," Harper mouthed. He was not sure which he found more interesting - the sound of the word, or the condensation that appeared on the mirror as he stood with his face as close to it as could be, without his nose touching it. He did not know what the word meant, and he had scowled when Mother had used it, but it sounded *great*. The 'ob' set the word off to a great start and the 'knock' running headlong into the 'shus' was just brilliant. 'Obknockshus' was how Mother had described his behaviour to the snotty guest that had visited them the day before.

To clear the condensation, he popped his finger into his mouth, and with a globule of spit, ran his finger across the narrow breadth of the mirror making a slimy trail that would put a snail to shame.

Mother was in the kitchen executing a plan that she had decided upon the day before; making tarts and scones. Later, she would be hand-painting miniature wooden boats and buses for sale.

Harper forced his feet into his boots, leaving the laces untied. His boots gaped at the toes but they were very comfortable once he got them on.

It was time for play - *out* of the house. Mother would be in a foul mood this afternoon, she always was when she tried her hand at baking because her wares nearly *always* burned or dried out even though she practically stood vigil by the oven. If they did not burn, they tasted average to nasty, but Mother's motto seemed to be 'if for the hundredth time you don't succeed, try, try and try again'!

He pulled himself together and ran down the stairs - well, threw himself really, with the odd ordered step to prevent him breaking his neck. He did want to play out after all and breaking his neck would put paid to that!

Mother dashed from the kitchen on hearing him but, keen to keep one eye on the oven and the other on her son, she stopped short of leaving the kitchen and merely stuck her head through the doorway. "And where are you going?" she breathed, the words tripping off her tongue at lightning speed. She was not in the mood for trouble or insolence, but she would rise to it if necessary – that is what *that* tone meant.

#Harper hurried to the front door tossing over his shoulder "I'm off ow' ter see Robin'".

He heard a low growl, and his eyes grew as he noted that it came not from a bear in nearby woods, but his Mother's throat – "out" "to" she enunciated, with such force that droplets of spittle escaped her lips, "ou*t* *t*o see - say *t*". "I've no time for an English lesson now Mother, Robin is wai'in for me". Her mind raced – is *this* what he learned at school? How to drop consonants? Mother decided that having the ghastly Robin arrive at the house was a fate she would rather avoid and so she dropped the matter.

The front door opened and shut, then the garden fence opened and so protested against the kick Harper gave to shut it, that it ricocheted open. Harper was off and Mother promptly went back to guarding her tarts and scones. She did not hear Harper shouting '*out*' as he ran down the footpath beside the house.

When he crept back into the house in the afternoon with just enough time to wash his hands ready for his own lunch, he could hear that Mother's luncheon meeting was still very much in sway. He stopped halfway up the long staircase, tugging at his boots, remonstrating with himself for not staying out for longer – "*I could 'ave go' away wiv it an' all*" he reasoned. He could hear Mother and a friend chatting away. The door was ajar and so he could also *see* the guest Petunia Thorsop: "*Yes,* 'Mr' *studied to become a 'Dr', studied for years more and promptly became a* 'Mr' *again...*" how Mrs Thorsop laughed at this contribution to the conversation. She laughed so hard that she did not hear Mother's wistful remark that she had gone from Miss to Dr to Mrs through her career as an Orthopaedic Consultant. Harper was now peering through the balustrades and straight at Mrs Thorsop. "*Petunia Thorsop, what a big gob you've got...* all the better to gobble lots of nasty jam tarts with" he mumbled as he took himself off to wash his hands.

Now he was clean and presentable for Mother, guest and tea - or so he thought. He either did not notice, or was wholly indifferent to the large streak of mud that ran from his chest to his waist, disappeared and then re-appeared on his right knee.

Harper sat at tea ignoring Mother's anxious glances as she tried to instruct him with her eyes not to pack his mouth *quite* so full with jam tarts, to mind the jam on the end of his chin and not to seek to play such an active part in the adults' conversation.

After playing obtuse to all such instructions; wiping his eye-brow instead of his nose (with a jammy finger) and putting yet another square of tart in his mouth rather than chewing the two he had already stuffed in, Harper eventually avoided all eye contact with Mother. He later explained that because he could not think straight for trying to read her expressions, he had decided to be polite and concentrate on the guest instead.

Harper was accustomed to adult company and conversation living alone with Mother and spending most of his time with her and her charitable friends. They spent most of their time chatting, making and painting toys, baking and eating so far as he could see but he had it on good authority that they also raised a lot of money for a lot of people. It was the same when Daddy lived at home with them - there was a lot of talk about charitable work. Daddy had joined an organisation that sent doctors and scientists to different parts of the world to help find cures for vicious but common diseases.

Back to England and Mother's luncheon; Petunia Thorsop announced that she was leaving ... and then loitered for an age afterwards; it was an unfortunate habit.

After a few minutes of watching them both, turning his head from one to the other to listen to their offerings to the conversation, Harper left the room. He loitered outside of the closed door, standing to the left hand side of it. A few minutes more and Harper saw the door handle turn and stood quietly on the other side of it. Mrs Thorsop was finally ready to leave and stepped out. Harper shouted "BOO"!

Mrs Thorsop nearly leaped out of her skin, or would have if her sturdy frame had not kept her rooted to the ground. She shook and nearly dropped her handbag. Her hair pinned in a mercilessly tight bun also shook but the pin piercing it through its centre kept it in place.

Mother missed the drama and was used to Harper's noise and so she followed a few seconds later wearing an amiable and satisfied smile. She looked at both of them contentedly; a beaming Harper and a flushed Mrs Thorsop. "Goodbye Mrs Thorsop," he called sweetly. "Do come again soon". "Yes, goodbye" Mrs Thorsop said setting her face towards the great outdoors. "The awful monkey needs to be brought in hand," she mumbled to herself.

Chapter Two

Harper Hepplesthwaite: It's all fine and dandy

Harper sat at the bottom of the staircase trying to force his feet into his shoes without untying the laces. It was Saturday and the October half term was about to start.

"And where are you off to young man?"

"Out. Out of your way Mother, out from under your feet".

"Don't stay out for too long dear, it's perishing out there - brrrrrrr" Mother said, rubbing her arms and feeling guilty that she was not able to find the words to say that Harper did *not* get in her way, or under her feet;

that she *liked* him knocking about the house while she set about her own business. Today, she was baking and researching content for a medical journal.

"I won't Mother"

"Keep your jumper on or you'll catch your death of cold"

"I will Mother"

"And don't stray ……"

"beyond the Common - I won't Mother." Harper knew the trio of conditions that usually came before he was allowed out to play and so completed Mother's sentence for her. The common had such a heavy job for a relatively small piece of land; keeping the horrible away from the nice, keeping the nice from the horrible, and keeping the nice together and the horrible together.

"I'll be back, washed and scrubbed before your pies are baked". "No mischief Harper, please Harper, *no* mischief". "I'll not get up to mischief Mother any more than you'll burn your pies." Harper said, giving a final and successful tug at his left shoe.

Bannersgate Common was the beautiful gated green that separated pleasant genteel Bannersgate Bow from Bannersgate. Bannersgate Bow took its name from the shape of the area from an aerial view. Bannersgate Bow was a well-established, very old area, while Bannersgate was fairly new, although over fifty years old!

Historically, the land had been used by local horse owners. However a wealthy brewery owner had built rows of cottages for its workers to get to work on the other side of town more easily and these cottages now occupied a large area of the land. Robin lived in one such cottage.

As Harper slammed the gate shut behind him, Robin approached the house and Mother watched them walk towards the footpath. Robin was wearing shorts with huge bulging pockets, a shirt and a jumper with a massive hole in the right elbow. Her hair looked as if she had been dragged through a hedge of prickles by a fox a week previously, her feet were sock-less and her shoelaces were undone.

With the ever-mischievous Harper out of the way, Mother pulled a big brown envelope from a dusty alcove in the kitchen where she had cosseted it from his sight. She took the envelope and turned it over, admiring the familiar writing for a few seconds. "Ah" she said briskly, tapping the envelope as if it were a shoulder. The letter was from her husband, Harper's father.

She reached into a drawer, shoving forks and knives here and dessert spoons and teaspoons there, until she found the letter opener. She was about to open it and then decided to put the kettle on. She might just need a cup of tea!

She sat down at last with a cup of tea, a slice of cheese and savoury biscuits made by her own fair hands. She took a bite of the biscuit (or tried to) and then used her two hands to snap it in half instead of exercising her teeth. The poppy seeds that she had sprinkled on too liberally (and too late in the baking process) scattered about the table and into her lap.

She pulled a long letter and a thin journal from the envelope. The journal had a note on it attached with a tiny pin. The note read - '*See page four for a photograph of your dearest*' with a hand drawn smiling face. Mother pushed the letter aside straight away. She opened the journal to page 4 and there he was squinting away, most likely because of the harsh sun, and looking leathern but well. As if reading an extract from the journal, although she certainly was not, Mother said "*Hilary Hepplesthwaite. Marvellous, clever doctor and scientist, wonderful writer of medical journals. Absent from home, wife and son. Hhhhmmmppphhhh*"! Mother finished abruptly and tucked into the rest of the biscuit, better able now to break it with her teeth! Daddy would not be home for Christmas yet again this year, his letter explained. Mother kissed the letter and put it back into the envelope with the journal, note and pin.

She would make sure Harper read the letter later on - but not the part about the plans for Christmas - she would tell him herself. Harper loved getting letters from his Daddy, even if he could not understand half of them.

Mother set to work opening a cupboard full of pots of lurid paint and paint brushes of various sizes. She would bake another day after all, she decided.

At the same time, just about a mile away, Harper's hands went into the deep pockets of his jumper and felt the coarse twine wound into a rudimentary ball. He pulled it out and showed it to Robin who grunted and nodded her approval. Harper grunted and nodded in return. For Harper, the twine was a toy offering, he did not really have toys anymore. He had outgrown them all and he could not lug one of his encyclopaedias about, or get his chemistry set past the front door under Mother's scrutiny. Mother eschewed all modern toys and gadgets.

Prompted by Harper's toy offerings, Robin pulled out the content of her bulging left pocket. As if revealing precious stones, she opened a wrinkled tissue slowly to reveal a lump of cheese, a lump of sponge cake, a lump of marshmallows and a quarter of an apple which oxygen had changed to a shade of brown. They were all squashed together and had been gently warmed by Robin's body temperature!

They had a kick about with Robin's new ball. It was a gleaming navy blue, white and red affair. Robin set aside the pouch of large marbles that she had brought to add to the games quotient as they set up a make-shift goal-post, using their pull-overs. The marbles were items inherited from Robin's grandfather. They were small perfectly round balls made of glass. Most were clear glass with swirls of colour - red, blue, white or green set in them.

Mother would be furious if she knew that Harper was dashing about in his vest but he would absolutely *roast* if he kept it on, and they needed *something* as a goal-post. It was not exactly new; it had been a Christmas gift from Daddy from some years prior.

Harper had the ball and ran as if for dear life towards the goalpost, trying to head off Robin before she even got anywhere near it. Excited by what seemed to be an invitation to join the game, a dog bounded towards

Harper in the opposite direction - *really* fast, and with its mouth agape. Harper quite liked dogs. They were his sort of animal, especially as lions and tigers were ruled out as pets. Mother had been very definite about that.

Well, he was not too sure if this dog was fun or fiendish but its owner's increasingly desperate calls were really not reassuring *at all*! At first, Harper was just struck by the dog's daft name but then, when Dandy's owner called with more and more alarm, *Harper* became alarmed.

The dog kept bounding towards him at such speed that he may as well have been flying. Harper stopped caring about the ball and making it to the goal-post. He just wanted to be out of the dog's path of sure terror and destruction, but he could not stop his legs running and he could not get them to change course and run *away* from Dandy either. In his mind, he was shouting "arrrrrgghhhh, arrrggggghhhh, aaaaaarrrrrrrrrrrrrrr-rrrrgggggggggggghhhhhhhh," but not a sound left his mouth. The shouting in his head seemed to be fuel to his short legs.

The dog owner shouted "Dandy get here immediately, I will never let you off your lead again if this is how you respond to the grant of freedom, HEEL *immediately!*" From the corner of his eye, Harper noticed another dog joining the chase, racing towards him and Dandy. He gave a quick glance and noted that it seemed a lot less ferocious than Dandy and most likely looking for innocent fun, rather than blood from boys' ankles. "*Fiiiiine*" the owner called to the other dog in a warning manner much more relaxed than the frantic calls to Dandy. "Fine - stop, heel - you too; Dandy, come here immediately."

Fine stopped the chase but Dandy did not listen to his owner any more than Harper's legs stopped going. In desperation, Fine and Dandy's owner called out to Harper instead of the dogs: "Excuse me, excuse me little boy, stop running and Dandy will stop too, *please stop running.*"

Harper did stop running; not because Dandy's owner told him to but because Dandy caught up with him and tugged at his trouser leg with his teeth. Grateful for Mother's advice that he wear trousers rather than shorts on account of the cold, Harper was a little nervous of his ankles being bitten but petrified that Dandy might just succeed in pulling his trousers down if he did not put up a fight to keep them on - this fight would require him to stop running and so his legs, as if they had been waiting patiently and willingly for the command, suddenly stopped. Even Dandy was taken by surprise by the sudden halt. He growled and bared his teeth, not sure of why Harper had stopped or what he intended to do next. There was a stand-off of a few seconds, both sizing the other up, one definitely more frightened than the other, only one baring teeth and growling but both willing to set about the other if required.

The stand-off was broken by the presence of Robin, and the owner of Fine and Dandy. For some strange reason, the owner gave both the unruly Dandy *and* Harper a furious glare. He bent down to snap the lead on to Dandy's collar and suddenly the vicious Dandy was meek, mild and making sport with Fine. Harper was suddenly furious and pointed at Dandy; "Fancy a person not keeping a *beast* on a lead given that it doesn't know how to behave in public." Dandy growled threateningly and Harper withdrew his accusing finger. "Dandy is *not* a beast; what sort of foolish boy runs *at* a dog? A *beast*? How *dare* you!" The stranger turned on his heel and walked off muttering to himself - and *soothing Dandy*!

Fine was barking playfully at the boys, blissfully unaware of the verbal blood that had been drawn between Harper and his master.

"Fancy calling me a little boy!" Once the fear of having his ankles bitten and modesty exposed disappeared, Harper's attention and rage turned to that slur! Robin started to laugh and Harper soon followed.

They both scrambled up a tree. Robin grazed her legs and Harper damaged his trousers. Then they both sat on different limbs of the tree, masters of all they surveyed from the great height. "Wow!" Robin declared, "I wouldn't mind a house up here meself – lucky birds"

Chapter Three

Harper Hepplesthwaite: Treats and trouble

Comfortably settled, Robin reached into her pocket and pulled out the rum treats that she had either salvaged or scavenged from home. She generously handed the warm parcel to Harper who unwrapped it gingerly. It all looked revolting and Harper thought that it would probably kill him but he took a generous bite at a piece of cheese squashed against the lump of cake and then handed the parcel back to Robin.

Suitably fed, the two climbed down the tree. Harper pulled the ball of twine until it fell straight with no knots or snags and then bent to his knees by a bench on the other side of the narrow pathway. He tied the twine to a leg of the bench and then crossed the path and tied the other side to the narrow trunk of a tree that stood opposite to the bench. He had not seen the twine used quite like this before - Mother tended to use it in the garden to train together tall plant stems but it worked a treat for his game.

"What's the idea then?" Robin asked.

"We're going to have a marble race. Let's be having them" Harper said, extending his hand to Robin. Robin extracted from her pocket the pouch that held the large round glassy balls.

"The marble that crosses the finish line first by rolling *under* the string, wins" Harper continued. "Best of seven?"

"Deal!" they agreed striking hands.

Next came the tricky part of the game - they bargained for the marbles that they wanted. The marbles were magnificent and to look inside some was to look into a deep ocean; clear swirling water with hints of blue and green reflecting blue sky and green sea leaves. Well, ships and pirates were missing from the marbles, but Harper's mind placed them right there in the eye of the marble with great crashing waves and so he always shunned the more colourful ones for the seemingly plain ones. Robin wanted at least one of the clear marbles as she liked a range. The bargaining was interrupted by a shrill voice.

"Kooo-eeeee - you there! That's most dangerous, untie it immediately - you cannot obstruct a public pathway like this. Someone is bound to fall - *I* nearly did!" The passer-by was right; if her dog had not pulled ahead on its lead, the woman would not have seen the twine before she tripped over it.

"Yes Miss," Harper and Robin chorused obediently, even though they fully intended to start the game as soon as she had turned her back. However, before they had finished bargaining for their preferred marbles, calamity struck.

An elderly man who was passing by got his walking stick tangled in the twine and tumbled to the hard floor. The elderly man was Mr Mowbray – a retired Judge.

Chapter Four

Harper Hepplesthwaite: A toast

A few people appeared from nowhere to help. Mr Mowbray lay still, very still indeed and calls were made for an ambulance to be summoned straight away.

Harper and Robin had no idea what to do when they realised what had happened. They traipsed out of the Common, stunned into absolute silence. They only spoke when they came to the crossroads dividing their respective areas. Harper's steps faltered; he really did not want to go home. "You'd better come home with me for a while," Robin said.

The rain poured and Harper was pleased to have the covering of his jumper. They walked with their heads bowed to the ground until they got to Robin's front door. Robin rapped the door with her knuckles.

After a few minutes the door swung open and Robin's mother, Alice stood in the doorway. Her expression said that she would not have opened the door had she known that Robin had company. Robin walked past passing under her arm and then looked back over her shoulder at Harper, beckoning him in with a nod of her head.

Alice stood with her arms akimbo. "Tell me what's happened...... *now!*" she ordered loudly and with finality as Robin tried a doomed protest.

"We were just playing a game. This old gent fell over, bumped his head and now he's probably dead ... I saw some blood. It's all our fault... *we've killed a man...!*" Robin concluded dramatically.

Robin had *no* reason other than her lively imagination to assume that Mr Mowbray was actually dead. Alice pulled both of Harper and Robin to her side and they clung to her like monkeys. "You ain't killed no one, I'm sure" They both nodded but remained unconvinced.

"Get outta my sight now ... both of you," she instructed. "I need to find out exactly what is going on."

They obliged, Robin taking the lead as she dashed up the stairs to her bedroom. They both slumped to the floor with their backs resting against a wall.

Harper really wanted to cry. Robin did too but, instead, she stood suddenly and declared that they both needed a drink to steady their nerves. As she went down the stairs, the odd tear escaped her eyes. "Poor mister," she said as she poured a lurid blackcurrant juice drink into two plastic cups. She snubbed the tart lemon juice - it seemed inappropriate somehow.

Robin took the drinks to her bedroom, pushing the door open with a bare foot. Harper stood to attention without really knowing why, then they both sat again and remained in silence for a while. Robin raised her cup towards Harper and said nobly; "A toast - to the old mister, may his soul rest in peace."

"To the old mister," Harper parroted solemnly ... respectfully. He had seen toasts at home when Daddy lived with them, never on account of someone being dead though – and, of course, never by his hand! "You don't *really* think he's dead do you?" In answer, Robin reached across to Harper and gave him a moderately hard whack across the head.

Alice appeared and brought the solemn assembly at an end. “You’d best be off home mister. Your ma will be worried sick and the evening’s closing in“.

Robin asked permission to walk Harper home. “Of course not,” Alice snapped “fink you should be allowed out alone *ever* again after today? That poor man’s in ‘ospital – a Judge an’ all! You‘ll give me grey hairs you will.” Harper agreed that they were perhaps a danger to the public but he was certainly not a magician and, if he was, he would certainly not waste time dabbling in hair colours!

They walked in silence, Alice making streams of smoke in the cold air as she drew on a cigarette.

They arrived at the grand front door of Harper’s home. Harper noticed that the drawing room light was on. The children instinctively fell back and Alice stepped forward rapping on the door. Mother would be horrified; the door had a perfectly good door-knocker – a bronze lion’s head in fact.

When the door opened cautiously, Mother looked more worried than cross and it dawned on Harper that he had been out of the house for hours. Mother must have started to worry. She did not say anything; she just looked with surprise at Alice, taking her in from head to toe and then she looked past her to seek out Harper's face.

"Hallo?" Mother said still wondering what was going on and why her son stood at the door like a visitor while the uninvited guests moved boldly to step in, Robin now at the front of the short queue.

"Ar, ar, ar, no we don't little girl!" Mother said putting up her hand to stop Robin walking into the wide and long corridor.

"There's bin a terrible accident so I've come round to explain but I can go 'ome and let 'Arper tell you the lot if you like". Alice stepped away from the door as she spoke.

"There's been an accident Mother - we were only playing," Harper translated. Mother turned a drained face in his direction. "Are you alright Harper?" She asked. "*He's* fine, it's the old Judge what's gonna be pushing up the daises," Robin intervened.

They had all spoken now but Mother was not really any the wiser. All this talk of an accident, an elderly Judge and daisies made no sense whatsoever. It had nothing to do with Harper surely. "You had better come in," Mother said. She wanted them to wipe their feet thoroughly on the door-mat provided for the purpose but could not find the words.

"Now, someone please tell me *exactly* what is going on *immediately*," Mother said commandingly, snapping on the light.

"Well it's like I said. The boys got carried away in a game and an old gent, a Judge, fell over and hit his head. He's in 'ospital, but alrigh' I'm sure," Alice offered. Harper explained where he had been since the incident, omitting the detail of the lurid toast to Mr Mowbray.

"I'll need you and Robin to leave now please if you don't mind. Thank you for escorting Harper home," Mother stood to signal the end of the unwanted visit.

"Chin up," Robin encouraged Harper, pressing two marbles into his hands - they might just cheer him and heaven knew when she would see him again. Robin and her mother stepped out of the house and into the autumnal evening.

Mother shut the front door after them. She went about the expansive ground floor of the house, locking doors and closing windows and then she turned off all of the lights and took to her room. She did not say a word to Harper, not even to remind him to brush his teeth and turn his bedroom light out. He was in his room with the light on waiting to be summoned, when he heard the door of her bedroom click closed. That was that. Mother must be furious, worse still – she was likely to be 'disappointed'! She was not just sparing with her words; she was silent.

Harper did not brush his teeth but he did turn off his bedroom light. He eventually fell asleep but not before uttering a hurried prayer in which he asked that Mr Mowbray was made to see how sorry he and Robin were, how they had just been out to play a game of marbles and not trip up a dear old fellow like him. Then in direct petition to Mr Mowbray's soul, Harper explained that he was better off where he was now anyway and would *definitely* not be tripped over *up there*. He probably would not even need his walking stick any more Harper threw in as a triumphant after-thought. He then promptly fell asleep.

Chapter Five

Harper Hepplesthwaite: The banishment

When Harper woke the following morning, Mother was sitting at the edge of his bed. "Oh good, at last; I need to speak to you, and we have a busy day ahead."

Harper sat up in bed rubbing his tired eyes so that he would stay awake and concentrate. 'You're going to live with Great-Aunt in the country Harper'.

Harper finally settled on looking aghast after opening his eyes to their fullest extent, and closing them as tightly as possible thrice in quick succession. He needed to check that he was indeed awake and not caught up in an unhappy dream in which Mother was saying beserk things that made no sense at all.

"The time is right and, most importantly it's for the best... for all of us." Harper felt as if he should give a very grown-up reply to this, but he could not. He was full of questions and they all spilled out of his mouth while tears spilled out of his eyes.

What a thing Harper thought! "Going to live with Great-Aunt in the country" she said, as if Great-Aunt was a familiar relative, but he had never met her, not so as to be conscious of it anyway. He must have been a mere babe when they met if he had set eyes on her at all. More than that, any talk about her had always been whispers behind hands and raised eyebrows. Harper decided that he must speak up. "Great-Aunt?" he questioned. "Isn't she the weird one? You and Daddy always said that ...". "We have never said any such thing," Mother interrupted. "She is eccentric, very slightly eccentric, that is all".

"Why Mother? Is it because of Mr Mowbray? It was an accident - I promise."

"I'm sure it was but that's not good enough Harper. Going away will help you to settle down and mature into a nice boy. If you stay here, you'll grow *wild*."

"I'll pack your bags while you use the bathroom."

"What?"

Mother sighed. *'Pardon,'* she corrected.

"What?" Harper asked – this time because he was genuinely incredulous that Mother was being military about his manners at such a time.

"When am I going Mother..."?

"Today. My mind is made up Harper and Great-Aunt is expecting you." Mother got up and left his room. Harper heard her go back into his bedroom while he was in the bathroom.

By the time he had finished in the bathroom, Mother had folded most of the contents of his draws into a suitcase. She handed him a singlet, shirt and jumper. "Put these on, it'll be cold."

He did not really know what to say and he knew that pleading with Mother would be pointless. A thought suddenly struck him, and he yelled; "Does Daddy think I should go away too - does he *KNOW*?"

Mother felt uncomfortable, she had not even had a chance to let Harper read Daddy's letter. It was too late, it would only upset the calm and so she just said a short and simple, "Yes."

This was not strictly true. Rather, Mother believed that, once Daddy knew that his only son's acquaintance with a local girl had nearly caused the death of an elderly neighbour – a Judge, he would certainly agree that Harper should leave for quieter more spacious climes with fewer people, as soon as possible. Harper was devastated. Who would have thought it when he had tripped out of the house yesterday?

"I'll go and say goodbye to Robin," Harper said. Even as he said it, he knew Mother was not likely to go for it at all but he had to try. "don' ask you don' get" as Robin would say.

The colour drained from Mother's face. "Don't be absurd," she said in a slow and deadly near-whisper.

As for Great-Aunt, soon to be Harper's host, she was sufficiently unconventional and her house sufficiently big to accommodate Harper even at such short notice, Mother reasoned.

Harper trundled down the stairs and noticed that two suitcases were at the bottom of the staircase together with Mother's handbag. He walked into the breakfast room and found Mother sitting at tea, toast and marmalade and a boiled egg. No milk in her tea today, Harper thought as if it mattered at all. A bowl of cereal was set at the table opposite her and Harper sat down. He had no appetite.

"We've a long journey ahead and so I suggest you eat all of that young man - every last morsel." Harper obeyed.

"How long are we away for *exactly* Mother? You've got *all* of my clothes in those cases out there."

"Do not speak with food in your mouth Harper. How many times do you need to be told that?"

Harper promptly bolted the remainder of his breakfast, except a tall glass of milk, and immediately he had swallowed the last mouthful, the questions began again. "Mother, where are we off to then?" He had no idea how near or far the suddenly 'wonderful-for-sending-little-naughty-boys-to' Great-Aunt lived. It could be as far as Timbuktu, or just over the common for all he knew.

"The country Harper. So many questions, but you didn't ask yourself *any* yesterday did you? Is it sensible to create a near invisible hazard across a public path... ummm?" One utensil was placed into the ceramic sink with a clunk. "Is this the best place to play this game... ummm?" And a second utensil sounded against the ceramic sink. "Will anyone be affected by my decision to play this game here... ummm?" And a third utensil clunked into the sink. This continued until Mother had cleared the breakfast table and placed all of the washing up into the sink. Harper counted ten items - and ten questions.

Harper hung his head and his shoulders slumped.

The telephone rang and broke into the silence. He could not hear all of Mother's contribution to the very short conversation, strained as he might to hear.

Mother bent to his height and, looking into his eyes, told him that Mr Mowbray was improving and not expected to be in hospital for too many days. The beginning of tears seemed to well in her eyes and she patted Harper on the shoulder. Tears stung his eyes and dribbled down his cheeks.

"I'm so happy Mother. To think that me and Robin drank a toast to his death yesterday."

"You did what?" Mother asked briskly, withdrawing from him. "You took *alcohol*" Mother exclaimed, making a statement now rather than asking a question.

"No ... *Mother.*"

Mother continued to look at him, now in bewilderment.

"I'm only *a boy.* What would I want with alcohol?"

Mother was persuaded by this protest.

"I don't suppose I can let Robin know that Mowbray's alive..."? Harper asked.

"*Mister* Mowbray to you Harper, *Mister, Judge! No you cannot.*"

Harper abandoned that line of request and, after a few moments of silence, launched another - after a fashion of his own.

He pushed the empty glass of milk away from him and pushed his chair away from the table - both quite deliberately. He pulled up his sleeves as he stood and walked from the breakfast room to the corridor. Reaching down to lift one of the suitcases, he called over his shoulder to Mother. She was pottering; watering plants and flowers, and checking that doors and windows were securely closed. "I'll take these back upstairs, before you can say '*Great-Aunt*'."

However, the suitcase was heavier than Harper bargained for and so he mumbled to himself and Mother that he would empty the contents a few contents at a time and then carry the empty, lighter suitcase back upstairs.

Poor Harper started to unbuckle the suitcase - all was well after all. He would not be going to live with Great-Aunt in goodness knows where for goodness knows how long. He would visit Robin once Mother was less angry and let her know that Mr Mowbray was alive. Robin would be horrified that he had nearly been banished to "the country" - wherever that was!

"What are you doing ...?" Mother's question broke into Harper's cheerful reverie.

Harper continued without turning to look at his Mother and so missed the clue held in her eyes that he had misunderstood the position so fundamentally.

"Harper, no" Mother said softly but firmly.

This got Harper's attention and he turned to face Mother. She studied the floor for what seemed like hours and then she told Harper: "You are still going Harper - nothing has changed."

Harper's mind was reeling. *Everything* had changed; Mowbray was alive and bound to be out of hospital before long.

"I'll visit him Mother. That's what I'll do. I'll visit Mr Mowbray and take a newspaper along, so that he knows *everything* that has happened in the whole wide world while he's been in hospital. I'll tell him that I'll never play such a game again. I can take him some of your scones"

"Harper........"

"That's a relief." Harper said chirpily starting up the staircase, his heavy tread making a racket.

"Harper," Mother called. Her voice was deadly low but somehow managed to cut through the noise of his footsteps.

Harper turned on his heel and trudged down the few stairs he had climbed.

"Come on now." She said putting the items back into the suitcase and closing it. Harper stood watching Mother. He was surprised and very sad.

Chapter Six

Harper Hepplesthwaite: Off to the country and Great-Aunt it is

Harper and Mother bundled themselves and the suitcases into the car.

Harper sat in the rear of the car, tight against the door, clinging on to its handle. Mother noticed this through the rear view mirror and winced. Her busy mind settled on the fact that she had packed two marbles that she had found in his room, in Harper's luggage. She guessed that they were a gift from Robin and this gave her some comfort. A prescient gift now that they would not see each other for a very long time.

Harper's warm breath created a patch of steam on the window but not long enough to obscure his view of the familiar turning into the unfamiliar. He knew the point of no return was nigh when he noticed the gold, red and greens of a wood, streams and narrow lanes replace dense rows of houses, broad roads and the odd skeletal tree.

He must have fallen asleep with little prior warning. He certainly did not see the bridge that arched itself over the brook filled with black slate and rock, or the huge field dotted with clusters of cows, sheep, horses and on the other side, the wild grass. Nor did he see the woodland that seemed to go on for an age.

They were now in the country – Eldersham to be precise.

Mother drove down a very long narrow lane and came to a rather abrupt halt which woke Harper. Mother had been forced to stop to make way for a passing tractor. After a while the lane forked into two and Mother took the turn westward. A forest was ahead on the left and Harper noticed a Church spire in the background protruding high above the trees. They passed a few houses in an area of green land, scattered like sultanas in a bun. Most were painted white, one was a sage green, another sky blue and others were stone. A few had white painted push-gates, the others were natural wood.

They finally slowed at the end of the lane and came to a stop outside a square, symmetrically shaped cottage that was white in colour. It had pale pink evergreen roses all around the front of it and some climbed up the sides and across the front of the house. There was another building on the left hand side but detached from the main house. On the right, there was a narrow gate that led to a huge back garden.

There were five windows at the front of the house, two on either side of the wide front door and a further two above them. One stood alone in the centre of the top of the house immediately under the chimney. There two big flower pots filled with the same pale pink evergreen roses that climbed the cottage.

All this Harper would take in, in the days to come. It was Mother that noticed all of this as she had not visited Great-Aunt for years.

The pillar box red door opened and Great-Aunt stood in the doorway and gave a wave. She then walked down the path to meet them. She shook hands with Mother and then, bending to Harper's height and looking deep into his eyes, said "So *this* is Harper. What a delight - I think we are going to have a thoroughly enjoyable life together here!"

Harper wanted to cry. A brusque pat on the back would have served him better than this. The soft, small hand patting his cheek and the deep twinkling eyes smiling into his were too much.

"How d'you do?"

"Well, thank you." Harper said bravely although his wary widened eyes said otherwise.

Great-Aunt nodded to acknowledge his answer but corrected "How d'you do!" Harper frowned, now was not the time for games and repeating greetings was it? He thought with some irritation.

Mother rubbed her forehead and in a tired voice explained to Harper that when asked "how d'you do", the correct answer was "how d'you do."

"You must be famished - will shepherd's pie do?" Great-Aunt asked him. Harper did not answer. Here we go again with the "dos" he thought. Was he supposed to repeat what Great-Aunt had said? "Shepherd's pie do-do!" He stared at the fan of hair that framed her dainty sparrow-like face until his tea was set before him.

Shepherd's pie, followed by pear tart and custard. Harper thoroughly approved of the pear tart and had seconds.

Maybe it was a satisfied tummy, or maybe it was the long journey but within three hours of his arrival, Harper promptly fell asleep and took to his new room relatively peacefully.

Mother wanted to leave as soon as possible but torrential rain made driving conditions quite treacherous and Great-Aunt persuaded her to stay for the night. She knew that this change of plan would make the separation even more difficult for Harper but Great-Aunt's reasoning was sound.

So passed the first day and night of Harper's stay at number 2 Pear Tree Lane, Eldersham.

He was not aware yet but he had stepped into another world; an altogether different time and age in all respects.

The next morning, Harper woke and took in the bedroom that he had been too exhausted to take in the night before: wooden floors painted white, three rows of books on wooden shelves also painted white, a navy, yellow and pillar-box red rug, pale blue walls and a large standing grandfather clock. The many artefacts that Great-Aunt had accumulated over the years were in the room for storage rather than for his use. In the corner stood a shiny rocking horse with its nostrils flared and mane flowing as if fresh from a race in its wooden world. He lay in a generous single-bed, well-padded with a coloured patchwork blanket.

Mother left early that morning after bidding a rather hasty and inadequate good-bye to Harper. She cried virtually all the way home - but Harper had no way of knowing that.

After the first week in the house, he wondered why Great-Aunt believed they would have a thoroughly enjoyable time together. It was all very nice but terrifically boring, and he did not really see an awful lot of Great-Aunt. She was an artist and spent hours at a time in a studio room in the cottage, or out of the house altogether at exhibitions and art fairs.

"Oh well" Harper thought – "that's adults for you." Not everything they said was literal. He had found that out at a tender age and with great disappointment. He had been looking forward to an outing to a fair. The promised day arrived at last and Mother explained that they could not go after all because it was raining 'cats and dogs' outside. Well, who needed to go to the fair when such a fantastic spectacle had come to his door step? He raced to the ceiling-to-floor glass doors at the back of the kitchen to see the air borne animals form a zoo in his very own garden. Alas, all there was to see were plump drops of rain pelting the glass and the lawn. Not only were there no cats and dogs hurtling to the ground from the sky, the rain drops were not even *shaped* like cats and dogs! Nothing about the scene had *anything* to do with cats or dogs unless you cheated and counted the neighbours' ginger tabby cat skulking across the wall. There was not a dog in sight. Harper had twisted his face into the most furious scowl that chubby cheeks could summon. Mother had had the audacity to laugh!

Chapter Seven

Harper Hepplesthwaite: Home is where fun, friends and your favourite foods are

Days turned to weeks and weeks to months and Harper settled into life at number 2 Pear Tree Lane, Eldersham and his new school - Bishop Challoner Boys' School. He also discovered a well-kept family secret - Great-Aunt's name, which was Millicent. Not that he used it; as she was introduced to him, so she remained.

Bishop Challoner was established as an all boys' school; however girls had been admitted in the last ten years. Its tradition as a boys' school stuck fast in local minds however, and so their numbers were still few and far between when Harper joined the school.

Like most of the villagers who went about on bicycle, Harper explored Eldersham on the bicycle Great-Aunt had bought for him in the first week of his arrival, cycling the length and breadth of the interesting western area. Great-Aunt had a basket attached to the front of her bicycle and used it to carry shopping and other wares. She always had pots of jam for delivery to neighbours and friends. Harper was absolutely taken aback the first time he saw Great-Aunt making jam. She used a huge pot - big enough to boil a child in and filled it with what must have been a field-full of strawberries and more sugar than he believed an adult would admit to liking the taste of! Before he realised the tradition of its distribution, he had announced with a firmness born of his alarm, "I aint eating all that!"

After the first month, the villagers stopped staring at him. Most smiled at him and asked if he was Millicent's grandson. He always gave a thrifty smile and mostly answered '*may*be'. It was too complicated to explain the relationship from across the road *and* they knew the answer before asking. His reply was sometimes impolite - but perfectly in line with his interpretation of Mother's advice that he should not talk to strangers. It had served him pretty well so far.

That was one of the many and vexing idiosyncrasies he had noticed about adults; asking questions that they already knew the answer to. Have you finished your home-work? Have you washed behind your ears? Is that the way to speak to your elders? What have you done with the 't' at the end of such and such a word? Blaaaah, blaaah, blaaah!

Harper made two particularly good friends at school, called Hugo and Agatha. The three friends were kindred spirits - always on the look-out for mischief and sport. Happily, they also lived in the lanes that led to school and so walked to and from school together.

Over time, Robin became a mere occasional visitor to his thoughts but Harper knew that they would be friends forever.

Hugo was a stocky little fellow, shorter than both Harper and Agatha. He had a mop of dark (almost black) hair and twinkling brown eyes which were in a perpetual squint because he refused to wear his spectacles all of the times that he should. Hugo was determined that the braces holding his unruly teeth in safe and tidy custody were enough for him by way of contraptions. He only wore them in English and science lessons because both Miss Honeywhistle who taught English and Mr Burnsom who taught science insisted on it.

Miss Honeywhistle was a very nice teacher. She floated about the classroom in brightly coloured skirts and cardigans and made the classes interesting. She often read stories that she had written herself and did not get cross - even when Harper interrupted her to guess the endings!

Miss Honeywhistle was very firm about Hugo wearing his glasses however. She told him that he could not delve into the magical world of stories if he struggled to see the words weave a tale on the page.

Mr Burnsom was a medium sized, medium height, rotund man. He had fleshy cheeks, a bulbous nose, a shiny rounded forehead and two tufts of wild grey hair that sprouted on either side of his head, just behind his ears. He wore glasses, which he often took off and misplaced somewhere in the science laboratory. Sometimes they were perched on his head, sometimes they were in one of the four pockets on his laboratory coat, at other times they were left behind on the desk of one of his little pupils. He would pad up and down the laboratory, up one row of desks and down the other, across to the next and up and down another row... again and again looking for his glasses. The children took delight in watching Mr Burnsom stoop and squint at each and every desk, mumbling and ruffling his already wild hair; "*Just where have they got to now?*" he would ask. The children never directed him to look in his pockets, or to reach for them where they lay perched on his head. In fact, on one occasion, Harper rather unhelpfully shouted in pantomime fashion: "they're behind you," just when Mr Burnsom's concentration was most focused, making him jump and the children laugh. Mr Burnsom never reacted angrily. Perhaps he saw the funny side himself. It was also entirely possible that he put on the performance quite deliberately!

Mr Burnsom performed fantastic experiments and expected the children to be actively involved. There were experiments with fire, effervescent and colourful liquids and powders, complete with magnificent explanation and sound effects.

Mr Burnsom said that Hugo needed his glasses "to see the fantastical in science". Harper thought that they often saw the fantastical in science, at closer quarters than their parents and Headmistress Pickering would like - and he fully approved. He found the possibility of leaving a science class with a sliced or burned finger, or singed eyebrows quite a thrill!

Last but not least of the trio of friends was Agatha. Agatha was a gangly child - all legs and arms with unruly hair. She bore the brunt of teachers' despair at their tom-foolery because her height made her appear older than she was.

Life with Great-Aunt at number Two Pear Tree Lane had its benefits. Great-Aunt was in fact Mother's oldest cousin. She inherited the pet title and it had stuck. She was actually a well-respected Artist. Harper and Great-Aunt grew to know each other through their time together - either cooking or eating.

Harper absolutely adored her puddings. Pear crumble was a simple favourite - partly because he was allowed to help make the crumble and partly because it tasted delicious. He was sure that Great-Aunt added a magic and secret ingredient. The pears tasted more like the best sweets in the world than fruit from the trees in the garden. Great-Aunt had also shown him the art of preserving pears so that they could be used all of the year round.

"So what was it like before I moved in then?" Harper asked wielding a raw carrot in a closed fist.

"It must have been really quiet. The house is always quiet except when Laurie visits. He's..."

Great-Aunt stopped Harper in his tracks. "It's Mr Beauchamp to you my dear..."

"Mr Beauchamp," Harper said, feigning appreciation for the correction, with a patronising nod of his head at Great-Aunt. "His voice makes the whole house shake," he continued, trembling to demonstrate his point, rattling his cutlery. His full mouth just about kept its content intact.

Laurie was Great-Aunt's partner in crime. They drove about in his classic motor-cars to shows, fairs, auctions and antique shops in the nearest towns and cities. Since retiring, he was a kind helper to the villagers but he had his favourites and Great-Aunt was at the top of the list.

Harper quite liked *Laurie*, not that Laurie or Great-Aunt could have guessed it. In fact the only thing that Harper did not like about Laurie was his grandson Matthew. They were not quite sworn enemies but they were awkward friends and even their first meeting had got off to a bad start:

"Wha?" Harper had said with a jerk of his chin and a squaring of his chest to Matthew - this new boy on his patch.

Matthew stared with a combination of irritation and curiosity, wondering who on earth this cheeky young monkey was.

"Have I got something of yours I wonder?" Harper asked cheekily looking about himself with mock earnest. Fearless Harper did not mind squaring up to this boy who was at least four years his senior and probably twice as many inches taller. Harper wondered why this *string-bean* was walking about Great-Aunt's garden as if he owned it!

Harper walked around Matthew, just as Matthew had boldly walked around what was now effectively, *his* garden. Matthew stood still initially - and then he mirrored Harper's steps, continuing to watch Harper with surprise. Harper continued to walk around Matthew in an ever decreasing circle.

"I think *I'm* going to do that one day," Harper said and did not mind the awkward pause that followed his statement.

"Do what?" Matthew asked when Harper made no offering.

"*Wander* into someone else's garden without so much as asking, *just* because I feel like it and have no manners."

"Hello? I'm Matthew, I've lived here for ages and I've been coming to this garden for years. My grandfather looks after it..."

Harper stopped in his tracks and walked backwards in an awkward semi-circle so that he and Matthew were facing each other.

"Oh I see, *you're* Laurie's grandson!" Matthew looked a little taken aback. He had *never* heard his grandfather called 'Laurie' by a mere boy.

"And you are?" Matthew asked.

"Someone who is meant to be on this land, someone who lives here........ Harper's the name if you must know," Harper replied.

The ice had eventually thawed between them but the awkward friendship was not necessarily for the best.

Matthew helped with the garden for pocket-money, cakes, pies or, best of all – for a chance to play on Great Aunt's grand old piano. Great-Aunt was always pleased to have the old relic used by someone of his generation. He was two years older than Harper.

Their second encounter (which followed the next day) ended more positively despite the frosty start. Matthew had appeared again. He stood in the garden and whistled up at Harper's window. Harper opened the sash window and leaned out so that most of his torso was hanging out of it. It was a crisp winter morning but he did not seem to notice the cold. Matthew, standing with a foot leaning against the willow tree, waved Harper down. "Come down, there's something you've got to see," he had called up.

Harper closed the window loudly and without a word, leaving Matthew wondering whether he was coming at all. He suddenly appeared some moments later, with his head down and his hands in his pockets. Robin would have asked Matthew "how on earth he knew which winder was his," Harper considered but, if Matthew had been knocking around the house for as long as he had said, it stood to reason that he could make a guess that Harper also lived at the back of the house.

After exchanging reluctant nods of the head by way of a greeting, Matthew explained that Great-Aunt had a bunker at the very back of the garden. Matthew knew where the key was if Harper was bold enough to fetch it. Harper fought back his indignation that Matthew knew secrets that he had not uncovered himself because he was really curious and excited at the prospect of having an underground play area.

Harper fetched the key and, before they knew it, Matthew was lifting the small covering of the entrance. They walked gingerly down the steps into the bunker, blinking rapidly as their eyes adjusted to the relative darkness. They looked around and took in a short ladder, presumably leading to another entrance long sealed off, a kerosene lantern hanging on a pretty rusty nail and spiders' webs. There was silence other than the sound of damp leaves under their feet. Nothing more and nothing less! They were disappointed and so they had a squabble about which of them would return the key. Matthew believed that Harper should return it as it was his house. That way, if he was caught, he would have a reasonable explanation for having the key. Harper believed that Matthew should return it as he had fetched it. "It's a wonder that you've been poking around this house what's not yours for so long and you didn't know what was down there" Harper said with exaggerated surprise and disgust as they stumbled out.

Matthew protested for so long that Harper did return the key in the end. Fortunately Great-Aunt was in her studio and would, therefore, not hear or notice - even if both boys ran around the house shouting blue murder. Great-Aunt took her art very seriously indeed and she was very good at it. A few of her pieces were displayed in prominent public buildings.

The boys agreed that the garden had more to offer than the bunker. They could find some interesting insects and perhaps some frogs if they were patient and looked hard enough. The rich damp soil and lush perennial shrubs of Great-Aunt's garden definitely delivered but they had to persevere at their search because it was cold.

Harper gasped when he saw a spider with unusual dappled colouring to its exoskeleton. He set it on a nearby stone and watched it with a wonder that would have pleased Mr Burnsom. He cupped his hands around it forming a boundary to hem it in. A tiny particle clung to the tiny hairs on one of its hind legs. Harper tried to blow it away and nearly blew the spider across the surface of the stone and over the edge but it clung still. Harper made a pincer of his forefinger and thumb and tried to pluck it off, but this did not work either. Eventually, a despairing Harper did a most terrible thing. He pulled off the *leg*. The spider continued to crawl away from Harper's cupped hand. Harper pulled off another leg, this time on the opposite side. He continued until he had pulled off all of the legs altogether!

Matthew was busy frog hunting in vain but he would happily have settled for anything slippery - a snail or slug would have been just fine.

Soon it was time to go indoors and get washed ready for tea.

Once he was excused from tea Harper dashed upstairs to the attic room at the rear of the fourth storey of the house. This is where he stored the model construction site set that Laurie had given to him together with a collection of miniature model cars. Laurie had gone up in Harper's estimation with this gift.

He set about building a bridge with a view to running the model cars over it. This was how he intended to spend his time when he was not in the great outdoors. Harper was concentrating so hard on his task that he did not hear the sound of tiny bits of coal falling from the grate and on to the hearth. Even if he had, he would not have paid a blind bit of notice. When they came thick and fast, he still continued his building.

Chapter Eight

Harper Hepplesthwaite: Has he lost his marbles or what on earth ...?

Harper, Agatha and Hugo had been out in the local woodlands leaving their homes early, and not returning until they were ravenous.

Harper raided the biscuit tin, grabbing three biscuits in each hand. It did not matter to him that he had dried insect juice on his hands – he ate with grubby hands quite literally, followed with milk which he drank from a brandy snifter. Great-Aunt was not there to forbid it – she was exhibiting at an art fair. He stuffed some of the biscuits into his pocket where they crumbled nicely around the glass marble that he had deposited there earlier. He ate another as he climbed the stairs, leaving a trail of crumbs that Hansel and Gretel would have marveled at.

He ran up the stairs, past his bedroom, up the next flight of stairs, past the third floor where the small library was and up the next flight of stairs to the attic. It was time to resume work on the model bridge he was constructing there.

The attic room was fairly large with parquet flooring and sparsely furnished with just a large rug in primary colours, a large beautiful fireplace that Harper was too young to appreciate, a trunk and a rocking chair with a custard yellow cushion on it. The walls were a pale blue and there were hollow casements on either side of the large window. Great-Aunt had said that they were used to black-out light so that homes were invisible from the air during the worst of the bombing raids in the war years. Harper was desperate to know what was inside the casements. They could have been used by criminals as secret storage for stolen booty – a hideaway from the eyes and hands of the police. How exciting would that be! He tucked the tips of his fingers into the tiny gap between the frame and the shutter and tugged with all of his might. The force jolted him, and the marble in his pocket fell to the wooden floor with a clunk. He clambered to his hands and knees but, as marbles are wont, it rolled out of his reach. When he accidentally flicked it onto the hearth with his finger, it just kept on rolling. Harper hoped that it would not disappear into one of the crevices in the skirting boards.

Unless the milk he had drunk had turned and was giving him wild day dreams, Harper was sure he could hear a very quiet and high pitched shrieking: aaaarrrrrrrrggggggggghhhhhhh, hhhhhhgggggrrrrraaaa, aaaarrrrrrgggghhhh. Weirder still, it seemed to be coming *from* the marble - well he always looked into them in wonder, imagining the worlds that existed in them, pirates, sailors, aliens and so on but *this* was something else. Something else altogether!

On his hands and knees he followed the marble around trying to catch it as it had gathered a momentum of its own. It eventually rolled back towards the hearth and he caught it, or rather stretched out his hand to stop it rolling, just as it threatened to ricochet off the corner.

'*Goodness graaaaaaacious me, oh my goodness, oh my, oh my, of all the devilment.... aarrrrggghhhhh, how awful, how very awful indeed and who'd have thought it – step out to do an honest day's work in all innocence and nearly get dashed to pieces and rolled and crushed and squeezed.* Ohhhhhh *my goodness, well I never...*' and then a burst of anger: '*well I never got my hands around a human-boy-neck to wring it before but this, this is uuuuuunacceptable, wwwicked, ww-wicked, wiiicked provocation to do just that*'!

By now Harper was lying flat on his tummy. His eyes started out of his head, and his mouth flew open. For pressed against the marble and slowly prising itself off it, was a tiny creature that looked like a chubby elderly man dressed in scruffy royal blue short trousers, a baggy cream shirt rolled up at the sleeves to reveal knobbly elbows, a ragged corduroy brown waistcoat and a black belt with a huge buckle that must have begun its journey at his navel but was now twisted askance after the roller-coaster ride on the marble. There were no shoes on his feet to describe; thick calves and thick ankles led to chubby, short and hairy toes. That was the bottom half. As for the top, Harper's eyes took in a bristly head of reddish brown hair, a rubbery face with absolutely huge ears but, *most* arresting of all, were the pair of piercing purple eyes that looked at him with shock and anger all at once!

Suddenly, as both pairs of eyes settled on each other, creature and boy screamed their lungs out. The screams started off as short bursts of alarm and then became longer and longer. Harper's grew more intense, his mouth stretching to the very furthest possible extent, when he noted that the creature had grown somewhat and was now standing a good head and shoulders taller above the height of his hand!

Harper's scream gave way to a yelp as the creature bit his hand to escape its loose barricade. The creature retreated gingerly to the fireplace with as much speed as could be got up when walking backwards. The creature splattered the air with admonishments, shaking a tiny clenched fist at Harper; "*miiiiiiiscreant, viiiiiiiolent one, foul, wiiiiiicked creature - ought to be ashamed, should be hanging your head in ignominy, NOT staring*'. Harper finally let his big eyes blink as he saw the creature disappearing into the grate and up the chimney breast.

As if that was not enough to make a boy faint clean off, Harper then heard something else. It was not particularly loud but it was very near; too near.

He shook his head forcefully in an attempt to clear it and then he trod cautiously to the middle of the room. Suddenly there were more sounds, quiet, but definite.

Harper heard whistling. He was too young to recognise the tune of 'The Great Escape'. He turned around slowly. The whistling was now joined with a clunking sound and small particles of debris falling to the floor.

Harper stepped towards the fireplace and scrambled to his knees faster than he could say his surname - 'Hepplesthwaite'. Then, being the intrepid character that he was, he stuck his head into the fireplace as far as it would go, looking up into the dark recess of the chimney breast.

Harper pulled his head back out and took a sharp intake of breath. The colour drained from his face, leaving the freckles that decorated his nose and cheeks to show off their colour without the usual competition from the flush in his cheeks. He knelt stock-still and barely breathed. His eyes darted warily to the fireplace because *that* was where the noise was coming from. What looked like a tiny man with a huge head was half holding and half pulling a table that must have been more than five times his size from the chimney breast. He then lifted it over the logs and grate of the fireplace and, having slid from the last rung of the grate, pulled the table away from the fireplace, and set it on the hearth.

His head was broad and round at the top and his forehead was a series of deep folds that gave way to grey bushy eyebrows. Unaware of Harper's presence, or at least seemingly unaware, the stocky little creature continued whistling as he set the table on its feet, dragged it a few inches this way and a half inch in that way, until he was content that it was neatly in just the right place. He clapped his hands with satisfaction as he walked this way and that and finally came to stand with his hands on his hips. Harper noticed that his bottom was *huge* - like a misshapen peach. So huge in fact that it made his mustard coloured trousers hang short so that the pink socks he wore could be seen, just shy of his ankles.

Then more rustling in the fireplace. A tiny creature with huge hands followed next carrying books in both hands and under both arms. Then one tiny creature followed another, both bearing tiny chairs. These characters were less fastidious than the first and planted the chairs about the table, not particularly careful of their positioning. No sooner had they placed one chair, they walked back to the fireplace, scaled the grate and a short while later appeared with another chair in tow. Harper counted seven creatures - but he could have been wrong about that.

After about the seventh trip, Harper heard a voice ask from deep within the grate; "how many more chairs do we need?" Then a muscular creature appeared with two chairs; one tucked under each arm. He tripped nimbly from rung to rung and landed on the hearth with a heavy tread. This was Hercules (he had chosen the name for himself). "Well, ask yourself how many we have taken down and you'll find your answer," another shouted up a little testily, cupping his hands at his mouth to channel his voice. This was Grotshaw - a less than delightful character!

"We'll be needing five more, and the bench of course," another creature shouted back more helpfully.

Harper was just about to catch his breath and his fists were nearly at his eyes to rub them to make sure he was not just imagining things, when he noticed *even more.* Harper noticed that once the furniture *and creatures* emerged from the grate they grew a few inches, just like the creature he had stumbled upon earlier.

He was taking all of this in when he heard three short dry coughs coming from the chimney-breast.

Suddenly, the whistling and jostling stopped. The creatures picked up a-pace as they set about their work and the chairs were promptly settled tidily around the rather grand wooden table.

A creature, as flat, narrow and straight as a ruler emerged from the fireplace in a pristine black suit, crisp white shirt and a black tie. He was responsible for the dry cough. He had extremely long narrow feet and a narrow face. His dark hair was parted just oblique of the centre of his forehead and clung closely to his scalp. His nose was a long, perfect ninety degree angle, and his lips were razor thin. He descended the fireplace with admirable grace and his nose in the air. His thin chest was puffed out and his long feet were poised at right angles to each other. He looked about what had taken shape as a miniature room within a room, without saying a word, or even acknowledging any of the busy workers still bustling under what they knew was his keenly observant eye. He rubbed the thumb and forefinger of his right hand together as he surveyed the room, whether as an aid to his concentration, or to rub away some imaginary grime - the watching workers were left to fathom. After strutting about the room, he walked away and disappeared into the chimney breast. This self-important creature was called, Pinikerty.

Shortly after, Hercules disappeared and returned with a small square table under one arm and a chair under the other. The chair was solid wood with emerald green upholstery on both the high rounded head of the chair, and its broad seat. He disappeared again and returned with what appeared to be a podium. He stood this up and the others rallied to position it at the very centre of the hearth. The two responsible for bringing the chairs then disappeared off and returned with a magnificent item of furniture and the largest chair of the set. It had an ornate gold surround at its head which was upholstered in a pillar box red with emerald green and gold figures. Gold tassels hung from the seat.

The podium and bench were arranged with plenty of shifting and shoving until they were just so. Finally, a very thin and wiry creature appeared carrying what seemed to be a gavel and a sound block. Both items must have been four times his size but he carried them as if they were a matchstick and a box, and placed them on the podium.

Then all of the creatures filed off onto the hearth ready to climb the grate, the one with the huge bottom bringing up the rear.

"What on earth...?" Harper thought. He did not have time to think anything else ... he fainted off. It was simply all too much for him to take in.

What he did not know (and would never know) was that even more odd things happened while he was out for the count. Had he stayed lively, he would have had a warning that these strange creatures had just set up a court-room ready for a criminal trial - but he would soon find out when he came to!

When Harper slumped to the floor, the grate in the fireplace trembled and the small dust and coal particles created quite a cloud for the creatures. The creatures coughed and spluttered, one more than all of the others. They looked over their shoulders to see what was responsible for the terrifying noise. There they saw Harper laid out on the floor as still as ever. "*Oh goodness he's dead, he's dead,*" Hobnails wailed, throwing his head back and holding on to the grate as if his life was in peril. "*You didn't know 'im,*" piped a creature called Skulkins, challenging the sincerity of Hobnail's lament. He then turned to his companion and repeated the sentiment: "*he didn't know him ... s'not as if he knew him,*" and a general rumble of comments and questions followed. "Stop the racket," Hercules ordered. "*Stop the racket at once, there's nowt wrong with the lad; he'll come to soon enough. These 'umans 'blot-out' sometimes - no sense or reason to it. They just - 'blot-out'. I've seen it before, many a-time in fact"* he said with unbridled pride.

"*Ar, blot out*!" ghoulish Grotshaw mumbled as if the idea was delicious - well it was delicious to him. He would not be surprised if there was some *blood* about - the thump had been a very loud one! "*Permanent is it?*" He asked, "*What?*" Hercules asked Grotshaw. "*The blot-out*,"' he said as he poked at Sculkin's shoulder with his knobbly forefinger, edging him out of his line of vision. "*Not necessarily*," Hercules answered.

"*Blot-out*," Prattles repeated with a knowing tone and a toothy grin but he had no clue what it really meant. Prattles' teeth were spectacularly big. They were so big in fact that his lips politely stood back allowing the teeth to overhang their boundary and touch his chin!

Hercules climbed down the grate as casually as you like and grew *smaller* as he did so. Then he climbed on to Harper's chest using his jumper as a strong-hold. He travelled from Harper's chest to his chin, for what seemed an age to the more nervous of the creatures observing from the hearth.

"*I'll swear on oath that he's dead,*" Hobnails offered, breaking into the silence suddenly and loudly. Hercules was so stunned by Hobnails' sudden outburst that he lost his grip, just as his right foot was mid-air, ready to land on Harper's chin. Hobnails continued oblivious to the peril he had caused: "*But if he's not, he'll dash you to pieces when his 'blot-off' comes to an end. Leave him alone and let's get out of here - I warn you*'.

After a lot of struggling, straining, damning of Hobnails and re-climbing, the danger was over... well the danger of Hercules falling at least. With both hands firmly gripping Harper's lower lip, Hercules continued his journey from Harper's chin, to his philtrum. When he got there, he placed his hands on his hips, bent so that he was level with Harper's nostrils and looked inside. As if surveying a drain-pipe, he looked inside as deeply as he could from the outside and gave a report to his fellows, calling over his shoulder:

"*He's certainly alive.*"

Sculkins crept away with suspicious disgust. How could Hercules work that out, just from looking into the human's nose!

"A *bit of a blockage, a little bit cold,*" Hercules said - now resting a hand on the tip of Harper's nose. "*Take about twelve of us to sit him up, just a few more minutes for him to come to ...*"

Sculkins was *really* sceptical now but he did not care enough to challenge Hercules.

"Oh *no, noooooo, no, noooo, no, no,*" - there was a general rumble of agreement amongst the creatures that they should not even venture too near, let alone get involved with rousing the human. Who knows what he would do, fresh from a blot-out? Sculkins led the mini - and very short-lived - rebellion. Hercules did not insist.

"A*ny bluuud?*" Grotshaw interrupted testily, wondering why they were given the bothersome, boring details rather than juicy ones.

"*No blood,*" Hercules reported patiently, dusting off his hands and starting the sojourn off Harper's chest, over to the hearth and up the grate.

Grotshaw huffed and tutted – "*waste of time*" he thought and lead the tiny troop back into the fireplace and beyond to who knows where, mumbling and grumbling as he went.

Harper had now met *some* of the Wighorns of number two Pear Tree Lane; well they were now acquainted with him at least!

It was all very well to have fainted off, but time waits for no man and it certainly did not wait for the boy Harper to come round though he did within seconds of the Wighorns disappearing into the fireplace.

The weird happenings were by no means over though; they had only just begun...

Chapter Nine

Harper Hepplesthwaite: A gathering in his name

Harper was about to find out that the attic room was now a courtroom. The Wighorns, for that is the name of the creatures, were gathering to hold a trial. Here they were; lawyers, twelve members of a jury, a Judge and all! They made it their business to ensure that any human child that circumstance put in their path stayed on the right side of their most important rule book: **"The Code of The Right and The Good and Miscellaneous Breaches Thereof"**.

They would not tolerate naughtiness and mischief.

A total of eighteen Wighorns filled the room, well nineteen to be precise - all at the rightful time, not all at once.

First one Wighorn and then a second, placing two in the room at the same time.

The first one traipsed down the grate with untidy foppish light brown hair parted down the middle. He wore a flimsy long black cloak about drooping shoulders which *nearly* hid dusty black shoes that wanted polishing but did not know how to ask. He stood at the grate as if manning a door. The outer corners of his eyes dipped to touch the tops of his cheeks, giving him a look of perpetual tiredness. This was Crouchlow, the Court Usher, and so responsible for marshalling everyone into the court-room. Crouchlow's colleagues called him 'Lightning' on account that he would never set the world ablaze with his sharpness. *No one* knew that he used this reputation to his advantage. Well *no one* except the Court Stenographer who was the second to make an entrance. Crouchlow would sometimes 'lose' the court papers of parties that he did not like on account of their lawyers being unreasonably proud and obnoxious...

The stenographer's job was to type every single word that was said in the Court. He hovered for a few moments. He was young and his eyes were extremely small and darting, taking in everything at an extraordinary pace. His eyes appeared even more tiny because of the full-moon roundness of his face. He shuffled the batch of papers in his hands before setting them in order on a table. He then retreated to a very small table beside the podium which had an old-fashioned machine called a typewriter on it. *This* was Earall-Seeall. His name was shortened and tidied to 'Cyril'.

Then entered another two.

As they entered the room, Harper heard music again. He did not recognize it as The Dance of the Knights, but it put him in fear of an outbreak of war or battle at any minute. One entered the scene on foot, the other with aplomb in nothing less than Harper's miniature red Bentley!

Both placed themselves at opposite ends of the very long table at the front of the chamber. They occasionally looked at the other in the most pleasant manner possible when scowling. When they were not looking at each other, they gave a surreptitious look at the papers the other had placed on the table before them with a breezy confident air. Both were dressed in suits but one was certainly more dapper than the other and seemed to be very, very aware of it. He who had arrived in the red Bentley was like a peacock strutting about the small space between the centre and right hand corner of the table he shared with the other gentleman. Wherever he walked, both his bulbous nose and tummy went ahead of him, almost as if to introduce themselves first. He looked as if his face were made up of too much fabric; too much fabric and too thick a fabric. He suddenly turned to look squarely at the other gentleman, draping his thumb casually in the loop of the watch and chain that hung from his pocket.

"Domble-bluff - you've heard the name."

The other gentleman, unsure of whether this was a question to be answered, or a statement to be accepted, put out a limp hand with extraordinarily chubby sausage-like fingers, even though his body was very thin. He gave his name as Pryson. Pryson cut off any further conversation by leaning deeply into his well-worn briefcase and bringing out a multitude of books and papers; his fat fingers enveloping all but the largest papers. The last extraction which was a heavy thick book, he planted on the table with a bang and a flourish. In reply,

Domble-bluff walked around the table and cleared his throat loudly just as he passed behind Pryson. Pryson made a point of not jumping. Domble-bluff then pulled an equally heavy and thick book from his briefcase placing it quietly and casually to the far side of the rest of his papers as if he may not bother to look at it at all.

So there were four Wighorns in the room together.

Domble-bluff and Pryson were lawyers. Domble-bluff would represent his client and Pryson would represent his.

Then twelve Wighorns came out from the fireplace and one by one took a seat in one of the twelve chairs. Accompanying the twelve was music that warned Harper of an imminent and certain doom. It was horrendous but, again, Harper did not recognise it as the aptly named: 'The Approaching Menace'.

The twelve were the members of the jury – the jurors. So twelve assembled together and there were then sixteen Wighorns in the room at the same time.

Then ruler-straight Pinikerty entered the room again, impeccably smart in his black suit with tail and white shirt. Pinikerty was the Court Clerk. He cleared a dry throat and as he moved about with deliberate and precise movements, reminded Harper of a stick insect, or the mosquito fly that Daddy had once told him about. He gave a brief tidy nod to Domble-bluff and Pryson.

Not one of them seemed to acknowledge the fact that Harper was in the room; not by speaking to him and not by looking at him!

Then the sound of a quick blast of a trumpet, followed by a deadly silence, as the last Wighorn descended the grate, with a slow and heavy tread. He was wearing a strange wig and flowing gown. Pinikerty cleared a dry throat and in a clipped nasal tone called out: "*All rise.*"

All Wighorns present stood to attention. This was no less than the Judge after all!

Unfortunately, the bundle of papers that Crouchlow held refused to be orderly and so they promptly fell from his hands. He bent to pick them up as quickly as he could. He stood and looked as hapless as possible his droopy eyes working a wonder in that effort, and so Pinikerty soon turned his frosty and disappointed gaze off him.

Judge walked with measured and authoritative steps over the hearth, finally taking his place in the high chair, at the podium.

So there were eighteen Wighorns in the room and Harper, of course.

This was an odd courtroom and, all in Great-Aunt's attic room at number two Pear Tree Lane! Here assembled were:

Crouchlow - Court Usher;

Earall-Seeal - Court Stenographer;

Pinikerty - the Court Clerk;

Twelve Jurors;

Domble-bluff - the lawyer representing a person not yet identified;

Pryson - the lawyer representing The Right and The Good; and

The Judge.

With all of these odd creatures already accounted for, there was no one in the room to actually stand trial and judgment ... was there?

"*Sit down, sit down,*" Judge said slowly with a deep rich voice. Everyone obeyed him of course... except Harper.

"Pinikerty," Judge said commandingly.

Pinikerty sprung to his feet.

"My Lord, case number 1020 - The Right and The Good against Harper Hepplesthwaite."

Earall-Seeall's hands flew across the keyboard of the antiquated typewriter machine, slamming the barrel back into its place after each complete line of typed words, while his busy tiny eyes roamed the faces of those speaking - and even the silent. Suddenly, *all* eyes and faces bent on Harper!

Judge spoke again; "Who is here for The Right and The Good?" Pryson leaped from his chair and bowed, "Mr Pryson, Lockaway Chambers my Lord?" He sat again.

"And for Harper Hepplesthwaite, the accused?" Judge asked.

Mr Domble-bluff rose quickly and immediately regretted his speed as his stomach bounced against the table: "Mr Domble-bluff, Freeham Mansions, M'Lud." He answered and then sat slowly.

"*Harper Hepplesthwaite - stand*" Pinikerty ordered.

As if he had been in a stupor, Harper suddenly came to. They were all gathered because of him! He stood bolt upright - but not in obedience to Pinikerty! He pushed past the open wooden enclosure that was erected around him (when - he did not know) and charged to the door as fast as his legs could manage. For the first time, he really did not appreciate the room's generous size. He reached for the door handle but it slid from his grasp and the door slammed shut. It was not the wind that shut it though. No, it was all so much more peculiar than that and so tug and pull as he might, Harper *could not* open the door!

Domble-bluff tried to contain his embarrassment and alarm. What sort of client was this? A first class miscreant! Trying to escape the courtroom - well this was a first!

Judge warned him: "*Take your client in hand Domble-bluff - Domble-bluff take your client in hand.*"

There was an uproar, the jurors loudly whispering that "*it was an outrage*", "*did not bode well*", "*not respectful to the Court*" and other such unhelpful observations.

"*Order in my Court,*" Judge commanded, hammering away at the sound block with his gavel. Immediately the Court fell silent.

"*MILLICENT!*" Harper suddenly yelled. It dawned on him that there was a source of help, a sure rescue. Great-Aunt would be home by now - maybe listening to classical music that was playing too loudly but she was home - and she was tough!

A few seconds passed and Harper heard nothing. He had silenced the court but that was all. "*MILLICENT!*" he shouted again, feeling less confident of imminent rescue. He realised that he had little hope of help because, even if Great-Aunt did hear him, she would count it a terrible impertinence to be called by her first name and never respond. He had no idea why he did not call out, "Great-Aunt" and he was even more confounded as to why he found himself unable to protest any further.

Judge turned to him and said, "*Keep order in my Court, or you will be taken down. You will be taken down if you do not keep in order in my Court.*" Under the force of Judge's glare, Harper traced his steps back into the dock, for that is what the wooden enclosure was!

Harper fell silent and waited for his fate. Judge struck the gavel once more. Fidgeting and elbowing by the thinnest of the twelve 'good' Wighorns continued as they settled down into order.

At that Pinikerty, extended his right hand and the ever so humble Crouchlow placed a scroll into it. He then bowed to Judge and backed away with great timidity until he had passed the corner square of the hearth and promptly stood still. Once he was out of sight and interest, Crouchlow mumbled dark, horrible things and wishes at both of the lawyers. 'Fat ignorant' he called one and 'ghastly scarecrow' he called the other; "may you both lose your case."

Pinikerty cleared his exceedingly dry throat, as a substitute for the drum roll he believed he deserved. Then with great ceremony, he opened the scroll which had written in large handsome handwriting in bold inky black: The Right and The Good -vs.- Harper Hepplesthwaite.

Pinikerty read from the scroll: "*The complaints against the human boy, My Lord.*"

Pinikerty checked that his rimless glasses were perfectly poised and then cleared his throat thriftily. He lifted his chin into the air and held the scroll delicately between the finger and thumb of both hands. He started to read and, as he read, the list and the scroll grew longer and longer.

"*The accused, Harper Hepplesthwaite is here to answer to the following most serious complaints made by The Right and The Good...*"

Harper's big eyes took in 'The Right and The Good' but he was too astonished to scoff.

"1. On the 30 November, the boy while at play in the garden at number two Pear Tree Lane, beset an insect with the most cruel games and finally tortured it by plucking orf it's legs one by one;

2. On the 27 November, the boy hurled a missile at a fox while it traipsed about its business;

3. On the 25 November the boy hid his class-mate's home-work book in the broom cupboard;

4. On the 30 November, the boy tied his legs to his school chair using his shoe laces;

Complaints 3 and 4 were done with the *full knowledge* that they would cause terrible trouble..."

Domble-bluff half stood and Judge turned his eyes on him... slowly of course. No-one apart from Pinikerty was allowed to stand and talk in Judge's court unless Judge gave permission and so Pinikerty looked very, very put out by this interruption. He hoped that Judge would beat Domble-bluff back into his seat (verbally of course) but Judge did not and so all Pinikerty could do was cast a withering look in the general vicinity of Domble-bluff.

"What is it Domble-bluff?" Judge stormed.

"My Lord, my decision to interrupt is not a decision lightly taken..."

"G*et* on with it Domble-bluff," Judge said.

Domble-bluff continued, "My Lord, the complaints against the boy are not being read in the order in which they occurred and this might disadvantage him. Further, the last two charges mention the boy's *intention* which *none* of us will *know* before the evidence is heard."

Judge frowned. The frown was the best and clearest invitation he was prepared to offer Domble-Bluff to try a better explanation for the interruption.

"My problem is with the words *'full knowledge',*" Domble-bluff said to clarify.

"What do you say to that Pryson?" Judge asked Pryson, slowly turning towards him and resting his hand under his chin as he waited for an answer.

Judge allowed Pryson to give his opinion on anything that Domble-bluff said and vice versa.

Pryson leapt to his feet, nearly upsetting the glass of water at his elbow. "My Lord, my learned friend's concern is unnecessary, and rather *curious,*" Pryson sat again.

"Well, *that's* your answer is it?" Judge asked, unimpressed with Pryson's answer -"curious *how?*"

Pryson jumped to his feet again: "My Lord, all possible complaints are listed in *The Code of The Right and The Good and Miscellaneous Breaches Thereof*. In the Code, complaints are not listed in order or categories of seriousness and so it does not matter if we do the same."

Judge did not care much for Pryson's answer but he gave a decision himself to move things along: "*Point one: It's for you, Domble-bluff, to defend the boy to the best of your ability. Point two: The order in which the complaints are read should not matter at all.*" Domble-bluff threw a sly scowl at his learned friend Pryson.

Before Pinikerty could resume the reading of the complaints, there was a noisy free-for-all from the jurors...

"M'lud, *excuse me, I appreciate that my interruption is highly irregular but how is the boy to remember all of these complaints ...?*" This question was from juror Ponderton, a solidly built Wighorn with rotund limbs, rotund tummy and rotund head. He had big red cheeks and his forefingers were very, very long. He pointed with his right forefinger at the note-book he had in front of him where he was writing down the complaints read out by Pinikerty.

"*Well, he can't escape justice 'cos he forgets his WICKEDNESS. What devilry would he get up to if he thought a loss of memory would save 'im? He's just got to keep up ... simple.*" This interruption was from juror Whizzle-grump. He was a waspish fellow; short and thin, with a very long crescent-moon shaped chin.

"*His wickedness...? We've not reached a verdict yet have we?*" Juror Weyall said, looking about him as if he may have fallen asleep, or bumped his head when the complaints were read, the evidence heard, considered and decided upon. Weyall had a huge forehead that looked like a cauliflower. Curly white hair sprouted around his head but wanted nothing to do with the front or middle of it.

"*Aaarrggghhhhh,*" Whizzle-grump grimaced, throwing down his pen and raising his head and eyes to the ceiling in despair. He could not cope with all the do-goodery coming from the opposite end of the grand table of twelve. Whizzle-grump looked to juror Snappernash for support but found him in an angry trance, grinding his teeth and nails at Harper. He elbowed him in the ribs with his thin pointed elbow but did not wait to see if the dig in the ribs had worked. He was too *furious.*

Whizzle-grump turned to juror Knapsley instead. Knapsley had been dosing-off but responded more quickly to a painful poke on the shoulder. He would do Whizzle-grump's bidding, no matter what it was, especially if there was a promise of a pork-pie for his trouble. Knapsley came to and Whizzle-grump leaned towards his perfectly round face. Knapsley was as thin as a locust but his face was as round as a ball. As Whizzle-grump whispered into his ear, his crescent-moon chin curved under Knapsley's round chin and his pincer-like nose looked as if it would pierce Knapsley's plump cheek but it did not - it just bent and leaned against it instead. Meanwhile the other jurors were busy having their say.

"*He is just a boy. That's what I want to emphasise - a mere boy and he can't be expected to keep up with all this, or to understand your windy explanations. Pinikerty - siiiiiiiim-plify it man!*" Weyall insisted. Ponderton nodded vigorously and rapped the table with his knuckles until a look from Judge silenced him.

Alas, Pinikerty would not and could not simplify it. He rattled on:

"*Complaint 12: on the 12 November, the boy did make a rude remark to a friend and neighbour of his Great-Aunt and did kick a stone after her heels.*"

Pinikerty disappeared into a wonderful world of words and refused to be brought out of it. He loved the sound of his own voice and the particular way that he rolled the letter 'r'. Being in Court helped him to indulge himself.

Harper was breathless with shock and convinced that he was dreaming. He stood looking aghast at Pinikerty and, as for the two 'learned friends' - well!

"*My Lord, the accused will give an answer to each single complaint one at a time in accordance with rule 4, subsection 3 of schedule 1 of the Code,*" Pinikerty said with a frosty glare at Ponderton.

Pinikerty read on - and on - and on. In fact, the scroll full of complaints was longer than he was tall. It extended to the floor and fell in folds and folds around his feet. Halfway through the reading of the complaints, he removed his glasses from his nose and let them rest on the waistcoat and tailed jacket.

Chapter Ten

Harper Hepplesthwaite: Rough justice

All of the jurors seemed particularly troubled by the complaints about Harper's treatment of the spider and fox.

Pinikerty started up again: "*Complaint one, that on the 30 November, the boy did ...*"

He was interrupted by Whizzle-grump who leaned to the very edge of his seat and growled: "*We've got a brain between us. We can remember the complaints against the boy. Why don't we join the first two together. They are more or less the same and can be dealt with sharpish. Good men of the Jury what do we say?*" Whizzle-grump looked along the table at his peers as if reading the mood but he was *not:* "*Off with his nails I say*," he shrieked, "*and hurl a rock at his head while we're at it - that'll deal with the first two matters. I warrant he won't go about pulling off spiders' legs or go a-throwing things at foxes again!*"

Having said his piece, he brushed his papery dry hands together as if dusting them off the matter and flung his body back in his chair. There was loud mumbling amongst the jurors.

With a long 'hhhhrrrrraaammmmpphhhh', having been so patient with the jurors, Judge spoke into the noise silencing it: "*We have not heard the case against Harper Hepplesthwaite yet, let alone the defence so how can we sentence him? Pryson, bring your evidence. After that, you are to call your witness Domble-bluff.*"

Harper was asked questions by Pryson and Domble-bluff.

Pryson was determined to show that Harper was guilty and that he knew he was doing wrong at the time. Domble-bluff was determined to dazzle the court with his magnificence and defending Harper had to be a part of that. He asked Harper questions so that he could explain that he had not done what he was being accused of at all, or if he had, that he did not know it was wrong and that he was very, very sorry indeed. *However*, Harper felt condemned by the questions of both lawyers. Worse still, what Domble-bluff thought were looks of encouragment looked like angry grimaces to Harper and so Harper said nothing to everything.

Domble-bluff became more and more red in the face and his eyes less and less kindly in their expression to Harper. The impression of a smile that creased his face but never reached his eyes stopped altogether too. At one point he was practically barking at Harper. It seemed Harper was doomed!

Domble-bluff summarised his defence of Harper, explaining why he should be found 'not guilty' of any of the complaints. As he gave his summary, Domble-bluff suddenly produced eye-glasses. He looked *under* them at the list of complaints on the table in front of him, *over* them at the jury, *through* them at Judge, *took them off* to look at Harper and let them hang importantly on his broad chest when he looked at Pryson.

He used a lot of flowery language and gestured elaborately with his right hand as he spoke. He started the short patrol from his side of the table to the centre of it but Judge soon put a stop to that with a wave of his fore-finger. It was amazing what Judge cottoned on to, for someone who looked as if he were fast asleep!

Then Pryson summarised the case against Harper, on and on he went about how serious all of the complaints were, how true they were, how Harper himself did not deny that they were true. He did his best to create scary visions in their minds of what Harper would do in one year, two years, three years' time if he was pelting innocent creatures and pulling off their legs *now*. Last of all he pointed out that it was clear that Harper *had known* that what he had done was wrong and was not even *remotely* sorry.

All that remained was for the Jury to make a decision – was Harper guilty or not guilty? If they found him guilty, he would need to be sentenced. If he was found innocent, he would be allowed to go free.

"A question that we've not answered is - *how did he know*" Weyall said.

"*What?*" Whizzle-grump shrieked, propelling his body to the edge of his seat again, so that he could see Weyall clearly. See if he had gone clean *mad*.

"*What?*" Whizzle-grump repeated.

Weyall explained: "*How did he know? How did Harper Hepplesthwaite know that what he did was wrong? Do we know the boy knew that he was doing wrong?* No, *no, no I tell you. So how can we bring any complaint at all - that's what I want to know - tell me that if you know*"! Weyall was really earnest as his very red cheeks testified. He would not let Whizzle-grump sweep away his concerns.

Ponderton piped in again. He was now getting quite exercised about the whole thing and took of his glasses, holding them in his right hand. His eyes were huge, grey and glassy - all the better to pore over lots and lots of rules with! With the glasses on, his eyes shrivelled to tiny pin-pricks; but here he was with the glasses off: "Surely *all of that* is only relevant to the punishment that should be given, *if* we find the boy guilty. It is not relevant to whether or not the complaints are true." His big eyeballs took in Pryson, Domble-bluff and Weyall as he said this.

Temperton who was sitting beside Weyall asked, "Does any of it *matter terribly* - is what the boy did SO wrong?" With that, he sat back waiting for the others to see his point and agree. His extremely long and plump chin nestled and relaxed on his chest.

"Oh *we have wrong by degrees now do we? Last time I looked at our law, wrong was wrong, was wrong - there was* *no 'wrong', and 'so' wrong - just your plain bad WRRRRRR-ROooooo*NG!" Whizzle-grump frothed.

Snappernash really got a dig in the ribs now! "*Uuuuuoooooohhhhhh!*" he exclaimed when Whizzle-grump's elbow hit its spot. Whizzle-grump leaned over to him to bring him up to speed with events. He whipped through what had happened so far.

While Snappernash's brain warmed, he cast his eye over the note Whizzle-grump had made of the charges. As he read, he clenched and unclenched his fists. He became very irritable and angry. His wild parker-straight black hair stood on end, a low rasping sound rose in his throat and he ground his teeth. He *despised* indiscipline in humans.

"The boy should be turned loose, even if these complaints are true ..." Juror Temperton started to say.

"*Off with his nails*!" Whizzle-grump shrieked for the benefit of the Court:

Temperton continued calmly "... even if these complaints are true, the boy should not be punished, he should be *taught* a better way."

That was enough for Snappernash, he had heard enough, ENOUGH!

Thin and wiry as he was, he clambered off his chair and over to Temperton. He grabbed Temperton's face, threw his head back and then prised his mouth open, using his two strong hands as a clamp to keep it so. Then he reached inside Temperton's mouth with his nose, to the wide open throat and then popped it out again to ask Temperton with a shriek, "Are you sober, or have you been at strong drink?"

"D'you want me to check the breath of the others in like manner?" Knapsley asked Whizzle-grump, obligingly. "*Of course not, we're in a Court of Law,"* Whizzle-grump hissed. *"No! Show some respect for his Lord-ship'.* To make sure Knapsley appreciated how poorly thought of his suggestion was, Whizzle-grump delivered him an eye-watering pinch. Oddly enough, Knapsley cast a deadly glare, not at Whizzle-grump the pincher, but at Snappernash who had shown himself quite the pioneer, venturing into Temperton's mouth and throat as he had.

Once his mouth and head were released, Temperton turned to Snappernash and with great calm and patience said, "Do not repeat that impertinence again." Snappernash scowled at him - he did not care for his softness or his threats. They were all one and the same to him; nonsense.

With forceful points made by Weyall, Temperton, and Ponderton, Harper was found not guilty.

With a very slow and deliberate manner, Judge turned to Harper and said; "Cruelty to innocent and defenceless creatures is wrong. You know that now so do not do any such thing again. Harper Hepplesthwaite, you are therefore free to leave this Court".

Down came Judge's gavel.

"All rise," Pinikerty said and all stood. Judge left the Court room as slowly as he had entered it.

Domble-bluff smiled at Harper like a smug Cheshire cat and a sly fox rolled into one. Then the smile disappeared as quickly as it had appeared as he turned to Pryson. Pryson was shuffling his papers together and throwing them roughly into his briefcase. "*You did not lose because of a lack of effort my friend...*" Domble-bluff said with a kindly expression and soothing voice. "*You did not win because I am a better adversary - good day to you.*" Then his rubbery face fell back into a smug smile; a smile which escaped his eyes.

Harper suddenly heard the sound of the room door swinging open on its hinges. The smell of freshly baked pear pie drifted in. Just this once, the delicious smell meant nothing to him. He dashed from the room as fast as he could and threw himself down the stairs as if his life depended on it.

When he caught his breath, he quietly decided that he would leave Eldersham and seek his fortune as an independent young man - it had worked for Dick Whittington and others.

He did not really eat. Rather, he pushed his tea around the plate. Even the pear crumble and clotted cream just about got the odd shove about the dish. Great-Aunt did not seem to say much - just that the trail of biscuit crumbs on the stairs explained his lack of appetite and that it was a tiresome nightmare to clear it all up.

Harper gave the occasional hard stare to Great-Aunt. His mind was nursing a grave suspicion that she knew about the Wighorns. Once he was released from the dining table, Harper took to bed. He pulled back the bed covers and threw himself into it, pulling the bed covers up and over his head. He lay there waiting for his breathing to settle which seemed to take forever. He suddenly threw the bed covers off and listened intently. There was a sealed fireplace in his room - the chimney breast was exposed in the brick-work. He was so very sure that he heard something, *those creatures* in *his* room, just behind or inside the chimney breast! It was awful. He threw the covers back over his head. He needed a clear head to plan his escape from number two Pear Tree Lane, Eldersham and the explanation he would give to Mother.

Mother could not have anticipated any of this when she banished him from home to the custody of Great-Aunt in the country. Daddy would be horrified and surely return from his wanderlust abroad to rescue him. "Egg-centric" Great-Aunt? They had no idea!

Harper had now met for the first time, the Wighorns of number two Pear Tree Lane.

He was no angel when he lived with Mother but he wondered how his life, so ordinary, had come to this ...!

Chapter Eleven

Harper Hepplesthwaite: Ten green-fingers

Despite his encounter with the Wighorns, Harper did not leave Eldersham after all. Spring found him at home at number two Pear Tree Lane.

He had gone home to Mother for the Christmas holidays. Sadly, Daddy had not been home but Harper spoke to him by telephone about all manner of both every-day and exciting things. Harper scowled at the telephone when Daddy told him tales about the *wonderful* children he was helping; he was the only *wonderful* child that Daddy knew - surely!

To compensate for his father's absence, Harper was allowed to spend time with Robin and this cheered them both no end. The condition was that they played *in* the house *and out* of Mother's way. Through a cloud of flour and bicarbonate of soda and with a paint-spattered pointing fore-finger, Mother laid out the terms and conditions of the visit.

They started well as always – making a maze of encyclopedias from which their competing toy soldiers had to escape.

Inevitably the play became less sedate and when Harper swung from a rope made of bed linen tied to a curtain rail, he kicked Robin in the eye with his heel. The curtain rail broke, Robin squealed and all that remained intact were Harper and the knot he had made in the make-shift rope. Mother promised that Robin would never cross the threshold of the house ever again. As Mother set out her promise, Harper contrived a plan to get Robin into the house when he was next home; he favoured the parlour window because the drop from window to floor was short. He was, therefore, able to respond to Mother's threat with the sweetest smile.

Great-Aunt was genuinely pleased to have Harper back after the Christmas holiday. The house had been quiet without him.

The noise soon resumed, especially when Matthew confronted Harper about his missing limited edition model ship. It had been months in the making but Harper blithely announced that he had given it to Robin as a Christmas gift! Matthew was outraged and Great-Aunt's lecture to Harper did not cool Matthew's fury.

However, anything could upset the delicate balance of their relationship. Harper did not like the fact that Matthew had his feet comfortably under the table at two Pear Tree Lane - and Matthew did not like sharing the attention which he had enjoyed exclusively before Harper's arrival. The reluctant gift incident caused a deep freeze in their relationship.

It was the first official day of Spring and time had sprung forward with the clocks being put forward. Birdsong woke Harper this bright morning - it was Saturday and so he was not disturbed by an alarm clock, or Great-Aunt.

By the time he had woken and had his typically brief spell with soap and water, Great-Aunt had made them both a sumptuous breakfast. The effort was lost on Harper. He loaded his fork with a lump of bread, scrambled eggs and smoked mackerel, as if the fork were a shovel and his mouth a wheel-barrow. Great-Aunt's patience expired after the first two mouthfuls.

"Are you in a race young man? If you are not rushing up and down the staircase, you are rushing your meal!"

"Wish I was Great-Aunt but I'm not."

"Well you are certainly eating much too quickly. You're barely chewing your food - don't you want to savour it?"

"It's the *newtrition* I'm after - some energy to keep me going while I help *you* with your *huge* garden, if you still want help with it that is?" With that, Harper again swallowed a heavily loaded fork of food without chewing it, closely followed with an almost desperate gulp of orange juice to help send it all down.

"Saaaavouring won't get the garden done Great-Aunt. The sooner I finish *this*, the sooner I can digest it all and have the *umph* to help. I think you said we were going out at lunchtime, so we should finish before noon - if we *both* hurry."

"Well, that's all very well, but you don't want unreasonably hard stools do you, and that's precisely what you will get if you bolt your food."

"*Arrrgghh!*" Harper exclaimed.

As if that thought was not sufficiently vile, she continued: “Matthew will be helping with the gardening as I have other business to tend to before tea. We have guests today – Laurie and Hilly Mainwaring.”

As usual, after breakfast Great-Aunt settled to read the newspapers. She always read at least two newspapers at the weekend; one local paper and one national newspaper. While Harper was still considering his response to the horrible announcement about Matthew, Great-Aunt rolled up one of the papers and passed it to him.

"Look through that while your stomach settles; it will help you get a good handle on your grammar and diction."

Harper was not remotely interested. What a rum morning for a boy, he thought. Reading boring papers and sweating over a great big garden all in the company of horrid Matthew and wasps that he could not even swat for fear of another ghastly encounter with the Wighorns!

"If it's all the same to you, I'd rather not read about murder and accidents straight after my breakfast ... well, at all really, seeing as I'm only a boy."

"I'm not asking you to read about murder and accidents Harper. It's a local paper about local news and events. We have not had a murder in Eldersham – *yet*! *I* have the paper filled with the stories of grisly murders and accidents." Great-Aunt said with deliberately irresponsible relish.

Accepting defeat, Harper flicked through the newspaper, turning each page noisily, not expecting to happen upon a story of interest. Well, he did not find one and so he turned to the classifieds and read every other word in a loud whisper so that Great-Aunt could make neither head nor tail of the advertisements he read, or concentrate on her own reading. Two-one to Harper!

Matthew appeared after another quarter of an hour, standing in the doorway beaming at Great-Aunt and looking freshly scrubbed, amiable and keen to get to work. "Here I am Miss. I'll fetch the tools and get cracking ... if that's ok with you of course?"

Harper felt bilious.

"Right-oh Matthew. Lovely to see you bright, early and ready to start. Your grandfather did the lion's share of the work in the back garden last week, so it's the front garden that I'd like you to weed please - especially the flower beds. Harper here will be helping you," Great-Aunt concluded breezily before she swept away.

Harper watched with his mouth agape as Matthew walked down the side of *his* house to *his* shed and back to the front garden with two pairs of gloves in his hands. He stood planted there near the front door and held a pair of gloves out to Harper.

Matthew was already driving Harper to distraction. He made Harper want to be *maddeningly* naughty.

Adopting a haughty gait, with shoulders pushed back, one hand draped casually in a pocket, head raised high and tilted backwards and so on (not unlike Domble-bluff in fact), Harper strolled past the flower beds which in a few weeks would be in full bloom with snow-drops, tulips, daisies, pink roses, begonias and the delicate cotton soft carnations but none of these softened his attitude. Not even the unwieldy thyme shrubs that brushed and tickled his ankles and shins softened him. It is fair to say that Harper's dimpled cheeks were the only soft thing about!

When he was a few yards away from Matthew, he stopped with both hands on his hips and with great condescension said, "We gotta start at the *front* of the garden - it's plain *stupid* to start at the back." Then he turned on his heels and started back up the garden.

To his surprise, Matthew followed the instruction like a lamb. Harper found it strange but with his pride like a train without brakes, he did not stop and wonder *why* it was that Matthew was playing the angel when there were no witnesses about.

"You start on that side and I'll start here," Harper said, in his stride now with the brusque patronage. Despite the broad path between them, the first few weeds Harper pulled were tossed so far out of his way that they just happened to land either on or around Matthew! Matthew bore it. In fact, after a few minutes he offered, "Do you want me to fetch a sack for all the weeds?" When Harper gave a grumpy reply that 'he jump to it', Matthew obliged. He took a fair while and Harper heard the tap running before Matthew returned. He positioned the sack between them but closer to Harper for his convenience.

"I've made up some water with plant food too." Matthew said. Harper was too busy contriving his next bossy instruction to notice Matthew blush. "I'll fetch the buckets when we're ready for them," Matthew offered after some minutes later.

"Good-oh," Harper said, struggling to keep up the hostilities.

The hostilities were made even more difficult to sustain when a bee started to buzz around and about the flower-beds that Harper was trying to weed. He tried to bat it away without too much force because the Wighorns sprang close to mind. His tolerance and brightly coloured t-shirt were misunderstood as invitations and the bee flew towards him, too close for comfort and buzzing too loudly. When it flew towards Harper's face without a hint of changing course, Harper fled down the garden yelling his lungs out!

He ran from the left to the right, his arms flaying about to ward off the bee without harming it, although it was clearly intent on harming him!

To his credit, Matthew only pointed and laughed for a *short* while. He soon fetched a small cloth from the shed, dampened it under the outdoor tap and, running after Harper, threw it over his head. The bee had long lost interest though - after all, there were the beginnings of buds elsewhere, vying for its attention. Matthew's bee-defeating tactic was absolutely useless of course but the gesture was golden and Harper calmed down.

After an awkward silence Harper spoke: "You know I didn't mean any harm giving away your ship. I am sorry but Robin *really is* top and she doesn't get nice presents. Her mother can't afford them - *even at Christmas.*

You really do need to get over it because by the time I go home again, it'll probably be broken - accidentally of course; so it's pointless us fighting about it."

"Uumm hhmmm!" Matthew mumbled still blushing but Harper did not notice or think anything amiss.

"But Great-Aunt won't see us if you *do* want to have a fight about it – clear the air once and for all and all that. That's how me and Robin always settle scores," Harper said with helpful enthusiasm, as he tugged and strained at the stubborn stalks of some weeds and dandelions. His face now very flushed but for a totally different reason to Matthew.

Matthew did not seem to want to fight and so Harper kept weeding and talking. He told Matthew all about Robin and the unfortunate incident with Judge Mowbray. Matthew did not say much but he roared when Harper regaled him with tales about his antics at school. Harper had no idea why Matthew found the anecdotes amusing!

Two hours flew by and, in that time, Harper had uprooted both plant and weed but the garden would hide his over-zealous efforts for a while. All that remained was watering.

"Right," Matthew said standing up and dusting his hands and knees of soil. "I've already filled the watering cans and *I'm* having the blue one with the long spout," he said bossily.

Harper's heckles rose and he declared that *he* was having the pick as it was *his* house and *his* garden. He stood to his feet too and Mathew seemed to try to step ahead of him to get to the buckets first - his elbows out to block Harper's path.

"I don't *think* so, do you?" Harper said as he barged past him.

Matthew relented with not much of a fight at all and Harper made for the blue bucket. He poured all of the content over his freshly weeded side of the front garden. Matthew poured the contents of the red bucket on his side of the garden, taking longer than Harper because of the shorter spout on the bucket.

When all was said and done - well done, Harper set about dismissing Matthew from the property:

"I'll fetch you a drink and then you'd better be off."

"Yes of course, if there's nothing else that you want me to do."

"No – that'll be all," Harper replied giving Matthew a hard and suspicious glare over the rim of his drinking glass. Tending *his* garden was a liberty enough!

Chapter Twelve

'Allo 'allo 'allo!

As a well-respected and local Artist, the Council Leader had commissioned a piece of art for the Town Hall. Great-Aunt was invited to a gathering with the Councillors and other local dignitaries to open a newly refurbished wing of the Town Hall, where the art was to be exhibited.

"Must I really come along?" Harper asked. "I could stay at home as usual."

"Yes, you must come. It'll be a pleasant trip - I'll be driving Mr Beauchamp's car. The one with the open roof – you will enjoy that. Wear something presentable please dear." Great-Aunt called after him as he bolted up the staircase.

Great-Aunt would arrive in style in Laurie's silver soft-topped MG. He had given her use of it for the day and she was thrilled.

After the hard work in the garden, Harper threw himself into the bathroom before changing his clothes. He may have had nothing more to do with the soap and water than wash his hands and scrub at his face while hanging his head under the tap for a few seconds but he did look fairly polished when he came down the stairs a short while later. He was wearing navy blue smart trousers and a blue jumper from under which the collar of a white shirt protruded. Before they left the house, he had taken off the jumper and held it in such a manner that rendered the pressing of it pointless. Nevertheless, he was dressed fit to meet any dignitary. He was not going to meet any in fact but Great-Aunt would wait to tell him as much en-route.

Harper came down the stairs and looked Great-Aunt up and down, just stopping short of walking around her as he made his silent assessment.

"You look very smart young man," Great-Aunt said. One of them had to break the silence after all!

"You look *exceedingly* smart Great-Aunt." Harper returned immediately, still staring."Is *Laurie* going to be there?"

"Mr Beauchamp, Harper," Great-Aunt corrected.

"No, he is not."

"*Well!*" Harper exclaimed. "So that strong smell of roses is just for my nose then?"

"It is not roses and it is not strong - but yes, it is *just* for your lovely little nose Harper."

"You've got tissues have you? Just in case I *vomit* in Laurie's car," Harper said stepping out of the front door, walking down the path towards the car and leaving Great-Aunt green-faced with alarm.

Laurie's car was in view just beyond the gate. It was magnificent and Harper was looking forward to the ride.

"This is exciting isn't it dear? It really is a cracking car."

Great-Aunt drove away from the house and down the lane towards the fork in the nearest trunk road. When she got to the junction, she made a right turn towards the Church to take the many small roads that led to the main road and out of the village.

Great-Aunt had given one hour and fifteen minutes for the one hour journey but a tractor and a small herd of cows on the road ahead of them slowed them. Great-Aunt fumed quietly, leaning out of the open window to see exactly what was going on. Harper was very relaxed about it all. He sat giving smug looks to his fellow road-users whom he was sure felt horribly cooped up in their closed-roof vehicles.

They were soon all out of the way and Great-Aunt stepped on the accelerator to make up for lost time.

"Yipeee!" Harper shouted as Great-Aunt sped down the winding road that stretched under the picturesque arches of Eldersham bridge. The wind blew his hair all about his face and tried to have a go at Great-Aunt's bun too - but with considerably less success. It had its way with the pretty scarf about her neck though.

"This is *great* isn't it dear? Laurie really must let us have use of this car more often!" Great-Aunt said as the countryside flew by. Harper agreed enthusiastically.

Alas, their enjoyment was curtailed by the short but loud demand of a police siren. A police officer indicated to Great-Aunt that she should pull over to the side of the road and stop immediately.

Being a law-abiding citizen, she did stop of course. She was mortified as she had never had an encounter with the law, well not on the wrong side of it anyway! Nevertheless, she was hopeful that they would be sent on their way after a brief lecture.

Harper turned around in his seat and watched a tall, bow-legged policeman walking towards the car. When he got to the car, he bent down and leaned on the open window on the driver's side.

"Good afternoon ma'am. Do you know why you've been stopped?"

Great-Aunt said nothing. What a silly question she thought.

PC Payne tried again: "Are you aware that you were driving *over* the legal speed limit?"

"No, I'm afraid I was not aware – no."

"What's the legal limit for this 'ere road ma'am, tell me that. Ma'am, what is the legal speed limit for this 'ere road?"

"Thirty miles per hour," Great-Aunt said. Harper could tell that she fuming as she was speaking through gritted teeth but her voice sounded very, very friendly and helpful.

"And what 'ave you got on your speed dial, what speed does it say you were driving at?" He said, leaning into the car and pointing at the speed dial. "So you understand why I had to stop you, seeing as you came tearing down the road at an illegal speed?" PC Payne persisted.

"I am very sorry officer, it will not happen again. Kindly remove your head from the car - it's not really big enough for both of our heads," Great-Aunt said, now quite flustered. "I have an appointment in Knoxham and I must not be late. Officer it will not happen again. Can I be on my way....?" Great-Aunt's polite rambling was cut short by PC Payne.

"On yer way?" Then PC Payne inhaled sharply through his teeth and stood to his full height. "It's not as simple as that madam. Do you know 'ow many miles *over* the limit you were madam?"

"Uuuummmm - let me think," Great-Aunt said. Her tone was suddenly very cold and clipped. "Let me think... uuuummm. The limit is thirty miles per hour..."

"Yes," PC Payne piped in.

"... and I was driving at forty miles per hour ... ," Great-Aunt continued.

"Corrrrect madam."

Harper's neck moved up and down like that of a lizard as he watched and listened to the conversation that to'd and fro'd between Great-Aunt and PC Payne - one head firmly in the car, the other now well out of it.

"Oh, I'm afraid you'll have to give me time to do the arithmetic officer." Great-Aunt was seething now!

"It won't pay to be *obstreperous* madam," PC Payne said, bouncing and rolling the word about in his mouth with some pride as if he had been waiting an age for an opportunity to use it.

"I beg your pardon?"

"*Obstreperous* madam! There is no need to be *obstreperous*."

"With due respect officer, this is a gross over-reaction. You have made your point, and I really should be allowed to be on my way."

"Ma'am, I'll ask you *once* to settle down, or I'm going to have to ask you to step *out and away* from the vehicle. *Ten* miles over the speed limit you were madam, a whole *ten* miles over."

By now, Harper had turned in his seat so that he was facing Great-Aunt and PC Payne full on. Then he docked an imaginary cap at PC Payne to show his respect, ... before his act of treachery!

"It's astonishing guv'nor," Harper said. Both adults turned to Harper in surprise. Harper continued pointing at Great-Aunt with his thumb: "You want to hear her letting me have it when I run up and down the stairs at 'ome. '*Harper, stop running, it's dangerous. It is not a race. How many times must I tell yoh - slow down immediately*'."

Harper said in the shrillest tone that he could manage. “Now here she is driving *TEN* miles faster than she should of - well I never!”

"Should *have*, should *have* Harper,” Great-Aunt said turning on Harper testily.

"... and not even *your* car Great-Aunt. Laurie won’t be very happy I bet,” Harper continued as if she had not spoken at all.

"Mr Beauchamp,” Great-Aunt snapped.

"What’s this ... not your car? Can I see your papers please madam?”

"No you can’t because, as the boy has said, it is not my car.....”

"Not your car,” PC Payne said whipping a little note book and pen from his pocket and making a note.

"... I do have the owner’s permission and I am included in the insurance. You can contact him to check - it’s a Lawrence Beauchamp of ...”

PC Payne interrupted. “Well, yes, with all due respect madam, I can’t take your word for it - *the rules* won’t allow it so I’ll need his full address and I’ll need you to produce the papers at the local police station tomorrow please.”

"Oh of course," she said - *the rules!* Great-Aunt was furious with PC Payne and herself - she knew she should not have been speeding; it was dangerous. She was not impressed with Harper either.

They eventually got away, and Great-Aunt announced to Harper (rather abruptly) that he would be staying with Hilda Mainwaring in a neighbouring village called Goldsbourne for the afternoon while she kept her appointment. Mrs Mainwaring would go back home with them for supper and so she would pick them up in another three to four hours. Harper pulled a face but Great-Aunt did not notice. "Let's just hope that your supper is not charred by the time we finally get back home after *that* delay!" Great-Aunt said as Harper got out of the car.

Mrs Mainwaring opened the door on the second knock and welcomed Harper in with a loud excitable voice. "Come on in, come on in, we shall have plenty of fun this afternoon." Then, addressing Great-Aunt, Mrs Mainwaring assured her, "You're not to worry dear. I'll look after him. Will he want feeding now? I have *just* cooled a batch of scones – no guest of Hilly's goes hungry." All this without a second glance at Great-Aunt, or a pause for an answer. She ushered Harper into the house and closed the door behind them.

Mrs Mainwaring continued her welcome of Harper as she bustled into the kitchen and started to smother locally made clotted cream and jam made by Great-Aunt onto seven scones.

"Thank you very much Miss," Harper said, "but I can't have all of those - I'm rather full actually."

"Nonsense dear, there's *always* room for a cream scone," she said, poking Harper's stomach playfully. "They're not all for *you* anyway," Mrs Mainwaring added more quietly.

Mrs Mainwaring set the scones on the dining table and, after handing Harper a glass of milk, she bustled about the kitchen making a pot of tea. She finally sat down and reached for a scone.

"Right young man. Tell me how you are settling into the delightful number two Pear Tree Lane."

Harper was polite and charming. He told stories about Hugo and Agatha and Mrs Mainwaring listened patiently, interrupting only occasionally with sonorous laughter. She sighed where adults would, tutted where they should, and reached for another scone. When he moved on to stories about Mr Burnsom, Mrs Mainwaring warmed to them and shared tales about her school days in boarding school. How she and a partner in crime had stolen onions from the pantry and sown them into the hem of their dormitory curtains on the last day of term before the *long* summer holidays. They left the teachers with a dreadfully smelly dormitory, as their skills of detection were not up to the girls' mischief and so they did not quickly identify the source of the smell. She had also glazed the tops of the wooden desks of her adversaries with honey or treacle while she was a trusted Class Prefect and planted a spider in a room-mate's pillow case which (by the morning) had marched on to and settled itself in the tidy parting in her hair.

Then, as if the story-telling was hard and thirsty work, Mrs Mainwaring made another cup of tea and sandwiches for two (and a half). Minutes later, she of course reached for another scone.

Harper was very impressed with Mrs Mainwaring. There and then, he made her a honorary child!

Great-Aunt arrived in the middle of the fun, looking pleased with herself. "Thank you so much Hilly, shall we leave..."

"Shall we *leave*? Dear, dear, no! Slow down and tell me all about it - come through, we are in here," she said pointing to the dining room. "Come on in and have a scone dear. I have just this minute put the kettle on."

Great-Aunt protested, "*Oh, I really cannot take on a scone now Hilly dear, I …*"

"*What's the point of life* if one cannot stop and enjoy a scone?" Mrs Mainwaring questioned, placing a hefty staying hand on Great-Aunt's fore-arm.

"Hilly, we will be having supper in another hour or so, I really cannot," Great-Aunt patted her slim stomach.

"Pause for a *grape* then dear. Surely you can manage one or two of *those*," she said firmly with a frown. Great-Aunt relented. Even she could not resist former Army Engineer Mainwaring!

Mrs Mainwaring bustled about and returned with a pretty glass bowl the size of a large human head, filled with plump purple and green grapes.

"Goodness me Hilly. This is *more* than a couple!"

"Oh hush dear and dig in. They are ab-so-lute-ly delicious *and* from you will not guess *where*!" Mrs Mainwaring ended in a lyrical tone.

"Oh – where?" Great-Aunt enquired.

"None other than the most garden-shy of fingers in the village - Brigitte Brockley. I have no idea how she did it, but she did.... or so she says and Mr Brockley attests to it, although he'd not dare do otherwise would he, hen-pecked soul that he is!"

Harper was captured by a vision of a grown man being pecked mercilessly by a hen. He wondered why Mr Brockley did not simply get rid of the pecking hen!

While Great-Aunt sampled the Brockley grapes and Mrs Mainwaring helped herself to another scone, Harper declared: "I wanna be a copper when I grow up. I'm gonna ... and that's tha'," he concluded pre-empting at least one objection from Great-Aunt.

"*Want* to, *going* to, tha_t_, Harper...," Great-Aunt corrected with irritation.

Then, as if he were not there, Great-Aunt launched into a complaint about his elocution. "He is unreasonably careless with his consonants and vowels Hilly, dropping them here, stretching and contracting them unreasonably there but, oddly enough, he speaks perfectly well a lot of the time. It is most frustrating." Great-Aunt gave Harper's unhelpful contribution to the police saga as another example, mimicking what he had said to PC Payne as best as she could.

Mrs Mainwaring gave Harper a conspiratorial wink. She found Great-Aunt's horror amusing but kept a straight face. "Harper is a *linguistic chameleon* Millicent dear, no, no, that's not it - uummm...' she considered looking out distractedly into the distance while rubbing her thumb and forefinger together. "...a linguistic *nomad*. That's it; a linguistic nomad!" Mrs Mainwaring was pleased with her evaluation and looked from face to face for approval before biting into yet another scone. "He wants those around him to feel comfortable and there is something quite *deliciously* hospitable about that I think," Mrs Mainwaring concluded with a reassuring smile at Harper.

Harper raised an eyebrow. She was not going to get her teeth into him; *delicious* or not! Great-Aunt did not react at all and Harper wondered why eating boys (which Hilly *clearly* intended to do) was more acceptable than supposedly not talking proper! Harper quickly leaned across the coffee table and handed Mrs Mainwaring the last scone - '*eat that and keep your eyes off me'* he thought, but all she saw was a sweet smile curving his chubby cheeks and a twinkle in his mischievous eyes!

"Oh my goodness! The slow-cooker has been on since this morning!" Great-Aunt suddenly exclaimed. "Hilly we *really* must go." They left more or less straight away. "We cannot have supper destroyed," Mrs Mainwaring said with concern as she pulled on her light coat.

Harper sat with the adults after supper. A tasty supper that was rounded off with poached pears.

Laurie and Mrs Mainwaring made an amusing team and unlike some of Mother's guests, they enjoyed Harper sitting with them and taking an active part in the conversation. There were very few codes or other indicators that the conversation was for adult ears only. In fact, once in a while (and particularly if Harper fell quiet), one of them would ask: '*what do you think about that young man?*' At one point, Mrs Mainwaring leaned forward and gave Great-Aunt's hand a pat: "You are doing an admirable job with the boy Millicent, an *admirable* job."

Of the four, Mrs Mainwaring did most of the talking and dispensed the most advice. Harper noticed Laurie and Great-Aunt exchange glances when Mrs Mainwaring was at her most talkative, blundering past their attempts to join in the conversation with determined verbal elbows.

Harper took advantage of the relaxed weekend atmosphere and, while the adults had cheese, biscuits and wine, he had milk. He also helped himself liberally to the contents of the biscuit tin during his trips between the kitchen and dining room as he had generously offered to help clear the dining table! Great-Aunt ignored the tell-tale signs of crumbs around his mouth and chest just this once.

For the first time that evening, when Harper re-entered the dining room from the kitchen, the adults fell into silence but Harper had heard the tail end of the conversation; "...Well-what-on-earth-has-happened-to-the-Hippocratic-oath?" Mrs Mainwaring was asking the ceiling incredulously. "It cannot be thrown off like an old *coat* - you *must* tell him that Millicent - *Sin Jun* must be *made* to remember."

"Doctor St John ..." Laurie said – "I haven't seen the old boy for an age ..."

"*Sin Jun,*" Mrs Mainwaring corrected. "St John is pronounced *Sin Jun.*"

Harper gave Mrs Mainwaring a conspiratorial wink and parked what he had heard in his memory for the time being at least. He would need to keep an eye out for this 'hypocrite' of a doctor!

Harper told them about Mr Mowbray and how he and Robin had been so scared and so sure that he had died as a result of their game, even going as far as drinking a toast to him.

Before he retired to bed, Harper made a final contribution to the conversation re-inventing history in his telling of the Great-Aunts run-in with the police officer. Great-Aunt cautioned him against shameless lies but he carried on, encouraged by the enthusiastic chuckles of Laurie and Hilly. He then retired to bed; it had been an eventful day and he had an early start the next day.

As members of the Boys Brigade, Harper and Hugo were due to take part in a special service at the village Church. Harper had failed to memorise the words of a recital and so he decided that he would conceal a tiny crib sheet in his palm or write the words directly on his palm.

The following morning, Harper presented himself for breakfast looking very smart in his Boy's Brigade uniform.

Great-Aunt bent to smell him as he sat to eat. Harper tried to hold his nose against the smell of the poached egg that Great-Aunt had for breakfast. He finally found that Great-Aunt was quite right - that he could choke or suffocate if he insisted on trying to eat at the same time as holding his nose. “You’ve got to hold your nose, *or* eat - you cannot do *both* safely dear,” she said.

When they were finally ready to leave the house, Harper squeezed his feet into his freshly polished shoes, avoiding the need to untie the laces first. After a short debate, they decided to walk to the Church rather than cycle. All was well for the few seconds that it took them to step out of the front door. Suddenly, Great-Aunt dropped her hand-bag and her hands flew to her mouth. Harper had no hand-bag to drop of course and so he just dropped his jaw – equally shocked. One whole side of the garden, the side that *he* had worked on, was a completely withered and ugly ruin.

"Harper, what on earth happened here yesterday? Were you *really* so unhappy about helping with the weeding? I really do wish you had said - instead of *this*. It’s years of work just ruined, *ruined!*”

"I didn’t do it - I mean I didn’t mean to do it...” Harper made a weak protest. One side, the side that Matthew had tended looked splendid and the contrast magnified the damage.

They walked to Church in silence. What Harper recalled of the recital diminished even further. It was a mitigated disaster, however, because he recited the lines that he remembered and extemporised through those that he did not. Unfortunately, this took the form of a jaunty limerick at high volume which he continued when his peers had stopped and so his voice alone rose to (and echoed in) the rafters for all to hear. Happily, the adult audience looked on the sea of cherubic boys with soft forgiving eyes, seeing all good, hearing all good - for the most part anyway. Harper caught the glance of one sour-faced curmudgeon who tutted and shook his head at Harper. '*Suffer* the children indeed' Harper thought!

Harper was glad when it was over. He wanted to solve the mystery of the ruined garden. Eventually, the truth dawned on Harper. Matthew was written all over it - the sneaky slithering snake!

Harper reported his findings to Great-Aunt but she remained an unbeliever. She said Matthew would not have put weed-killer in Harper's bucket of water and it was better that they both put the matter firmly behind them.

When it was time to prepare for tea, Great-Aunt considered allowing Harper to help make the pastry for the pie. The state of his finger nails dictated otherwise and so she encouraged him to watch the flour, butter, milk and other ingredients, turn into a ball of pastry. His attempt to pummel the pastry once the ingredients bound together, was also rebuffed. The pie was delicious nonetheless.

Before he knew it, it was bed-time.

Harper looked forward to getting back to school to tell Agatha and Hugo about Matthew the rat.

Chapter Thirteen

Harper Hepplesthwaite: The day of the angry bear and the charging bull

Harper woke up in a foul mood. As he left the house and walked through the wreck of a garden his mood darkened further.

He strolled ahead of Agatha and Hugo, kicking at sticks and stones as he trundled the path to school. His contribution to their excited recounting of their weekend was an occasional grunt, not his usual repartee of jokes and commentary. Harper decided that he would save his pocket money to buy some new flowers.

He would plant them and tend to them *every single day* of the rest of his life if necessary, until the garden was beautiful and full again. This thought occupied him all the way to school and cheered him a little but he was still quite grouchy.

During registration, Miss Honeywhistle commented that he was like a bear with a sore head. Harper was really *not* in the mood for lessons at all. Worse still, his first class was Geography with none other than Mr Hornby! The lesson was about physical structures made of bricks, stone and concrete. Their task was to draw a structure made of their material of choice. Mr Hornby gave the children some ideas: walls, roads, houses and bridges.

Harper was not the only one feeling grouchy. His classmate Humphrey, a spoiled horror of a boy, was in a particularly testy mood.

"You - pass me your eraser and make it snappy. *I want mine to stay new and clean*," he whispered to Harper. He was cheating at the exercise, tracing an image of a bridge from a book but he had made a mistake and needed to erase it. Harper could not believe his ears. Had *Humphrey*, really just called him '*you*'?

"Use your own," Harper replied indignantly, baring his small perfect teeth as if he really was a ferocious lion, or indeed a bear with a sore head.

"I don't want to use mine. Hand your eraser over – *now.*"

"It's a rubber," Harper said. He did not vent all that he *wanted* to say, in case Humphrey started to cry as he tended to when he found himself in a tight spot.

"Eraser is the *proper* word but what would you know - are you giving it to me or not? You'd better hurry up or ..."

"No it's a rubber," Harper said and then, as an after-thought, he answered without looking up, "and no, I'm not giving it to you!"

"Hand it over or I'll tell Sir."

"Tell him if you like. It's mine and I don't have to give it to you if I don't want to. Use your own!" Harper said looking over at him defiantly but not baring his teeth this time.

After hiding his own eraser in a pocket, Humphrey shrieked and took the quarrel to Mr Hornby. Harper watched Cry-baby-Humphrey walk to Mr Hornby's desk and make a bitter complaint. He watched him as he pointed a bony accusing finger in his direction and saw the easily-roused clouds of dark anger descend on Mr Hornby's face.

Mr Hornby stormed over to Harper's desk like an angry bull - a thunder-storm gathering in his face. Humphrey walked smugly beside him looking forward to seeing Harper face giant sized trouble. Mr Hornby stopped at Harper's desk and planted his hands firmly by his sides.

"Harper, do-you-have-an-eraser-in-your-pencil-case?" Mr Hornby asked quickly, each word tripping into the other as he spoke without pausing to take a breath.

"Yes Sir," Harper answered honestly.

"Why are you refusing to lend it to young Humphrey here?"

"Because he should have his own and he didn't ask me nicely."

Humphrey protested – "I did ask nicely, but he said 'no'." With that, Humphrey broke into a fresh lot of tears.

Mr Hornby had been at the rough-end of Humphrey's tears and complaints before, so he ignored them and cut to the chase.

"Harper, hand your eraser to Humphrey please."

"No I won't Sir."

Mr Hornby blushed with irritation.

"What do you mean? Why not?"

"He has his own, Sir, that he wants to keep clean."

"Harper, hand me your eraser immediately," Mr Hornby persisted.

"No, Sir, because you'll give it to him..."

"Now hand it over *immediately*," Mr Hornby was getting *really* angry now. Harper's disobedience was virtually sharpening his horns! The whole class had stopped drawing, sketching and paying attention to the task.

"Harper, I'll ask you once more. Hand me your eraser immediately."

"Yes, hand it over *you*," Humphrey said boldly, stirring the boiling pot of trouble.

"Sshhtttt," Mr Hornby snapped at Humphrey. Humphrey's bottom lipped trembled as he prepared to cry but a look from Harper dried the tears and stiffened his lip.

"Harper, we are supposed to *share* with others, *share*!" Mr Hornby said, trying a different tack. He would have taken delight in whacking Harper until his rebellion weakened but he knew that no one else would find such a reaction acceptable.

Harper took the eraser from his pencil case and clutched it in the palm of his right hand, as much to say 'if you want it, you must be prepared to wrestle it from my grasp'. He had no idea that Mr Hornby would have relished nothing more but instead he coaxed; "Harper what if we all took that attitude?"

Harper shrugged.

"Let's see shall we?" Mr Hornby said. "Take your things off the table Harper. It's not your table, it belongs to the school."

Harper packed his things away and put them on the floor.

"Do not lean on the table Harper - it is not yours. It belongs to the school." Harper moved his arms off the table and pushed his chair away from it.

"Stand up Harper. That chair is not yours - it belongs to the school," Mr Hornby continued. Harper stood to his feet. Humphrey clamped two bony hands over his mouth to stifle the sound of his giggles. His eyes twinkled with mirth as he wondered what Mr Hornby would say next.

Harper stepped away from the chair.

Mr Hornby's last instruction was outrageous and, this time, Humphrey could not stifle his laughter and neither could the more disloyal members of Harper's class.

"Get off the floor Harper. It is not your floor - it belongs to the school." With that, he scooped Harper up and threw him over his shoulder. Harper was livid and he showed it unfortunately. He pummelled Mr Hornby's back with his fists and protested: "Put me down you idiot!"

Harper found himself outside of Mrs Pickering's office before he could say 'Harper Hepplesthwaite'. Mr Hornby wanted to drag him to the office by his collar or ear so that his insolent feet did not touch the ground but he could not; *no one* else would approve of that either! Rather, he charged on along and around the corridors like a bull trained in the military. Harper broke into a trot to keep pace with him, his own mind brewing an angry storm. Mr Hornby *surely* had no right to put him over his shoulder!

Mrs Pickering shook her head when she heard the tale but Mr Hornby did not mention the little exercise he had engaged in before Harper pummelled him and Mrs Pickering did not ask how it was that Harper reached his back so as to pummel it! Mrs Pickering despaired. She imagined that Mr Hornby had been beaten in his own chair in full view of his pupils for giving a perfectly fair instruction to Harper; to share! She told Harper that he must write a letter of sincere apology to Mr Hornby by no later than Wednesday that week. He was to take time to reflect and think about what he had done before he wrote.

That evening, Harper set about writing the letter, and more or less filled a corner of the room with discarded drafts of the letter. He persevered until he was content with his final version. It read:

> Dear Mr Hornby
>
> I am sorry for hitting you and calling you names.
>
> *D*on't be cross with me please.
>
> I was cross with Humphrey. The last thing I wanted was to cause trouble.
>
> *O*nly last week, Simon shared his coloured pencils with Humphrey and he broke one.
>
> ***That's why I didn't want to share with him – and he has his own clean one too!***
>
> Yours most very sincerely
>
> Harper Hepplesthwaite

The following day, as instructed by Mrs Pickering, Harper went to the staff room straight after assembly to hand the letter to Mr Hornby. Miss Honeywhistle was pleased that Harper was putting things right. A letter of apology was a very good idea indeed she thought; just the sort of thing that Mr Hornby would appreciate as he really treasured discipline and respect.

Harper knocked on the door and waited for Mr Hornby's booming voice to instruct '*come in*', before pushing open the heavy door.

Mr Hornby was sitting in a large chair drinking a cup of tea. He was wearing a pair of glasses that made his eyes look huge. Harper was not used to seeing him in glasses and nearly made a comment concerning the unusual size of his eyes but thought better of it in all of the circumstances.

"I've got this for you, Sir," Harper said, staring at Mr Hornby's artificially huge eyes.

"Righto - off you go now," Mr Hornby said, shooing Harper away ungraciously.

Harper was tempted to say; "*... and what do we say then...? 'Thank you'*" but he did not of course. He tugged at the door handle, struggled with the heaviness of the door and eventually got out.

Harper had no idea, but Mr Hornby was not very far behind him. He had read the letter, once, twice and, on the third reading, he spluttered his tea on his papers and went a furious red. “Ooohhwww,” he fumed, “ooohhwww,” and he stormed to see Mrs Pickering in her office.

When he arrived there, Mrs Pickering was initially irritated and told him that she would not listen to a word until he calmed down. “Do calm down Mr Hornby. I told Harper to write this letter of apology. I really do not see what is wrong with that. I thought it was a lovely, helpful gesture and a chance for him to give a considered and genuine apology.”

Mr Hornby handed the letter to her – “Ooohhww, I am sure that you *did not* tell him to write *this*!” Mrs Pickering read the letter and said that she could not see what Mr Hornby was so cross about. Mr Hornby continued to fume without any further words and pointed to the left hand margin of the letter.

"This is not good. This is not good at all," Mrs Pickering said. Where Mr Hornby burned a furious red, Mrs Pickering’s blood drained away. The audacity of the boy!

There written in black and white was the word: **'Id-iot'**!!!!

Mrs Pickering sent for Harper and he was given a stiff telling off and a letter to hand to Great-Aunt.

When he got home and handed Great-Aunt the letter, she frog-marched him into the drawing room even before he changed out of his uniform.

"I want you to tell me everything young man – truthfully."

Harper told Great-Aunt what had happened with suitable embellishments. His emotions reached fever pitch when he relayed how Mr Hornby had thrown him over his shoulder so that he nearly fainted and vomited all at once. How Mr Hornby had more or less instructed the whole class to laugh at him; how he felt guilty for the rest of the day just for *walking* around the school, because the ground was not his. His final word was that his feet were still aching for walking on tip-toes!

Great-Aunt admonished him, explaining that it was very important that he showed respect for his teachers, both as figures of authority and as his elders.

"I'll be keeping a close eye on your behaviour for the rest of the week young man and I will come down on you *like a ton of bricks* if there is any hint of this insolence."

Harper looked at Great-Aunt's dainty frame and guessed that the phrase was of the *'raining cats and dog'* variety.

"I am sorry Great-Aunt," he said. It was going to be a *long* week he thought. All this and it was only Tuesday.

Great-Aunt was, in fact, also very cross with Mr Hornby and she sent a suitable letter to Mrs Pickering informing her that she expected a satisfactory reply to it.

That weekend, Mathew visited with Laurie. Harper's fury was rekindled and he confronted him in the presence of Great-Aunt and Laurie. Laurie seemed perfectly happy to leave the boys to iron out their differences but Great-Aunt intervened and sent them into the garden.

In the end, Harper relented and told Matthew about the week at school - the Humphrey incident and the 'idiot letter' being the main events. Matthew roared and the two were friends again (of sorts anyway)!

Unfortunately Great-Aunt heard – everything. Every proud chuckle, every flippant guffaw and details that Harper had withheld when she had asked him for the whole truth. She was not at all impressed and she banished Harper to the attic to contemplate his actions.

Harper obeyed, traipsing slowly up the stairs with his hands hanging at his sides, his head bent low.

Harper reached the attic and pushed the door with his foot. He slid to the floor crying. He worried that the family would eventually run out of places to banish him to. Drawing his knees up under his chin, he rubbed angry knuckles into his eyes; I miss Mother and I miss Robin. A single tear escaped the inadequate stop-gap of his fist and dropped to the wooden floor. He stretched out his left foot and smudged the wetness into the floor.

Chapter Fourteen

Harper Hepplesthwaite: A brush with justice

Harper heard a sigh. It was not loud and despite his current feelings, it was certainly not him!

He stood up, wiped his nose with the back of his hand and walked over to the window. The windows were firmly shut but they were single-glazed and therefore not sound proof. He peered out, narrowing his big eyes as he surveyed the large garden and as many of its nooks and crannies as he could from his vantage point. Maybe Matthew was in the garden.

Harper was not completely wrong. Matthew was still at the house but it was not him.

He heard the sigh again and he was sure that it came from the room, yet he peered even more keenly out of the window, pressing his nose against it. He scowled at the lead framing that obscured his view.

Another sigh which sounded closer by than the other two stopped Harper in his tracks. He turned around to face the room with his back to the window and his fingers gripping the window sill. A glance at the fireplace and the recollection of his last experience in the room consigned to history Great-Aunt's reprimand and all self-pity. He was *not* in the mood for to be bullied and judged by the Wighorns!

He made for the door but of course it slipped from his grasp and the door knob turned to close it firmly. He was trapped and there was nothing he could do about it. He did not expect help from Great-Aunt at the moment and he guessed (perhaps correctly) that Matthew would be of little or no use!

Harper slid to the floor in defeat.

He witnessed the workmen traipse from the fireplace bearing, lugging and swinging the furniture into the room; all were again seemingly oblivious to his presence. In turn, Crouchlow (Lightning), Pinikerty, Whizzle-grump, Snappernash, Knapsley, Ponderton,

Temperton and all of the others entered the room and took their places. Lawyers Domble-bluff and Pryson were also there of course. Domble-bluff looked very smug indeed and as sharp in dress as before. His watch chain draped from his pocket and the chain for his eye glasses hung about his neck and chest. Harper could see the miniature blue soft-topped MG parked to the left-hand side of the hearth and assumed that it was Domble-bluff's chosen mode of arrival to the trial. Pryson looked as weary as if he had just walked one hundred miles and his suit had slipped from the hot reach of an iron.

Harper was particularly aware of about three members of the jury that he had not noticed or heard much from before. He noticed them now because of their unusually lurid attire. One was wearing a crimson velveteen suit with a lilac shirt which had a profusion of frills. He had a narrow, long and stone grey face. His right eyeball was very large and protruded so much that it seemed to be set on a stalk. The left eye was a tiny pinprick in his face. He had very, very long and grey fingernails; fingernails so long that they curved at the edges and seemed to sharpen each other when he rubbed his hands together. This was Stonehard. He settled himself and sat between Whizzle-grump and Snappernash.

Another was wearing a pea-green jacket with a swallow-tail at the back and a shirt of spotted pink and yellow, which strained and gaped at the tummy because his tummy was as round as a football. His head was also as perfectly round as a football and his ears stood out from his head like large Portobello mushrooms. His face was very shiny and very red as if it had been polished with oil and strawberries. He had teeny tiny hands which were perpetually folded over his stomach. His eyes were the brightest purple that Harper had ever seen. *This* was Wellersay.

The last one was as round as humpty-dumpty but his arms and legs were as thin as pencils. His three front teeth were huge and he had a bushy yellow moustache. He wore a black and white pin striped suit, a lime green shirt and a bright yellow tie. This was Bumble-snore. He had taken his seat between Wellersay and Knapsley before Harper noticed him.

Judge made his appearance in due course.

Pinikerty called all to stand, Judge called all to sit, Seerall Hearall started to type every word that was said - and the trial began.

Crouchlow approached Pinikerty and handed him the scroll containing all of the charges against Harper. Crouchlow walked backwards away from Pinikerty in an unnecessary and insincere display of respect, nearly unhinging his hip as he walked into the sharp corner of a table. The table shook slightly, upsetting Pinikerty‘s fountain pen which rolled to the very edge of the desk before Pinikerty reached it preventing its fall. Seerall Hearall noticed this and his tiny eyes twinkled but the mirth did not reach his thin lips which remained in a tight thin line. Pinikerty winced with embarrassment; such occurrences were disorderly and he hated disorder in *his* court. He cleared his throat three to four times to settle his nerves.

Whizzle-grump hated the sound and groaned; "*aaar-rrgggggghhh - there he goes, grating on my nerves with his rasping throat.*"

Pinikerty continued as if he had not heard Whizzle-grump but he fixed Snappernash with a withering glare because Snappernash sniggered at Whizzle-grump's remark.

"My Lord, in case number one of the day: The matter of The Right and The Good against Harper

Hepplesthwaite. Harper Hepplesthwaite is accused of the following ..."

As if suddenly becoming aware of his presence, Stonehard turned his eyes on Harper and gasped as he pointed at him with a bony finger and long grey finger nail. All eyes followed the long finger nail and with varying expressions of horror on their faces, all of the jurors gasped and stared at Harper.

The colour drained from Harper's face. Something was very badly amiss but he did not know what. For all of the staring, not one of them expressed to Harper exactly what horrified them - not sufficiently promptly anyway.

Alas, Harper was still sitting on the floor instead of standing in the dock. Judge would surely hold him in contempt of court before the trial even started! There was a deathly silence and then a low rumble as if a storm was brewing. A storm was brewing alright and the room was shaken by it when Judge commanded:

"*On your feet young man, young man on your feet immediately.*" He did not raise his voice as such. Rather Judge's voice erupted like a volcano and filled the room with trepidation. In his rampage, Judge's eyes went from narrow slits to huge balls and back again before settling at a dimension somewhere between the two. He shot a warning glance at Domble-bluff and told him to take his client in hand.

So Harper *stood* before the august group and in the dock once again!

"Pinikerty," Judge called and Pinikerty continued to read the charges as if there had been no interruption at all. He did not mind when proceedings were disrupted by *Judge*.

"Harper Hepplesthwaite stands charged with the following:-

Number one: That on the 13 March, he did behave in a pompous and unkind manner to Matthew Beauchamp, friend and neighbour;

Number two: That he did plot to cheat and deceive at a Boys' Brigade service ..."

The juror Temperton interrupted: "He will not *remember* this I warn you. I am barely able to keep a note myself with the speed at which you are going. Remember, he has no pen and paper available to him."

"My concern is that he will not *understand* the accusations," Weyall added.

Snappernash started to grind his teeth - he was getting sick to his back teeth with the interruptions of the 'let-him-off" trio, Temperton, Ponderton and Weyall. Bumble-snore was nodding his approval of their comments too but Snappernash knew he would soon fall asleep as he always did and so did not trouble himself with administering a cautionary pinch or kick.

"I just hope that we are not wasting our time instead of hearing another case. *That's* my concern. Human boys will be human boys after all - there is no getting away from it,"Ponderton said.

Now Whizzle-grump's heckles were *really* rising.

Pinikerty coughed a dry cough and continued:

"Number three: That he did refuse to share his stationery with Humphrey Snitchkins;

Number four: That he did refuse to obey a teacher's instruction to share his stationery, with the said Humphrey;

Number five: That he did use a pejorative word to describe his teacher and ... "

"Simplify it man, 'pejorative' what does THAT mean?" Ponderton interrupted.

"Insulting. Rude. It means..." Pinikerty started.

I know what it means," Ponderton protested. "I'm thinking of the boy; does *he* know?"

"Are we going to be here all day again?" Bumbles-nore said wearily. In answer, Pinikerty quickly turned the scroll so that the Jurors could glance at the list of charges. "Harumph," Bumble-snore sighed; the list was very, very long!

Again, Harper saw his name written: "The Right and The Good -v- Harper Hepplesthwaite"

Bumble-snore decided to let his eyes *rest* for a few moments. Just a few moments ...

Pinikerty went back to his reading and Judge sat back in his chair looking barely awake as his chin rested on his chest.

"Number six: ... that Harper Hepplesthwaite did call his teacher an idiot;

Number seven: that Harper Hepplesthwaite did *angrily* pummel his teacher ..."

Ponderton exclaimed, "We cannot say he did anything *angrily* can we? We have not heard anything to suggest he was *angry*. The teacher's action could have been playful. The boy's response could also have been playful.

Angrily? I don't think that anyone can decide that *before* we hear from the boy."

Weyall nodded his agreement and Temperton gave a satisfied sigh. Common-sense might win, he thought.

Whizzle-grump despaired. His keen sense of justice was marooned in a sea of do-gooding sentiment and Judge did not seem to be doing anything to stop it. His gavel was relaxing on the sound block as if it had *nothing* to do. Stonehard rapped his nails on the table impatiently - he shared Whizzle-grump's concerns.

Judge spoke at last to inject some order into the proceedings. "We are just hearing the charges read at the moment. It is for Pryson to try and *prove* each charge in due course but we must hear them - without further interruption. That is correct is it not Pryson? Domble-bluff?"

Pryson stood to his feet as a mark of respect as he addressed Judge. Unfortunately, he banged his knee on the desk and squealed, "Yes M'Lud." Domble-bluff replied in a particularly authoritative tone, confirming that Judge was indeed correct. He actually disagreed fundamentally but the contrast of tone between his reply and Pryson's showed him off to better advantage. There was also the fact that the human boy was undeserving of the effort of disagreeing with Judge.

Judge addressed the jurors but his eyes focused on Temperton, Ponderton, and Weyall. All listened in respectful silence:

"I ask you all to remain quiet and let *Domble-bluff* do his job of defending Harper Hepplesthwaite."

The three jurors nodded cautiously. They were not confident of a fair trial but they would play their part committedly.

"Pinikerty," Judge called again, ordering him to continue reading the allegations.

At last, thought Pinikerty - it seemed everyone's voice but his was being heard in *his* court! He resumed reading the charges but not for long.

Ponderton interrupted, "I apologise but these additional allegations seem to be variations of what we have already heard."

Snappernash snapped: "Why don't we just ask the boy to lie down so that we can tickle him? I ask you, why don't we stop this charade immediately; ask the boy (*nicely of course*) to lie down and we'll rally the troops to tickle his tum and feed him as much ice-cream as his wretched heart desires."

As usual Bumble-snore fell asleep just as matters became entertaining. Stonehard was again sharpening his nails as he rubbed his hands together. They would probably sound like swords if Harper's hearing was sufficiently keen! Whizzle-grump gave a wheezy cough to waken Bumble-snore but he did not bat an eye. Only his eyebrows acknowledged the blast of air released by the cough, with a slight trembling. In the end, Whizzle-grump had no choice but to knock Bumble-snore's head with his notebook. "Waaaaahhhhhh," Bumble-snore groaned as he came round from his stupor. He smacked his lips as if he had just dined on a tasty meal and then, as if sleep had never shut his eyes, he was bolt upright and alert. Especially as Whizzle-grump shrieked his remedy for Harper's offences at the top of his voice: "*pummel his head... call him a worm and let's be done with it!*"

"Order! Order in my court!" Judge said and sent the gavel down with force. The court fell silent and Judge continued: "I happen to agree that the additional allegations are not new and so you should both proceed with charges one to seven only. Charges eight to fifty-seven should be struck from the record, unless you wish to address me on the point," Judge said bending his gaze on Pryson and Domble-bluff. Both shook their heads and Domble-bluff's jowls continued to shake for some time after he had given his answer.

Domble-bluff was, of course, keen to make sure that Harper Hepplesthwaite was again found 'not guilty'. Not for Harper's sake. Oh no - getting his clients off did wonders for his renown! He remembered Harper's lack of cooperation at the last hearing and so, thinking on his feet when Harper sneezed loudly and opportunely, he hatched a simple cunning plan.

Workmen Grotshaw and Hobnails who were eavesdropping from inside the fire place both clutched their throats and stuck their tongues out in disgust when they heard Harper sneeze. "*That 'uman will be the death of us - if not by another blot-out or glass boulders, then with a deadly disease. I just know it, I just know it.*" Hobnail wailed. "Oh belt-up," Grotshaw said. "It's dirty-filthy, yes but it's not as bad as all that." They soon settled down again, shuffling about until their bottoms made comfortable seats of the lumps of charcoal beneath them.

"My Lord, can I request a brief conference with my client given this sudden - uumm, fit. I need to ensure that the boy is well enough to continue," Domble-bluff requested.

"Pryson, do you have any objection?" Judge asked him.

Pryson stood slowly and carefully to his feet - his elbows avoided the glass of water and his knees the table.

"Well, my Lord, I don't see why a common sneeze should delay the proceedings.."

"Is that a yes or a no?" Judge interrupted.

"It is a no my Lord, I have no objection," Pryson said, retreating.

Domble-bluff approached Harper and Harper's eyes turned to saucers. Without thinking, or really meaning to, he sat so that he was as close to the floor as possible and, therefore, closer in height to Domble-bluff.

Harper stared and stared at Domble-bluff. Domble-bluff got down to the matter of business quickly because he knew that Judge could call a halt to the conference at any moment.

He lowered his voice to a whisper. "You are now going to face a series of questions. You *MUST* answer all of mine. Then I will give a speech. Now when I say "*Hooper Hopplesthorn is truly sorry*", you weep boy, *weep* your apology. You-bury-your-insolent-face-in-your-hands-and-you-weep and nod your agreement."

"*Harper Hepplesthwaite*," Harper whispered helpfully. "My name is Harper Hepplesthwaite."

"A silly name, Hopper Hepples*bane*, and I simply do not care." With that, Domble-bluff smiled, turned on his heel and took his place. Before he took his seat, he addressed Judge, "My Lord, my client has confirmed that he is fit and able to proceed."

Once Pryson and Domble-bluff had asked Harper all of the questions that they wanted him to answer, it was time for them both to explain to the Judge and the Jury why *their* case should be accepted instead of the other's. In other words, they were to give their windy 'submissions'!

Domble-bluff was the first to make his submissions. He stood and, for the entirety of his speech, held his glasses between his thumb and forefinger. His hand rested casually on his stomach.

As he came to a close, he said in sonorous voice: "I have seen Harper Hepplesnare, nay Hepplesthwaite, weep. I have seen his lips a-quiver and his eyes a-swollen with sorrow and so I can say to you that ***Harper Hepplesthwaite is truly sorry...***'

This was Harper's cue to weep, to-bury-his-insolent-face-in-his-hands and weep, and nod his agreement to Domble-bluff's statement. Alas, Harper did not, or rather his timing was completely off kilter. For at that moment, Bumble-snore stood from his seat and walked towards Temperton to hand him a note. As he walked, Harper caught his profile and noticed that he had an absolutely huge bottom and he had the longest feet he had ever seen.

Domble-bluff coughed and glared at Harper, repeating the cue. Harper took the cue and wailed insincerely, splaying his fingers over his 'insolent face' so that his large unrepentant and dry eyes were clearly visible between his fingers. He stared through his fingers at the Wighorns and they stared at him.

Domble-bluff was livid and his time was up. He was puce with fury. How he wished he could flog the roguish expression from his client's face but, alas, he could do nothing but fume – inwardly *and elegantly* of course. He puckered his mouth as if to whistle a jaunty tune, studied the ceiling above his head and masked his despair.

Now it was Pryson's turn to make submissions for The Right and The Good. Harper scowled as Pryson made serious and various unpleasant comments about his character, while describing Matthew, Humphrey and Mr Hornby as veritable angels! He was not unruly, or a danger as Pryson said he was and he wanted to overturn their tables and charge at them but he could not.

He became increasingly cross and the anger twisted his facial expression into that of an incorrigible rogue.

Pryson finally finished the character assassination and then Judge spoke.

"Harper Hepplesthwaite, we have heard all of the evidence and you will now be judged by twelve of your peers..."

"Not apples then?" Harper mumbled under his breath but loudly enough for Knapsley to hear. Trust him to be awake and alert for a change. "Contempt, contempt of court!" Knapsley shouted.

Questioning grunts were sounded from all quarters of the jury as they tried to establish what had led to the call of contempt.

Judge's gavel went down and the court fell silent. Knapsley sat shaking his head while hastily scribbling out a note to Snappernash and Whizzle-grump explaining exactly what he had heard.

Whizzle-grump hit the roof and Snappernash sarcastically called for Temperton, Ponderton and Weyall to be sure to check whether Harper preferred his feet to be tickled in preference to his tummy and whether he preferred chocolate ice-cream to vanilla.

Bumble-snore turned to juror Wellersay. "What do you make of all of this?"

"Well I say," Wellersay answered.

This was typical of him. He just warmed the court seat and said "well I say" when pushed to give an opinion.

Then Whizzle-grump turned to Wellersay hoping to rally support to find Harper guilty of all charges.

"Well I say," Wellersay said with a confused and nervous frown.

"Well I say WHAT? You've been 'well-I-saying' quite a lot. Well *what* do you say? You say *what*?" Whizzle-grump snapped.

"Well I say.... You know?"

"No I don't know and it seems that you don't either, so save your breath ... *especially as it's pretty sour,*" Whizzle-grump said, mainly to himself.

Harper was found guilty of all charges but he did not face a punishment as the jury, or rather Ponderton, Temperton and Weyall put their points across admirably and rallied another juror, called Biggles-Dream-Porter, to support their decision.

Another raucous episode nearly broke out as Snappernash, Whizzle-grump and Stonehard were furious.

Once it was unwaveringly on its way, Knapsley ran to catch up with the band-wagon and jumped on with enthusiasm. He accosted Ponderton by pinching his lips shut with both sets of finger tips: "*Don't utter a word,*" he said. "*Don't you utter another soft cuddly-wuddly, wishy-washy-do-goody-let-him-off-lightly word.*" Then he looked over his shoulder seeking out an approving nod from Whizzle-grump. However, it was Snappernash that gave him a surreptitious approving nod before loudly ordering: "Set his lips free at once."

Knapsley obeyed and Ponderton patted his lips until they assumed their normal dimension and shape.

Judge encouraged Harper to improve his behaviour as the jury may not be so lenient next time. All stood and Judge left the room, disappearing into the fireplace.

Before the rest started to file from the Court, Lightning announced that all should leave the court room quietly and respectfully as a funeral was to be held in the court-house and the mourners and guests were already present in the building.

Ponderton collared Harper and said that he had been pondering - and what he had been pondering was that Harper should do some pondering so that he need not see them again. He recommended that Harper ponder what would happen if no one shared and took to beating their teachers. Ponderton turned to another matter close to his heart – puddings. "What would happen if Great-Aunt decided not to share her food with you? Especially the puddings. The delights that she makes with pears – pie, crumble, poached ones..." Ponderton nearly continued dreamily but a paper missile thrown by Snappernash hit his cheek bringing him to. "*Ponder these things boy. Ponder. I ponder and it serves me well.*"

Weyall mumbled to Ponderton about Hornby's behaviour not being beyond reproach – "... not right surely, to have thrown the boy over his shoulder...," Harper heard him say.

The door clicked open and Harper fled from the room. He was soon back, however, lying on the floor in the doorway peeping through a gap in the door. Surely the room was not really used for funerals...?

Chapter Fifteen

Harper Hepplesthwaite: Have you ever seen such a thing in your life as...?

If Harper did not have a strong constitution and some experience of the extraordinary with the Wig-horns, he would have fainted off at what he saw as he lay in the corridor between the attic rooms. He peeped through the narrow gap of the open door-way and watched, mouth agape.

Pinikerty had spoken no word of a lie - a funeral was indeed taking place! Great-Aunt oblivious to all going on in the fourth storey of her dear cottage, was playing 'Speak softly love' on the grand piano.

There before Harper's big eyes were six tiny mice, marching with precision as if in time to a drum roll. Leading the procession was a mouse walking upright on his two hind feet as if he were born to it. He wore a charcoal grey three piece suit, a shirt in periwinkle blue and a white satin tie. Hanging from a chain about his neck was a pendulum from a grandfather clock which knocked against the shiny buttons of his waistcoat and jacket. Of course at the rear of the jacket was a meticulously cut hole to accommodate his tail which he held with poise as the spout of a tea-pot. Whether this was to add to his regal air, or to keep it from the tread of the mice following behind him did not matter; it held its poise for the whole procession.

The six bore on their shoulders an open small rectangular box across the hearth. In it lay a small mouse as stiff as a board and smaller than the length of Harper's open palm. The men were dressed in the darkest purple he had ever seen, with the most dazzling white shirts that he had ever seen. Their shoes matched their shirts.

The mice lowered the casket at last and rows of mourning mice filed past to look into it. All showed their respect and grief in their way. Some shook their heads as they looked on, others removed their hats dramatically and clasped them to their chests, still others dabbed gently and movingly at their eyes with white handkerchiefs. One passed and, lowering his head uncomfortably close to the body, blew a very full nose with a force wholly inappropriate for the occasion. A female mouse, perhaps his wife, delivered a sharp kick to his ankle causing him to yelp. Her long flowing gowns hid her dastardly act.

They marched the length of the hearth solemnly, looking neither to the left, nor to the right. They then did a sharp about turn and, slowly and carefully, mounted the fireplace grate and disappeared. Seconds later, Harper heard the sound of crying in the distance. The sound grew louder and closer. A procession of mourners emerged from the side of the hearth. They were wearing black flowing robes. Two seemed particularly sad as they walked side by side. They howled more loudly than all of the others, raising their heads to the skies (well, ceilings) as if to ask it 'why'? All of their actions were synchronized in fact. If he blew his tiny short nose, she blew hers a second later; if she beat her breast, he beat his a second later. Another pair immediately behind them looked at each other and thumbed their noses at the pair. Their ridicule only lasted for a moment.

They soon turned back to their mourning, for they were all four of them to be paid for it - they were professional mourners! In turn, they all filed into the fire-place and, moments later, it was as if they had never been there at all. Man alive!

Harper had two stark choices before him. He could excavate the fireplace to discover the world of these creatures once and for all, or he could give himself a firm pinch, run down the stairs, splash his head with cold water, throw himself under the bed covers and forget the whole horrid thing. He did the latter and finally fell asleep after a fitful start. It was not every day that an ordinary boy witnessed the funeral of a mouse but then it was not every day that a boy was taken to court - and certainly not by creatures living in the chimneybreast of his home! 'I've seen it all now' was the last thought that occurred to him before his closing eyelids shut him off from the weird world for another day.

Early the following morning, Harper started to write a letter. Not a letter to Mr Hornby but a letter to Mother. Not a letter of apology but a letter begging for rescue. It was not a short letter but a long one.

He described the madness of number two Pear Tree Lane and just how eggcentric Great-Aunt *really* was. He wrote everything he could remember about the trials with the weird and wicked Wighorns and the funeral procession of the mice. He scratched out the word mice, in favour of rats because he did not want the facts to stand in the way of his release. Mother was terrified of rats. He focused in on the merciless Domble-bluff, Whizzle-grump and Snapper-nash and how he could not sleep for nightmares about them sharpening their nails and teeth to shred him to pieces.

Unable to decide on which of five endings to use to close his letter, Harper decided to use all of them. He scratched out his home address on a scented envelope that he had squirreled from Great-Aunt's study and posted it on his way to school.

Alas, the arrival of Harper's letter relied on a kindly soul at the post office putting postage stamps on the envelope and a diligent postman tracing his address without the postcode. Both proved unreliable and so Harper waited and waited for days and weeks for Mother to arrive and take him home. She did not.

Harper knew that she would not believe him if he spoke to her by telephone. Mother was a scientist and so she needed hard evidence. Harper determined to supply it when he next wrote to her.

Chapter Sixteen

Harper Hepplethswaite: An extremely eggy Easter

Easter was on its way with the promise of chocolate eggs. There was a buzz of excitement in the school hall and Harper sat with the other two amigos Hugo and Agatha, whispering, elbowing, chuckling and only half listening. He was giddy with anticipation of the holidays. It was the last day of the school term before the Easter recess.

Mrs Pickering told the children the story of the first Easter. Harper found what he had heard of the story intriguing and he decided that he would read about it himself - and perhaps even re-enact it with Agatha and Hugo. The woods would make a perfect setting.

The mischievous and light mood lasted all day and heightened when the boys realised that they were not to be saddled with home-work over the holiday. As they made their way home, they played as if their young lives depended on it. Before going their separate ways, each dared the other to eat all of their Easter eggs in one go.

Great-Aunt had what she believed was a marvellous Easter Sunday planned for Harper. She had plenty of work to complete ready for an art exhibition and was, therefore, going to be very busy over the two week school holiday period. Harper initially took the view that Great-Aunt's idea was a rum one which would provide a dearth of entertaining stories when he returned to school but he found that it was not so bad after all.

Harper soon found out exactly why Great-Aunt boiled so many eggs that morning and why she was wearing an apron splashed with brightly coloured paints. "We shall have an Easter egg hunt Harper - a themed Easter egg hunt," Great-Aunt announced.

"I thought Easter *was* the theme. Is this a way of making me *work* for my Easter eggs?"Harper said, retreating from the kitchen to the garden. He hated the smell of boiled eggs. In fact, he had little time at all for eggs - unless they were hidden in delicious food such as cakes. Easter eggs were another obvious exception of course because they were made with chocolate. Great-Aunt knew this well and hoped that this would be the key to the success of her scheme. It was time she tackled Harper's elocution!

She had prepared two sets of eggs. The first set was chocolate eggs she had bought from local confectioner, "Pudimore's Sweets". She wrapped them in foil and sealed them with a circular seal of red, blue, green or yellow. For the second set, she had cooled boiled eggs in the fridge to help deodorise them and then wrapped them in foil with a white circular seal. The eggs with the coloured seals were genuine chocolate eggs and those with the white seals were the boiled eggs.

On each set of eggs, Great-Aunt wrote a word on a grey label. The chocolate eggs, with coloured seals, had correct spellings or single letters "h", "r" or "t" written on them. She placed the eggs with a single letter written on them in dainty china egg cups. The real eggs with the white seals on them had the words "wha'", "gonna" and "yer" written on them.

Harper's task was to find the eggs and match the letter or correct word to the correct eggs.

All eggs were strategically hidden in the garden for Harper to find. The prize was a large chocolate egg, hand-made by Mr Pudimore. It contained a compartment of luridly coloured soft sweets. Great-Aunt was thrilled with her idea. Her only sadness was that Harper would have to play the game alone.

With all arrangements set, Great-Aunt started the game.

"Right young man, here's a fun game for you." Harper was curious but skeptical that the game would be any fun at all.

Great-Aunt explained the game and then reclined in the rocking chair to watch as Harper set about it. "Don't forget." she called, "you *must* pick up the 't's' and 'h's'. They are precious like the china egg-cups holding them. *Too* precious to drop or ignore!"

Harper soon discovered the nasty side of Great-Aunt's game when he presented "wha'" as a correct word! She sent him out to look for a 't' in a china cup. He reluctantly admitted that the lone 't' belonged to the 'wha' and expected that to be the end of it –but it was not! Great-Aunt ordered him to eat the egg labelled 'wha'. Harper squeezed the egg and it seemed too soft to be made of chocolate. Before the foil wrapping was fully removed, the content was revealed because the fridge could only do so much!

Harper held his nose and took the tiniest bite possible of the *disgusting*, smelly boiled egg. Great-Aunt looked on without a trace of sympathy; "That'll help you to focus next time you are tempted to drop a letter."

To reinforce her point, Great-Aunt made Harper leaf through an Oxford dictionary bigger than his head, in search of the word "wha". Harper liked the game less and less. When he protested that "wha" would not be in the dictionary, Great-Aunt insisted that he look nonetheless.

He was awarded the prize after all. "It's for your perseverance, not your elocution," Great-Aunt said as she relieved his lap of the heavy dictionary.

Harper marvelled at the Easter egg. "Mr Pudimore is remarkably clever," he said dreamily. Great-Aunt agreed!

They spent a few more hours in the afternoon sunlight before venturing to the back of the garden to find fruit to make a pudding.

Chapter Seventeen

Harper Hepplesthwaite: Practice makes perfect

It was summer and, spurred on by Harper's spirit of adventure, the three friends discovered many of the interesting nooks and crannies of Eldersham. With the sun shining enticingly through the window-frames of the classroom, the sound of chalk on the blackboard was not enough to draw their attention back to the lesson. Instead it made their feet itch for a run in the woods, to scale a tree to a height that would make their parents take a sharp intake of breath!

They did not have too long a wait. It was the last week of the summer term and Harper's school year was to take part in a school play. Miss Honeywhistle and Mr Burnsom were responsible for the production.

The theme was the seasons of the year - "All glorious four of them" Miss Honeywhistle trilled with a theatrical voice when she first announced it. She said that the idea was inspired by the personalities of her 'clever, clever *childrun' as well as the subject of her PhD*.

Time flew and, with just two days before the assembly, there was an excited buzz of activity in the drama and crafts lessons. Mr Hornby had hammered his way into the arrangements, taking on the role of stage set-maker after denouncing Mr Burnsom's ideas as mortally dangerous. Mr Hornby was just as loud and strict in the rehearsals as he was generally.

The day's rehearsal started with a costume fitting. The costumes were made of card with carefully placed strips of Velcro to secure them in place.

There were huge blue rain-drops, grey and white fluffy clouds, large snowflakes, a sun so hot that it was golden yellow *and* orange, extremely tall daffodils and tulips – and leaves of gold, brown, red and green. They were all one dimensional, with long tabs on either side.

"Wow, they are *ginormous*," Hilary exclaimed. Miss Honeywhistle emerged from amongst the props and rounded on Hilary.

"It's either 'gigantic' *or* 'enormous', *ginormous* is not a word dear." She then disappeared from view amidst the props as quickly as she had appeared. From the same spot, Mr Burnsom and Mr Hornby suddenly appeared with breathtaking scenery that was to form the backdrop for the play.

With scenery and props in place and the children standing ready in their costumes, the rehearsal of the play started. Mr Hornby stood at the back of the hall to listen and observe. When Harper took to the stage, Mr Hornby interrupted him bellowing: "Project your voice boy, projeeeect your voice ...'

Harper felt thoroughly silly, strapped to a giant raindrop and surrounded by several classmates dressed up as huge daffodils - but at least they were all in the same dismal boat. Harper projected his voice but he did not act. Miss Honeywhistle refused to despair, they were only two seasons into the year after all.

"Spring is the most beautiful time of the year Harper. You are excited, the earth has shaken off the icicles of winter, grey has been pushed aside by soft blue and little green shoots are bravely pushing through the earth made soft by the rain, flowers are blooming just like the young daisy beside you. Look." (Hilary, a Daisy, looked smug behind the bright yellow card that he wore.) "Start again - and this time *express* yourself dearie.... *express Spring*." Harper expressed Spring after scowling at poor 'Daisy'.

Winter would have been more suitable for a boy like him, a boy as 'tough as old boots' as Great-Aunt sometimes described him. All of that biting frost, cold blasts of snow and the inky blue-black sky. An alternative was the lightning and thunder of an autumn storm. He would express himself alright is she let him at *that*!

During the autumn season one of the boys played clown and feigned slipping on a soggy brown leaf and a snow flake on stage in the wrong season fell over, landing rather heavily. However, never to have her spirits dampened, at the end of the rehearsal, Miss Honeywhistle trilled: "That was sublime children, *sublime*!"

After the rehearsal, Mr Burnsom and Miss Honeywhistle broke into enthusiastic applause. Mr Hornby shook his head slowly from side to side with his head bowed to the floor. He leaned towards Miss Honeywhistle but it was impossible to hear what he said. A frown worried her face for a few seconds but she soon brightened again.

Harper tripped home with his friends, walking with his head down and with big strides for his short legs. His hands were pushed deep into the pockets of his shorts.

"Hornby thinks we are going to make a bad job of the play and be an *embarrassment* to the school in front of the Mayor."

Happy to have dropped a bombshell on Hugo and Agatha, Harper broke into a whistle and kept on walking. They asked a series of three questions before he interrupted his whistling of Dance of the Knights, to answer them.

"I heard him tell Miss Honeywhistle *loud and clear*."

Harper continued with an impression of Mr Hornby.

"Stop loitering and get to your places NOW!"

"Tuck your shirt in you scruffy-little-boy."

"Harper, take yourself and your grubby little friends off to see Mrs Pickering at once."

"We'll just have to prove him wrong then," Hugo said, kicking a stone into the long grass.

"Noooo, we'll just have to prove him *right*," Harper and Agatha chimed.

The three stood in a make-shift circle, interlocked their thumbs and made a solemn pledge to prove Mr Hornby right.

"The last one to the cross-roads, let off a stink in English!" Harper yelled, taking off and thereby giving himself a generous head-start.

“Poooo-eeee!” Agatha yelled, steaming ahead of the boys.

Chapter Eighteen

The Mayor, young Harper and the vexed Stage-maker

Harper was woken, not by his alarm clock but by Great-Aunt dashing into his bedroom and whistling loudly before his alarm clock sounded. When she dropped his navy blue dressing gown on to his face, Harper thought that he was having a nightmare in which he was drowning in a deep and dark blue sea. He gasped for breath and knocked his head against the hard wood of the capsized ship as he tried to swim out of the dark depths.

"Wakey wakey dearie. You have a Mayor to entertain." She tied the curtains back and swept about the room collecting stray socks from its corners, while Harper snatched the deep dark blue sea and stretched his arms into its sleeves.

"Hurry, or you'll be late for school. I expect your teachers are in a frenzy of preparation. What a *palaver* for a man that likes dressing up in gaudy jewelry and ridiculous jackets."

"*It is* a palaver Great-Aunt but I'll bear it!" Harper replied.

He looked at Great-Aunt with a hand shading his still sleepy eyes from the glare of the sunshine that flooded his room - the brightness that was Great-Aunt herself with hair that resembled a field of unkempt barley.

He did not push the bedclothes aside and so he fell out of bed with the bed linen around and about his legs and feet. He stumbled out of them and into the bathroom.

He charged down the stairs and to the breakfast table where a bowl of nasty porridge waited for him. He pushed the bowl away from him.

"Eat every morsel, young man. An army marches on its stomach," Great-Aunt encouraged.

"No wonder the wars took so long. I'm not in the army anyway. We don't have a war on do we Great-Aunt?"

"Don't be silly," Great-Aunt chided mildly.

By the time Great-Aunt tugged at his collars, brushed his wet hair, polished his shoes and pulled his socks up to their full extent, Harper looked fit to set before the Mayor. If Great-Aunt's efforts did not survive the journey to school, the giant raindrop of a costume would cover any disgrace.

Harper and friends skulked into the school grounds and joined the line of fellow class mates prepared to file into class for registration.

"Now children, who do we have with us in assembly today?" Miss Honeywhistle asked the class.

"The Mayor."

"And why is he here?"

"To enjoy our play," most answered.

"Correct, so let's prepare to do a wonderful job for ourselves, our year and our school. Does anyone need any help with their lines? Winter...? Spring ...? Summer ...?" All droned, "No." They were excited and the buzz of excitement increased when they put their costumes on.

There was just enough time for Autumn to practice his lines under his breath. He walked in small circles with his hands behind his back.

Mr Hornby burst through the curtains to announce that they had three more minutes before the performance was to start. "Forget your lines at your *peril*," he encouraged before he disappeared behind the curtain.

Happily, Miss Honeywhistle had the final word: "Now my brilliant children, it's time for you to show all of your hard work. Do your *very best* and, most of all - have *fun*! That's what your families and the Mayor want to see - lovely children, having plenty of *fun*!"

A low and deep, "Testing, testing one-two-three," from Mr Hornby calling through a hand-made tannoy and the stage curtains opened to reveal a sea of faces. Mrs Pickering opened the proceedings with an introduction:

"Lord Mayor, teachers, families, children, good morning to you all. We are privileged today to welcome the *Mayor* to our school and this *special* end of year assembly. It is not often that we have the opportunity to join together in such a manner and I know how *diligently* the children have been working to make sure that you all enjoy the performance today. This is all possible, of course, due to the time and effort invested by our teachers - Miss Honeywhistle, Mr Burnsom and Mr Hornby. Kindly give them a round of applause!"

Then Miss Honeywhistle took to the stage. "Good morning everybody and thank you. Without further ado, I present to you our play: '**The *wonders* of the four seasons**'," and the performance began ...

Winter did valiantly, especially given that they were the first out. The wind blew and howled fairly realistically, even though it could be heard pausing to catch its breath. Mr Burnsom had done something wonderful and so the icy white cold of frost rose from the stage and into the air. The snow-flakes also stood a decent average of between 133 and 150 centimetres from the ground. A harsh winter indeed! Thunder and lightning burst on to the scene (two seasons early) with suitable flashes of light and loud clashing and banging fit to rend the ceiling of the assembly halls. They were magnificent and drew impressed gasps from the audience.

Spring represented by Harper and his friends were next.

He was happy for the shelter of the huge rain-drop. With his eyes only barely visible, he could stare at the Mayor to his heart's content. The mask of his costume made his staring eyes less staring and his open mouth not quite so open wide. Why the wide eyes and gaping mouth? Well, the Mayor was virtually opposite him and what a picture he was!

Mayor was wearing black predominantly and a white frilly shirt that buttoned right up to his chins. There were gold chains about a very short neck. He could not see the Mayor's eyes because Mayor was wearing a big smile that left them buried deep in his cheeks. Harper could see his nose. Oh yes! His nose was not hiding anywhere or from anything. In fact it very nearly hid narrow, compact purple lips from view. Leaving off the Mayor's head and dress, Harper's eyes travelled to Mayor's legs, because his trousers stopped short of his ankles and the huge and shiny metal buckle on his shoes begged for attention. What a palaver indeed thought Harper!

Minutes can seem like seconds and so Spring's start was delayed until Miss Honeywhistle prompted it.

Harper was magnificent. He seemed to inspire the other props of Spring to act out their parts with enthusiasm. He projected his voice superbly and his narration was captivating, helping the remaining props of Spring to act very well. He also delivered his lines with perfect recall - at least initially ...

Suddenly, Harper the giant raindrop strummed an air guitar with the fury of a summer storm and bellowed the chorus of a popular song that *all adults disapproved of*. A tall daffodil, otherwise known as Agatha swayed wildly, knocking snowdrops and tulips out of its way. A golden leaf, otherwise known as Hugo, stormed to the front of the stage and growled his best impression of thunder. His arms and fingers twisted and contorted in rhythm to the song, to portray lightning. As the wretched chorus came to an end, Harper made the Mayor its object by extending a pointing arm and forefinger to him.

There was a sharp intake of breath from Miss Honeywhistle, a gasp from Mrs Pickering and an unrestrained growl from Hornby. Mr Burnsom patted his pockets and head in search of his spectacles because he was sure that his natural eyes deceived him.

The Mayor's face went redder than a beetroot. He crossed, uncrossed and re-crossed his short legs and he huffed and puffed his cheeks. Then he seemed to round on Mrs Pickering, shifting in his chair so that he was as close as possible to facing her full on. He had no idea what Harper was singing but he guessed at something ribald.

Spring was ushered off stage and Summer rushed on. The muted applause must have been for the patient daffodils, puffs of blossom and lightly chirruping birds. They were certainly not for Harper!

Bumble-bees and butterflies flew about the stage in harmony, occasionally landing on a huge shoot of lavender or a sunflower. Huge sunbeams eclipsed three roses until a greenfinch elbowed them out of the way.

Almost immediately after red and gold leaves and bare trees filed off the stage, Mr Hornby grabbed Harper by the elbow and in furious silence marched him to Mrs Pickering's room for the inevitable dressing down. Harper thought about asking Mr Hornby if he was happy that his nasty little prophecy had come true but he thought better of it.

Harper waited outside of Mrs Pickering's office for an age. He did not hear her enter the office from the left wing of the school's building and so he jumped when she called him in.

Her tone was sharp and did not bode well. He approached the door which was now ajar. He pushed it open very slowly, expecting to find that Mrs Pickering had turned into an ogre. "If only you'd showed such trepidation in assembly young man," Mrs Pickering said with a very stern expression on her face. “Do you know why you are here Harper?”

"Yes Miss," he said meekly.

"What you did today was very silly and ruined assembly for your friends as well as our guests. Mr Hornby is clear that you were the ring-leader, the mastermind behind Agatha and Hugo's tomfoolery. This must *not* happen again. Now, I have arranged for you to meet the Mayor in about an hour. You are to apologise to him for the embarrassment that you have caused to him. I am now sending you back to your class and you are to apologise to Miss Honeywhistle and your class. Finally, by the end of the day, you are to apologise to Mr Burnsom and Mr Hornby.

Do you understand everything that I have said to you Harper?"

"Yes Miss."

"And do you understand *why* I have said it?"

"Yes Miss."

"Ok Harper- go back to your class now please. Miss Honeywhistle will accompany you to apologise to the Mayor."

"Yes Miss, thank you Miss," Harper said.

At eleven o'clock prompt, Harper bolted his milk and biscuits. At a quarter past eleven Miss Honeywhistle took him to Mrs Pickering's room and through to a rather grand antechamber. It was time for him to make his apology to the Mayor.

The Mayor was sitting in a large ornate chair. Mrs Pickering stood aside, to the Mayor's right-hand side and explained that Harper was there to apologise for his antics in the assembly that morning.

There was an impressive tower of neatly cut sandwiches and a platter of scrumptious looking cakes on a layered ornamental stand on the left hand side of the table but Harper's eyes went to the object of his visit.

He stood just a matter of feet away from the Lord Mayor and his eyes turned to saucers. As if playing his part in a performance, the Lord Mayor assumed a stern expression. He narrowed his eyes, bent his eyebrows into a frown and puckered his lips into a stern '0'. As if to drive his message home, the Mayor shook his head from side to side, wagged a short plump forefinger at Harper and tutted. He then looked from the platter of sandwiches and cakes to Mrs Pickering whose expression remained somewhat expectant. The Mayor started to speak again, "Young man, sedition is ..." However, the lure of luncheon was strong and so he left the sentence incomplete and gave a suppliant sigh as if to say, "Now that is over with, let's resume the *serious* business of eating."

Mrs Pickering then looked expectantly at Harper. "What have you got to say Harper?"

"I am very sorry indeed me Lud," Harper bellowed as if auditioning for a role as Town Crier. He then saluted, bowed and took one step backwards. Mrs Pickering despaired but she could see that Harper was sincere and the Mayor was clearly satisfied because he reached across the table for a cake before Harper's salute.

The apology to Mr Hornby was an entirely different affair. After shouting for Harper to enter the room, Mr Hornby sprung out of his chair and thereafter, Harper could not get a word in edgeways. He circulated Harper with his hands clasped behind his back and asked him an endless series of rhetorical questions. At last he concluded:"...Thought you were clever didn't you but who is the silly one now, missing-his-classes-to-go-about-different-offices *squealing* 'sorry'? Get out – grubby little boy!"

The ordeal had lasted five hours by Harper's reckoning but he was, in fact, back in his seat in class within nine minutes and thirty-nine seconds of leaving it, including walking time. Hugo and Agatha watched him as he walked to his seat. Using his eyes, he told them what a nightmare it had all been. They replied with sympathetic looks and Agatha winked to indicate that they would listen to the whole dreadful tale after school. Harper nodded his agreement and, on the way home, he did just that - leaving no stone unturned. Agatha and Hugo had also had a stiff telling-off from Mrs Pickering but they were spared the 'Hornby-treatment'.

Mrs Pickering and Mrs Honeywhistle also agreed that Harper's mischief could be curbed with additional English and Music lessons which were to start before the Summer holidays began. When the news was broken to Harper, he smiled sweetly but resolved in his heart that he would be as uncooperative as humanly possible!

As he pushed open the gate of number two Pear Tree Lane, Harper decided that his account of the day would lead with the Mayor. He would only touch on his antics in the play if Great-Aunt had already learned of it.

He was about to knock on the front door, reaching for the handle that would beat at the dog's nose to summon Great-Aunt, when the door swung open.

Great-Aunt welcomed him in. They both said 'hello' and asked the other about their day. "Just the usual," Harper said, fussing with the buckle of his satchel as if it was a wicked obstacle to his getting at his homework.

Great-Aunt swept on with details of her day; how she had gone into the village to buy some fresh yeast from the village baker and nearly had her ankle taken off by Mr Bishop on his new bike. How unsafe he was on his own two-legs and what madness it was that he was getting about on two wheels, and so on and so forth. Harper breathed a sigh of relief.

"That is madness Great-Aunt. I do hope your ankle is not too sore," he said, showing an uncommon interest in all she had to say and relieved that Great-Aunt had forgotten about the Mayor's visit to his school.

"What about the man in trinkets? *He* doesn't visit your school every day now does he – now tell me all about that?"

Harper's eyes turned to saucers and he became animated as he walked to the kitchen telling Great-Aunt *exactly* what he had made of the Mayor and his clothes. His enthusiasm waned when he got to the sticky part of the actual play and so he stopped it short by drinking down a glass of milk. "Milk is so *newtritious*," he said when he had drained the glass to its dregs and made his way to the sink to deposit the glass in it "... all the better to do my homework."

"You don't have any homework and you know it. Now tell me about the guitar business and the mayhem you and your friends caused!" Great-Aunt said determinedly.

"Now, *I'm* in a right *palaver*," he mumbled to himself.

"I was in the village at lunch-time and saw Mrs... Mrs... Mrs - what's the name of that teacher of yours? Short, straw-like hair, enormous eye glasses, tiny feet," Great-Aunt enquired. Harper wished she did not insist on the minor details of Mrs Titchell's identity in the circumstances. He was in trouble and he wished she would just get on with it.

"Oh," he said, smelling certain defeat.

"Yes, 'oh' Harper. 'Oh' indeed! I heard all about the needless embarrassment you caused. Hours of hard work and rehearsals thrown away in favour of mischief. After supper, you are to go to the blue room where you are to sit for thirty minutes thinking about what you have done."

"Not the *blue* room, please Great-Aunt!"

"To the blue room Harper - you are in no position to bargain," Great-Aunt said with finality.

Harper looked askance at Great-Aunt. He wondered if she knew about the Wighorns. She had virtually been born and bred in the house, having lived there from the age of six years old and the Wighorns clearly preyed on children!

Harper ate his sandwich supper in silence – well, apart from chewing very loudly and clapping his mouth at the end of the meal to compliment the chef but it was, of course, an unwanted and unpleasant sound.

Great-Aunt felt some sympathy for Harper; however, he needed discipline and reinforcing the standards that the school had impressed on him was important, for his own good. Consistency was the other side of the coin of discipline after all.

Harper traipsed up the seemingly endless staircase. He was being punished and the long trek to the fourth floor seemed part of it. He thought about stopping off at his bedroom to collect bits and bobs to keep him entertained, or perhaps a poker to see off the Wighorns. However, his bedroom was immediately above the drawing room and had a creaky floorboard and so Great-Aunt would surely hear him and be even more disappointed with him.

Harper's spell in the blue room was uneventful on this occasion. In fact, he thumbed his nose at the chimney-breast as he left the room.

Great-Aunt summoned him for a cup of hot chocolate, perhaps as a peace offering. After ordering him to brush his teeth to avoid the chocolate monsters plucking them from his gums while he slept, she sent him to bed so that he was sharp for the last day at school. Harper laughed extravagantly, pointing at Great-Aunt and shaking his head as he did so. How old did she think he was - chocolate *monsters*! He did not add a word to the laughter but Great-Aunt somewhat regretted resorting to the unrealistic threat.

Chapter Nineteen

Harper Hepplesthwaite: A word in time...

The next week brought Harper's first additional English comprehension lesson. They could not have chosen a worse day.

Miss Wordsworth breezed into the room, "Good-afternoon, Hepplesthwaite. You do remember why you are here don't you?" Without waiting for an answer, Miss Wordsworth continued, "You are *very* privileged you know. Many children would give their *right arm* to have additional tuition in language and comprehension."

This last statement riled Harper and got the lesson off to a bad start.

"Well it won't do 'em much good will it Miss - losing a righ' arm? I'd rather have a righ' arm than speak proper." Spread before his mind's eye was an image of a daft boy offering a bloody arm torn off at the shoulder to Miss Wordsworth. She, in turn, stood before the said daft boy with an open box full of words, some lying peacefully in the box, others leaping from it towards him, letter by letter.

Miss Wordsworth refused to engage in a battle of wills with him. She sniffed as if to dismiss his riposte and pressed on.

"Hepplesthwaite, I'm going to introduce you to a wonderful world of words. Let us make a start then. Take note of the following; I want you to imagine yourself swimming in a pool of words, when I speak I want you to pay attention to what I say, how I use words, when I use the words - the *context*. First, however, tell me about your week. How has it been thus far?"

"Thus far...," Harper began.

When he had finished, or rather when Miss Wordsworth brought Harper's litany to an end, she had two simple instructions for him, "Hepplesthwaite, you *must* pronounce consonants unless they are silent and you *must not* stretch your vowels. They are not *elastic bands*."

"Right, Hepplesthwaite." she continued after a pause, "I have compiled, that is, *put together*, a list of absolutely fabulous words for your first lesson. The first one is 'rebellious'. What do you suppose it means?"

"No idea Miss but it's a good enough word," Harper said.

"I will walk you through some examples."

Harper's lively imagination took flight again and he had visions of 'walking' through corridors of words bumping into some of them and some of them bumping into him as he walked along.

A sharp snapping of Miss Wordsworth's fingers close to his right ear brought him to.

"So tell me Miss. What do I say - 'orrible or *h*orrible, orrid or *h*orrid, onestly or *h*onestly?" Harper said, putting too heavy an emphasis on the 'h'!

"You pronounce the 'h' in 'horrible' and 'horrid' but not in 'honestly'." Pay attention to this example Hepplesthwaite...

"David's 'ill'" – now, what do I mean Hepplesthwaite? Am I referring to a place called David's Hill, because there is such a place, or do I mean that someone called David is ill – unwell?"

"No idea Miss. You'd know best, cos you're the one saying it. I've no idea if David is ill 'cos he looked well when I last saw 'im, *h*im, and I never knew there was a place called David's 'ill until you just said, so I can't help you Miss..."

Miss Wordsworth sighed, "You would need to know the 'context' wouldn't you Hepplethswaite? And do you see that without *context*, the letter '*h*' in the statement could cause alarm?"

"Why of course Miss, especially if you looked alarmed as you said it," Harper demonstrated, putting his hands to his head and drawing his forehead into a worried frown!

"But they would *not* be alarmed if I said David's Hill would they?" Miss Wordsworth persevered.

"Be odd if they did Miss."

"So, Hepplesthwaite, there are reasons for rules and we must follow them mustn't we?"

"I suppose so Miss," Harper said. His face displayed a deep sense of scepticism which Miss Wordsworth did not see, having turned to the blackboard.

"Right, let's see if we can also expand your vocabulary," Miss Wordsworth said as she wrote some words on the blackboard.

"Obnoxious," Harper shouted from behind her.

"I beg your pardon!" Miss Wordsworth whispered, aghast.

"Obnoxious," Harper repeated. "That's already part of my *vo-cab-ula-ry,*" Harper stuttered.

On realising that Harper was not being insolent, Miss Wordsworth continued.

"Very good, Hepplesthwaite! Now, I am going to use the word 'rebellious' in a sentence and then you will try and compose a sentence of your own."

Harper started to relax and enjoy the exercise - there really were some excellent words going!

So continued Miss Wordsworth, introducing Harper to words, meanings and contexts. Miss Wordsworth pronounced each word phonetically to help Harper:

1. Copious; 2. Odious; 3. Audacious; 4. Intrepid; 5. Tepid; 6. Consequence; 7. Sequence; 8. Manner; 9. Manor; and 10. Honour.

"This is all very confusing, Miss. Pretend some letters *are* there when they aren't, pretend others *aren't* there even when you can see them clear as day.... if you've got eyes what work...." Harper said with exasperation.

"You will get to grips with it in no time at all, Hepplesthwaite. Do not despair. It will all come with practice. It is just the same with vowels. You know what vowels are don't you?"

"*Course* I do Miss – 'a, e, i, o, u'," Harper said, stretching and contracting his face as he pronounced each one.

Miss Wordsworth continued "... some vowels, depending on *where* they appear in a word, are meant to be tripped over quickly - silenced, *not* emphasised. The 'a's in 'extraordinary' are such an example. The treatment of 'e's' in 'interest' is another one. So we pronounce 'extraordinary' 'exstraw-dunry' *not* ex-trah-ordi-nairy. Do you see Hepplesthwaite?"

"What I see is letters put in a word when they're not supposed to be there - that's what I see!" Harper exclaimed.

"Come, come now Hepplesthwaite....," Miss Wordsworth said, smiling and patting Harper on the cheek.

The rest of the lesson went off well and Harper did enjoy it, even if he was not ready or willing to admit the fact to Miss Wordsworth... just yet; it was only one lesson after all.

From then on, Harper more or less embraced the wonderful world of words. He continued to drop the occasional letter sometimes by mistake (and often by design) but Miss Wordsworth so stretched him with words and expressions that he would have stood six foot tall had words been a device for physical stretching!

The first music lesson with Mr Bell was significantly less successful and it was, therefore, the last, although Harper's voice was as that of an angel. Harper distorted the instructive doh - re - me - fa - soh - lah – te - doh, to a thankless: 'Bo - ring - me - so - please - let - me – go'. Therefore, a mere four minutes and twenty-nine seconds into the lesson, Mr Bell strode to the door and held it open for Harper to exit. Fast on Harper's heels, Mr Bell also left the room - his destination, Mrs Pickering's room. He told her in no uncertain terms that he was unwilling to cast his musical pearls on the 'Hepplesthwaite horror'. Thus, Mr Bell withdrew from the scheme to improve Harper using music!

From that day onwards, Mr Hornby and Mr Bell mended their long standing hostilities, united by their dislike of Harper. They no longer took a dim view of the other's subject and went so far as to decide that there was an inextricable link between music and mathematics which extended beyond the letter with which both words began!

The summer holidays were in full swing and Harper accompanied Great-Aunt and Laurie into the neighbouring Knoxham and Goldsbourne to look at antiques. They also looked around the museums and ruins that the local towns, villages and hamlets offered. Harper loved the indulgent lunches that they had when they were out and about, especially the sweet treats.

Laurie taught Harper a few limericks and Matthew taught him how to play a tune on the piano. Harper determined to write a limerick and an original tune by the end of the summer.

Chapter Twenty

Harper Hepplesthwaite: Food glorious food

By the third week of the summer holiday, Harper was left to make his own entertainment. Great-Aunt and other members of the Committee for the Enhancement of Life in Eldersham were exceedingly busy arranging the annual Summer Fete. Great-Aunt had plenty of overall responsibility for the event as Social Secretary.

The day of the Summer Fete soon arrived. It was an important and well-loved tradition, not least because it brought past and current residents of Eldersham from near and far. Visitors included Marjory Meldrum's niece from Paris, Matthew's aunt from Yorkshire, the former village doctor, Dr St John (now of Exeter) and the Mayor. The fete was also an opportunity for existing local traders and those considering trade in the village to market their wares and products. Mr Buchanan, the butcher, was going to display his prize sausages, for example. If the visitors from the surrounding areas liked what they tasted, they would be sure to patronise him, particularly at Christmas. He had struck a bargain with Mr Greening the village grocer for the supply of apples, sage and leeks for a premier range of sausages. Great-Aunt had enthused about the fete but Harper responded with a poorly veiled yawn and so she had left him at home for a few hours for boredom and curiosity to set in.

At eleven o'clock sharp, Harper was interrupted by an unfamiliar voice calling him. "Harper? Haaarper?" He abandoned the model train set to interrogate the audacious intruder.

"Who goes there?" Harper shouted, standing at the bottom of the staircase with both arms akimbo and his short legs spread apart.

"Penelope," was the polite reply from a lady that resembled an angel - aside from the scarlet red of her dress and shoes... and perhaps her accent.

Harper tried to stifle the instinct to correct her pronunciation of her name but instinct won. He repeated her name slowly and phonetically, before pressing for better details of her identity and the purpose of her presence in his home.

"I am Penelope, Mrs Meldrum's niece from Paris." She repeated her name pronouncing the 'lope' as it is pronounced in envelope and omitting the 's' from Paris. What would Miss Wordsworth make of that!

"Penelo*pe*, Pari*s*," Harper insisted. Raising his voice as if she was deaf, Harper admonished that being from Paris, or anywhere else in the world, was not a licence to speak poorly.

English lesson over, Harper moved on to the nub of the matter: "Right, enough of that. *Who* let you in, and *what* are *you* doing here?"

"*Quel morveux*," Penelope mumbled and then, more loudly, "The door was open. Millicent sent me here to collect you for the fete. Change your clothing and we can then be on our way."

Harper was outraged. Great-Aunt had not breathed a word of this arrangement to him in all her ramblings about the fete. He was also already suitably dressed by his reckoning *and* Great-Aunt's, he told *Penelope* with a defiant pursing of his lips.

Penelope saw that Harper had lied when Great-Aunt's eyes first fell on Harper. His shabbiness looked all the more stark because Penelope was so perfectly groomed herself. Her red dress was well starched and stopped just shy of her knees. Her shoes and hand-bag matched her dress perfectly. She walked elegantly beside Harper who looked ready to storm a field full of mad cows. His shirt looked exhausted and his shorts had conspicuous holes in them.

"Look at you Harper. Of all the many clothes you have, you wear *this?* They are only fit for dusting!" Great-Aunt declared. "You must stop going about as if no one in the world cares for you."

"Yes Great-Aunt."

A few people looked at Harper with pity, others with surprise. Most acknowledged that boys will be boys. They were caught up in chatter and the beauty of Penelope's hair and dress. "Mmmh," Harper thought; "It's all very well to admire a fairy dress but the great big feet are the spectacle."

One villager, Emily Davenport, arrived quite deliberately late, bearing an enormous and impressive platter of quivering cheese soufflés. This image of culinary perfection drew the admiration that she sought. Hands reaching for chests in surprise, hands raised to mouths shaped into a delighted '0', the sound of sharp in-takes of breath and murmurs of delight. Another villager, Lily Molsome, exclaimed "Goodness gracious - they are *incredible*, *did* you make them yourself? You have the patience and calm of *a saint* if you did!"

Mrs Davenport's chubby cheeks trembled with pride as she replied: "Oh, they're nothing, *honestly*. I made them this morning while Donald was gardening. You know the pollen de*feats* me at close range and so I thought I'd *idle* the time away while he toiled."

Betsy and Mable, the village's only set of twins, exchanged a knowing glance. Souffles will collapse without mercy or consideration for the most diligent cook, even when they do get *plenty* of attention. Daisy must have been in a flutter all night and all morning to turn out the perfect soufflés; not one of them had flopped.

Great-Aunt had put together a platter for Harper so that he did not miss any of the treats.

"Here we are Harper. I put some excellent treats aside for you. That," she said, pointing at an elaborately decorated cup cake, "is one of Mrs Pudimore's creations; deeeelicious!" Harper was not paying a jot of attention - his eyes were fixed on a generous slice of spinach, leek, and mushroom flan.

"What's that Great-Aunt?"

"Flan, Harper. Nutritious, full of good things, tasty, try it ..." Great-Aunt was not fully persuaded by the combination of ingredients but it did taste alright - but shy of 'delicious' perhaps!

Apart from looking absolutely awful with green and brown streaks staining it, Harper knew that the innocently named 'flan' was heavily laden with eggs - lots and lots of them!

"I don't eat things what look ghastly...?"

"Wrong, wrong, wrong, Harper," Great-Aunt whispered close against his ear. "Grammar, wrong; manners, wrong; volume of your voice, wrong. We discussed this yesterday did we not, and we agreed that you would behave nicely..."

"I've been perfectly nice I think Great-Aunt but it's quite another thing to eat food that..."

"Harper, stop immediately! Leave it on your plate and keep quiet about it."

Harper inclined his head towards Great-Aunt with a tight-lipped fleeting smile. Great-Aunt was nearly overcome with the urge to box his ears, especially as the shy cook was sitting nearby and had, in all probability heard the exchange.

Harper poked about the plate and looked about him to see if there was any fun to be had once the eating was over. He stopped short at 11 o'clock on the opposite side of the table because he noticed a lady wearing a deep pink that matched her cheeks and nose, staring at him intently and not with the most kindly expression. "Are you going to waste that perfectly good plate of food young man?" Harper looked about him as if he did not know where the question came from, or to whom it was addressed. Then he looked back at the very large lady that he decided *must* be called Mrs Tomato-Head. She continued looking at him, expectant of an answer. Harper decided that he would be 'nice' and answer the question.

"*Oh no* Miss, I won't waste it! I'll leave it be on my plate, *just* in case *someone else* wants it." With that, he gave a conspiratorial wink and nod indicating that *she* was angling to be the '*someone*'. He went on, "It's just that I can't eat things what look ghastly just in case it's a useful hint that they *taste* ghastly." Harper gave his reply with polite earnest. If Miss Tomato-Head was red before their conversation, she was a beetroot when Harper had finished with her. She threw her napkin down and turned her body a full 180 degrees away from Harper and his impertinent face. All he could see was her back.

Harper saw hours of boredom spread ahead of him until his mind chanced upon an idea for an experimental magic trick that did not require a captive audience or a glamorous assistant. Hugo and Agatha were away in Dorset on holiday after all.

He would remove the red and white gingham tablecloth from under the tray of Mrs Davenport's souffles with a swift sleight of hand.

Alas, Harper was not a magician, the villagers refused to taste deconstructed soufflé encrusted with mud and grass and they all learned that Mrs Davenport was certainly not a saint. Great-Aunt's shoulder absorbed the blow that she aimed at Harper's ears.

Chapter Twenty-one

Harper Hepplesthwaite: The sweet smell of freedom

When they finally arrived home that evening, Great-Aunt sent Harper to the blue room. "Stay out of my sight for a while young man - off with you to the blue room. I will call you when tea is ready, not that you deserve any food after your performance today. Shocking, simply shocking." Harper protested, "Not that room please, Great-Aunt."

"Why ever not? Don't be silly." Harper was not sure if there really was a twinkle in Great-Aunt's eye.

"I'll go to my own room," he offered.

"You're to go to the blue room as I have instructed Harper - now please."

"I'll go to *any* other room Great-Aunt. I'll-even-stand-on-one-leg-with-an-encyclopedia on-my-head-and-facing-a-wall-for-*hours*."

"Harper, go now – *immediately*!"

Great-Aunt would not relent and so Harper decided that he should perhaps direct his attention to conquering the Wighorns, rather than pleading with Great-Aunt to no avail.

Perhaps the problem was that he had always entered the blue room with trepidation but it was *his* house, he was a *human* and he was *bigger* than the Wighorns. Harper had a plan as a result of this assessment of the situation; he would have to consider a forceful offensive. He stopped in Great-Aunt's bedroom and pulled a poker from its hold as he continued up the stairs. He held it out before him, ready to charge into the room, charge at the fireplace and charge a Wighorn through if necessary ... only *absolutely* necessary he considered as the long staircase fell away to just a few steps from the blue room.

He walked to the window, facing the fireplace at all times. He was in the room for about four minutes and there was not a sound, not a speck of charcoal falling onto the hearth, not a pin drop. He had kept the poker by his side as he sat on a metal trunk by the window but he decided to brandish it just once for good measure. The trunk was a new addition to the room. Great-Aunt had taken a liking to it on one of her shopping trips with Laurie.

Harper settled the poker against the wall beside him and sat waiting for Great-Aunt's summons for tea. His patience lasted a second or two. He became cross at the banishment and considered storming down the stairs in defiance. He would simply *refuse* to stay in the room any longer. If Great-Aunt persisted, he would run away. He had, after all, discovered a short route to the main road to Knoxham. That thought evaporated after a mere twelve seconds.

Bored and nervous, Harper did the only logical thing that he could - he stood to his feet and with a phantom adversary, set about fencing! He moved deftly from left foot to right foot, his leg bent at the knee and an arm folded behind his back as he stabbed at the air with the poker. This lasted for about two minutes.

Before he had time to stop and consider his actions, Harper's head was poking into the fireplace as he kneeled on the hearth as close to the grate as possible to assist his exploration. Harper's head was about as far in as it could go without it becoming stuck, when he perceived that a tiny clump of coal had landed on his nose but it did not fall off its narrow surface; rather, another piece landed and again remained firm. Just as he paused stock still to consider this phenomenon, he felt a light tugging on his hairline, just above his forehead. While his brain caught up with the reality of the situation, Harper's ears picked up the sound of a sharp in-take of breath, followed fairly closely by a long, and very alarmed, "'Elppppp! 'elppppppp!" Harper reached up to touch his nose and his hand closed on a teeny, tiny... body - for he had chanced upon Grotshaw, or rather Grotshaw had chanced upon his nose!

Harper screamed and clawed at his face. *Nearly* in the nick of time, Hercules reached down and grabbed Grotshaw's left hand, which still held a few strands of Harper's hair! Grotshaw's rescue came before he was smashed to the hard ground by Harper's clawing hands but, unfortunately, *after* Harper's clawing hands had beaten at his little body. Both Grotshaw and Hercules retreated further up the chimney breast and Harper collected himself sufficiently to make his way across the room to fetch the poker which was resting against the narrow edge of the window pane.

Grotshaw looked worse for wear. He pulled at Hercules' collar, drawing his ear towards his lips so that he could utter some final wishes; his preferred attire for his funeral, what his family were to be told of the manner of his death, the music that must certainly *not* be played at his funeral (unless the organisers wanted haunting) and such other wise words and concerns that one would utter, if one had the privilege of knowing the time of one's own death. His final words were not instructions but a statement. He also made a humble apology to be passed on to Hobnails who had predicted that the boy would be the death of them. His death-bed speech was cut short by Skulkins who gave him a sharp prod in the back and said, "Get out of it, you're not dying, 'twas only a jostle, now get to your feet there's work to be done. Take this chair, or I'll stand it on your big head."

"Oohhhhhhhwwwwwwwww!" Grotshaw whined, "'arsh in life, WICKED in death," and he shook his fists at Skulkins.

"Ar there you go. If you've energy for that, you've energy for these," Skulkins said and he swung a chair at

Grotshaw who had no choice but to take it! He stood cowering amongst the small lumps of coal in the fireplace, mind too shaken, body too weak, to do anything but stand, barely able to take the weight of the chair. The other workmen passed him with the odd curious or sympathetic glance but only Hercules released him from his burden. He skulked back up into the chimney breast to check his wounds and howl while his colleagues worked.

In the meantime, Harper considered his next move. He saw the workmen spilling out of the fireplace at double-speed, perhaps to make up for the delay that ensued from his close encounter with Grotshaw. He could charge at them, as he had the poker to hand now but they seemed a feisty, strong bunch and he considered that they might just be up to the task of overpowering him, encouraged by the twin motivations of loyalty and outrage. Harper realised that he could not deliberately harm them; not when it actually came to it.

Nevertheless, Harper kept the poker close to hand though out of sight; he would not court danger but he would defend himself if necessary ... perhaps.

He watched the usual scene unfold, tables and chairs brought out of the fireplace and set in their rightful places. There was a general hullabaloo with the workmen making small protests about bearing the burden of Grotshaw's tasks but Hercules soon waded in carrying more than his share of the required furnishings. For the first time, Harper noticed the workmen sweat under their labour. It must have been the weather as it was a particularly balmy summer's day. He felt the odd bead of sweat on his nose too but that was more on account of his nerves. Hercules gave a couple of the men an approving pat on the back before they disappeared onto the hearth, up the grate, into the fire-place and beyond.

Crouchlow shuffled into the room next and seemed to be remonstrating with himself with mumblings, gritting of teeth and the clenching and unclenching of fists. He even punched the air at a height suggestive that he had a certain person's head in mind. However, he assumed his usual ostensibly docile attitude when Hearall Seeall entered the room. Hearall Seeall set the tools of his craft neatly on his desk, checked for the sixth time that his typewriter had no want of ink, that the barrel had no intention of jarring, that his notepad lay at a forty-five degree angle from his left elbow and then sat down with his hands behind his head, with the complete repose that only one thoroughly prepared for every eventuality could afford to adopt. In the shade of the corner of the hearth where he sat, his face resembled the face of the moon tilting very slowly to and fro with the shifting motion of the night clouds. He noted Crouchlow's discomfiture and gave a private, dry smile - perhaps 'Lightning' there had failed to strike yet again and had been chastised for it. Hearall Seeall was not too far wrong!

The very grand Pinikerty came in then, looking impeccably perfect in a black three piece suit with pale blue piping running through the waistcoat. This ensemble was set off with a crisp white shirt that had his neck in a death grip that he seemed to bear with pride. His shoes shone particularly brightly and announced themselves with a smart tap with each step that he took. Pinikerty was generally concerned that too many grubby and horrible things could be observed if one looked down. This day, however, he held his nose even higher than usual, because he knew that he had turned himself out particularly well. He checked that his pen was full of ink and the nib clear of any excess ink. Then he tested both ink and nib by signing his name on a piece of paper with an elaborate flourish of the wrist. All was in order. He was never tempted to look in any great detail at the list of complaints against an accused before court formally started and so he had nothing to say to Crouchlow. He only needed to know the general nature of the allegations so that he could paraphrase to his vanity's content.

Pryson and Domble-bluff entered the room next and took their places. Pryson sat, Domble-bluff stood. Domble-bluff captured one of his thumbs in the chain of his glasses that hung about his neck, Pryson's thumb steadied his grip on the jug of water on his side of the table as he filled his drinking glass. Domble-bluff cleared his throat with a delicate force that demanded attention; Pryson settled the tickle in his throat with a gulp of water. Domble-bluff looked slowly and pompously about the court-room avoiding the eyes and persons of all others in it; Pryson kept his head bent over his papers. Of course, Domble-bluff looked as if he had spent every single penny of Pryson's monthly wage on his shirt alone and Pryson looked as if he had spent a penny on his suit, shirt and shoes. Harper noticed a model train carriage to his left and his miniature white Rolls Royce to his right. Pryson had arrived at court by train and Domble-bluff by car. However, Harper did not have another second to muse about that.

The jurors filed into the room. All twelve of them. Harper studied them all but it was Whizzle-grump, Snappernash and Stonehard that arrested his attention.

Why Harper was particularly intrigued was that they were dressed bizarrely; dressed bizarrely even for the odd creatures that they were!

They had been in conference since the last trial, planning for this one as they knew for a surety that Harper would be back. In that conference they had made a conspiracy! A conspiracy with a three-pronged approach in the form of a Plan A, Plan B and Plan C in ascending order of the chaos they would cause. One plan would be deployed after the other if they were forced to!

Whizzle-grump was wearing a suit of purple with large pale blue spots on both the trousers and the jacket. He also wore a waist-coat of pale blue with large purple spots all over it. For all its oddity, the suit was remarkably well cut; Domble-bluff's tailor could have had a hand in the making of it, if not for the busy fabric! As for Snappernash, his chosen hue was the *softest* pink that one could imagine outside of a baby's nursery! He wore a pale blue waist-coat and shirt. The shirt had pink frills and trills about the neck which must have tickled his chin. Stonehard was the most outrageous. He was wearing *short* trousers - they just grazed his ankles and it was likely that, when he took his seat, they would only just cast a shadow on his shins. Hairy, spindly legs were out for all to see, except where his lurid socks left off of course.

Knapsley was dressed in his customary fashion but he wore an absolutely queer hat on his head! It was similar to the one that Dickens' Ebenezer Scrooge wore in his night vigils but it had a solid red and yellow ball at its floppy point. He held a massive, impressive looking book in his hands and its cover was inscribed in large writing with the words: **"The Rule of Law: The Right and the Good (and sundry codes of practice)"** He placed it before Whizzle-grump and took his seat.

Pinikerty felt light-headed as he watched the trio parade into the room and take their seats, Cyril broke into a fit of hiccups that refused to end, Domble-bluff looked at the trio and then looked away, shaking his head vigorously at least eight times in succession, making his cheeks shudder. On spotting them, Pryson's lips formed a stunned '0' and he buried his head so deeply in his papers that his eyeballs were virtually on the desk before him.

In short, the trio's collective attire nearly brought proceedings to the point intended by Plan 'C'! Only Judge's entrance to the room ensured that order was maintained. Judge initially looked as sleepy as usual but even *his* senses were not left unscathed. Though the Court was silent, he hammered his gavel thrice after looking at the trio and uttered a very low, concerned, "hhhrrrraaammmppphhh," before he laid the gavel to rest.

Ponderton, Temperton and Weyall looked positively dull by comparison in their royal blue, navy blue and pale blue, set off with yellows, whites and greens! They had also held a conference and had decided that they would not interrupt the proceedings to express their concerns, or view-points. Rather they would wait until the proper order of the proceedings invited their comments.

The door slammed shut but only after something incredible occurred. The poker that Harper still held loosely in his hand escaped his grip and - by some magical means - and as if in a jaunty dance, left the room and settled against a wall outside it! Judge turned his eyes on Harper, they seemed to flash, but he did not say a word. Not a solitary word. Harper felt very nervous, very nervous indeed - perhaps the poker had been a really bad idea after all. Harper wished Judge would bellow at him, or something!

Proceedings commenced as usual with Pinikerty reading the case number and case name. Judge called for Pinikerty to call for the scroll so that the complaints against Harper could be read. Crouchlow ambled forward with the scroll and ambled backwards to his spot, mindful not to do himself an injury on the sharp points of any of the tables.

All eyes turned on Harper as Pinikerty announced that they were there to hear case 1036: **The Right and The Good -vs- Harper Hepplesthwaite:**

"The first charge: That Harper Hepplesthwaite did, on the 25 July, conspire to *ruin* a school play *deliberately* and with merriment. He carried out his plan, causing shame and embarrassment to a *distinguished* member of public office."

"The second charge: That Harper Hepplesthwaite did offend the sensibilities of the Lord Mayor, who was the said distinguished member of public office at the said assembly, by the actions hereto before mentioned."

Whizzle-grump huffed and puffed at the windy and unnecessary explanation and so, for once,

Whizzle-grump and Ponderton were in agreement but both held their peace for *very* different reasons. Stonehard started to sharpen his nails but Snappernash elbowed him. Left uninterrupted for a change, Pinikerty continued in his glory!

"The third charge: That Harper Hepplesthwaite did waste food at the said fete;

The fourth charge: That Harper Hepplesthwaite did at the said Summer fete make unkind, unnecessary, hostile and ungracious remarks;

The fifth charge: That Harper Hepplesthwaite did recklessly ruin a platter of perfectly formed souffles;

The sixth charge...," Pinikerty started. Pryson looked down hurriedly scanning his copy of the list of charges. There were no further allegations on his list but he said nothing and so Pinikerty continued.

"... My Lord it is irregular (not usual) to add another charge at this late stage, especially before the Advocate... umm lawyer for the defence has not had a chance to hear it - but the interests of justice *demand* that this is allowed. These are exceptional circumstances. The exceptional circumstances are that Harper Hepplesthwaite did immediately before these proceedings began, *beat black and blue* one of our diligent court staff..."

Temperton hastily jotted a note to Weyall: "*He surely cannot give evidence about the colours!!!*" The protest was mute and so Pinikerty continued.

"... and quite mercilessly too. The said member of staff, Grotshaw, is still suffering from his injuries and will do for the foreseeable future. Grotshaw is too badly injured to attend court to give evidence on his own account and is, indeed, still trembling so badly, so as to make his bed shake beneath him. An ear witness is too frightened to attend but the court can perhaps hear from the doctor who has attended the poor victim."

"Ear-witness?" Ponderton thought with alarm but he remained mute.

(Skulkins was the '*ear*'-witness who was supposedly too frightened to attend court to give evidence for his co-worker. Truth be told, he was not frightened at all. He just did not care a jot. He would rather eat toe-nails boiled with onions and Marmite, he had snapped when asked if he would attend the hearing as a witness!)

Carried away by the lack of interruption, Pinikerty exceeded his responsibility and added a summary all of his own:

"It seems "The Right and the Good" say that Harper Hepplesthwaite is a general tryer of patience, deliberate ignorer of social graces and beater of innocents M'Lud!"

Judge gave an exasperated "hhhhrrrrrraaammmmppphhh" at this and another when he noted that neither Pryson nor Domble-bluff took the last two matters up with him! "Back in your box Pinikerty, Pinikerty, back in your box," Judge said wearily.

Judge turned to Pryson, "What do you say to the last charge? Do you need time to prepare to deal with it?"

Pryson stood to his feet to answer, "In summary M'Lud, I have no objection to dealing with this last charge now. Two points my Lord if I may. Point 1 my Lord, to the last charge, I say disgraceful my Lord if proven true; Point 2 my Lord, the Right and The Good do not require additional time to deal with the sixth charge. Finally, my Lord, the doctor may be called as witness if it so please the court."

"Very well," Judge said and then he bent a surprisingly alert gaze on Domble-bluff.

Domble-bluff raised an objection to charge six being presented at the last minute and, therefore, objected to any witness being called to give evidence concerning it. However, this was not really true. The list was mercifully short for a change so it was not *time* that concerned Domble-bluff. What concerned him was that Harper Hepplesthwaite *was* guilty and that the doctor would deliver a damning description of the victim's injuries – confirming the *black* and the *blue*! Domble-bluff had a reputation to maintain and the human boy ruined it as his peril! At the moment, the hordes of junior members of his Chambers parted like the Red Sea when he, Domble-bluff entered the busy corridors. Even his peers were starting to do the same and he would not have that ruined by the wretch Harper! The tell-tale black and blue bruises needed time to fade!

Judge had to make the decision because Domble-bluff and Pryson had different opinions.

"While I note that charge six should ideally be heard at *this* hearing to save time and the costs involved in bringing *everyone* back to court *again* to hear it separately, my *decision* is that Grotshaw, Domble-bluff, Harper and the doctor need a proper opportunity to consider what they have to say about the charge."

That dealt with, Judge then turned to Pryson:

"Does The Right and The Good want to continue with charge six at another hearing, or do they want to withdraw it altogether?"

"The Right and The Good confirm that they *definitely* want to have the charge dealt with at another hearing, my Lord," Pryson answered determinedly.

"In that case, Pryson and Domble-bluff, you must meet with your witnesses promptly to gather evidence before their memories fade. They must be prepared for the next hearing."

Harper nodded vigorously to assure the whole court that he would *definitely* remember *all* of his evidence. He needed the charge dropped for today so that he could get out of the room as soon as possible. He had *no* intention of ever returning again in his *whole* life! He promised himself that he would be an angel of angels from that day forward.

Judge then ruled that neither Pryson nor Domble-bluff should refer to the charge during the current hearing. It would be dealt with at a separate hearing on another date.

"Now that we know where we are with *that*, let us hear the case for the five charges–Domble-bluff - call your witness, ordered Judge.

"They'll all have *clean forgotten* the five by *now,*" Crouchlow mumbled to himself with the most quiet and sardonic a chuckle possible.

Whizzle-grump, Snappernash and Stonehard prepared to execute Plan A.

"My Lord, if it please you," Whizzle-grump said, standing up and pressing to his point before his Lordship, or the monkey, Pinikerty, had a chance to object, "On account of the precious time of those here present and the money that these trials gobble up, we propose that the accused Harper Hepplesthwaite be called – called, my Lord, to tell us at once what he would have us do to *please* him. However, before that, he is to be hoisted above us all, in a chair not unlike your own, my Lord, and borne by the court staff, perhaps even the very one he beat to a pulp. Once upon their shoulders, a scribe, not just any scribe but the court's best, should set about enquiring after and recording in ink, what his heart so desires. As if from the boy's lips to the very ears of God, when the wish leaves his lips, those who work for The Right and The Good are to see his wish done. A baker is to be commissioned immediately to bake him a Victoria sponge cake for *if* it is his favourite; mind there is no scrimping with the butter cream and jam! Treacle is to be drizzled on his tongue at half hourly intervals, or until such time as he yells 'stop' in the ear of the drizzler; whichever event occurs sooner."

"Here, here," Snappernash and Stonehard called, with their fists banging on the table as they echoed their support.

Pryson, emboldened by the preposterous nature of the notion, stood to his feet and prayed his Lordship to perhaps, maybe consider calling the three to order.

Judge looked at the three sitting in their odd suits and smelt a rat. A rat that he would squash as soon as it ventured more boldly and clearly from it's hole. For now, he gave the order to Pryson to call the witness, Harper.

Pryson called Harper and asked him an initial set of questions designed to get him to admit that he had conspired to ruin the school play, that he was at the school play, that he knew the Mayor was there, deliberately ruined the said school play and had no remorse for his actions. Harper accepted all propositions and Domblebluff barely muffled a snarl. The billows of the Red Sea were closing around and about him but he would keep it parted yet!

Before moving to Plan B, Snappernash made an attempt to re-work Plan A. "My Lord, if it *please* you," he said rising to his feet, grinding his teeth and not caring a jot that he displeased his Lordship, "What we mean to say is that we may as well *get* to the verdict now rather than procrastinate, knowing that *it's all one and the same* whether we continue for hours or draw the line now."

'Ar' Judge thought to himself; it was just as he believed. He bent his eyes on Snappernash and told him in no uncertain terms, "In my court, justice will be *done*, and be *seen* to be done. The proceedings will continue *without any interruptions.*"

Snappernash sat down without any sign of having been beaten back at all. He looked to Whizzle-grump and Stonehard - Plan B it was then!

Whizzle-grump reached for the large book that Knapsley had brought into the court room. It was, in fact, a book full of empty pages that a willing work-man had made at their request, not knowing what their purpose was. Stonehard had crafted the top cover, writing the words **The Right and the Good: The Rule of Law (and sundry codes of practice)**.

Whizzle-grump tore the book with a reckless delight passing sections of it to Snappernash and Stonehard who followed suit, making an absolute din as they tore at the pages.

"What, what, *what* are you doing?" Judge asked in a dangerously quiet voice. He was not the only one to wonder! His gavel was raised high but was not sent crashing down while he made his enquiries.

They all spoke at once but Whizzle-grump's voice prevailed as the loudest, as Snappernash was hindered by the grinding of his teeth and Stonehard by the sharpening of his nails. Maybe it was the weather - but there was mutiny in the court!

"Why, my Lord, if it please you, we are tearing up the Rule Book and, if we had a horse and motor-cart, we would run that through the rule book too for that is what we see done *time after time* with this most *abominable* human boy, let orf for the most horrid things by the *soft* pleadings, of these, these, '*mercy-merchants' and 'grace guerillas'*," Whizzle-grump shrieked as he pointed a gnarled forefinger at Ponderton, Temperton and Weyall. The alleged mercy merchants and grace guerillas exchanged surprised and disappointed glances.

Once he had satisfied himself that the jurors hadn't the temerity to use his white Rolls Royce as a substitute horse and cart to run through the Rule Book,

Domble-bluff relaxed in the knowledge that Judge would do his job and bring them in hand.

Whizzle-grump was set to continue his tirade and Judge still held the gavel suspended in the air ...

"Stop this outrage, stop this outrage at once!" Pinikerty exclaimed, very close to hysteria. This brought a silence that only Judge's gavel could. Judge was silent for a few seconds - of all the outbursts, Pinikerty's had most surprised him.

"Collect yourself Pinikerty. This outburst is most disconcerting, most disconcerting. Pinikerty, do collect yourself at once!"

Snappernash could no longer bear it. "What *ought* to be done is quite clear. We have heard of his deceit, embarrassing behavior and vile language. We are not allowed to mention the most *cruel* beating yet are we? Well, there's only one thing for it ..." Before he could say that Harper should be marked indelibly on his hand or left cheek to indicate that he was a deceiver, a causer of embarrassment and a user of vile, insulting language and starved until he agrees not to waste food anymore, Ponderton interjected.

"I sense a sinister attempt to ruin the boy's character and his chance of a fair trial by suggesting there is some devilment in his behavior. I call on all to *think* on the words of Snappernash. I ask you; *D*eceiver? *E*mbarrassment? *V*ile? *I*nsulting *l*anguage? Does anyone else see the *devil* in it? If they do, which they must for it is clear, his words must be struck from the record."

However, there was no record, not an accurate one at any rate; Cyril had long given up his attempt to give a full, clear and complete typed account of the court proceedings on account of shock! He would be forced into the disgraceful act of making it all up afterwards. If only he had been kinder to Crouchlow, he may well have helped with the confabulation!

Weyall spoke now, "Surely we are all here to see *justice* done and *mercy* is the other side of the coin of *true justice*..." Knapsley came to at this point of course and asked incredulously, "*Mercy* - what's *that*?" He spat as if the very word tasted disgusting.

Whizzle-grump and Stonehard then shouted their suggestions as to suitable punishments for the boy Harper.

Judge's gavel went down and order was restored again - but not for long.

It was Domble-bluff's turn to question Harper.

As Domble-bluff put his questions, Whizzlegrump, Snappernash and Stonehard deployed Plan 'C'.

They elbowed and nudged each other. Then, in turn, they pointed at the Rule of Law on Pinikerty's desk, the Judge's stand and both Advocates while rolling about in their chairs with feigned hysterical laughter.

Judge's gavel went down with force and his voice was a storm, "Whizzle-grump, Snappernash, Stonehard - put a stop to this now or you will be made to stand down. You will be made to stand down if you do not stop this now Stonehard, Snappernash and Whizzlegrump!"

"We are merely making a *mockery* of the court which is done and tolerated here by those guerillas *time and time again* my Lord, *if it so please you!*" Whizzle-grump shrieked, the laughter drying up even more quickly than it had started. He was exhausted, now that all plans A, B and C had been deployed!

Knapsley, making an attempt at a self-styled Plan D, suggested in hushed whispers in Whizzle-grump's ear that he make a show of pulling at the very elasticated waist of his trousers. Whether because he was fatigued, disappointed with the failure of plans A, B, and C, or simply because he missed Knapsley's point. Whizzle-grump's response was to pull mercilessly at

Knapsley's nose. He only relented when Knapsley gasped his explanation that the prank was to show the inappropriately loose grip of the law shown by the court again and again. Whizzle-grump's fingers immediately relented and, while he did not agree to take up the idea, he whispered calmly that the point could be quite horribly misunderstood.

Judge raised the gavel in warning and all were silent again. He then looked to Domble-bluff to give his speech to close the proceedings before the jury reached their decision. It was a below average bungling performance for, alas by this time, the mutinous mood had totally devastated Domble-bluff's attempt to demonstrate his court-craft. No, today, it seemed that the award for top performance would go to Pryson, and the 'jackals for justice' but he did try amidst further interruptions from the said jackals.

Harper was found guilty of all charges and sentenced to half an hour a day in the blue room for two weeks. This was a disaster, more so for Harper than Domble-bluff's reputation, although Domble-bluff was adamant that the disaster fell on him. The merchants and guerillas were not disappointed with the result; Pryson had made his case well and Harper's character would benefit from *reasonable* discipline.

Harper was left with the prospect of facing the creatures each and every day for a whole two weeks. He knew there was no escape; any notions he had to the contrary disappeared at the same time that the poker skipped out of the room earlier. He would not be able to stop going to the room, or get himself out once in!

The door clicked open and Harper left the room, too exhausted to run.

It really was time to go, to leave number two Pear Tree Lane - and Eldersham once and for all. Harper would not rely on a lift from Laurie. He would just leave and first thing in the morning too. He could not bear the thought of an afternoon or evening with the creatures.

As he went about the rest of the day, Harper's actions spoke a fond goodbye. He stared at Great-Aunt all through tea. She had no idea what it all meant and so, after initially meeting him head-on with a steely gaze of her own, she avoided all eye contact. 'If only you knew,' he thought to himself and focused his attention on his hearty meal of shepherds' pie and green beans.

Harper did not wake as early as he intended the following morning. He planned to wake before Great-Aunt - but failed to.

He made the briefest of trips to the bathroom before dressing and packing for his journey. With Great-Aunt buzzing about on the ground floor, he had no opportunity to pack any food and there was not even a cube of cheese in his bedroom; not even under his bed! No matter, the fields would feed him he mused, full of self-pity.

While Great-Aunt went out to water the recovering front garden, Harper left the house through the door in the kitchen. He had a few items in his school satchel, including a marble that Mother had packed for him when she first brought him to Eldersham. Harper ripped through the gate and tripped down the long dirt lane that led to the crossroad flanked by woods on either side. Left to school, right to Church. He buried his hands deep into his pockets, head bent low as he kicked stones and headed right; and nearly headed for the Church.

Harper made for the huge field from which Mrs Mainwaring had said she got supplies of oil. At the time, he had found it a strange thing for her to have said but he was not really interested to know what she meant.

He remembered a route to the field but it seemed to take an age. It had been so much quicker when he was a passenger in Laurie's motor-car. Harper saw the field in the distance - it was a sea of purple. His heart skipped with nerves and excitement. He wondered whether Great-Aunt had noticed his absence; perhaps not but she would feel wretched when she did, he thought, with a pang of guilt.

Harper crossed the narrow road, took a running jump over the brook and then followed the path to the northerly entrance to the field. He walked into the field and kept on walking, imagining the route he would take to get to the main road to hitch-hike to the nearby town without a villager seeing him and reporting the fact to Great-Aunt or, worse still, insisting on escorting him home by the ear or scruff of the neck.

Harper had made good progress for one with short legs and was well into the field and all wistful thoughts were cast aside. He was suddenly aware of a scent in the air around him. The smell was pungent and it was everywhere. He sniffed his clothes, wondering if Great-Aunt had gone wild with the washing detergent. His clothes were *not* the culprit however and he *certainly* was not, although he was sure that he would absorb the strong smell through his pores if he hung around!

It was the flowers all around him, for Harper was in a field of lavender! He had to return to number two Pear Tree Lane after all - an intrepid young traveller could not, or rather *should* not, embark on an adventure of independence smelling of flowers!

When he arrived home, Harper realised that his feelings of guilt were misplaced - Great-Aunt had not noticed his absence.

Harper did have to go to the blue room for thirty minutes every day for two weeks but nothing at all occurred; all was as still as could be. It was a mystery!

Chapter Twenty-two

Harper Hepplesthwaite: Chestnuts roasting on an open fire...

The balmy summer days soon came to an end and the lush greens of the many trees soon became rather glorious rubies and golds before withering and falling from glory altogether, trampled underfoot by the busy adults and children of Eldersham. Harper, Agatha and Hugo loved to walk home through the smaller of the two woods that led a direct path from the school grounds to the east of Eldersham where they lived. In the early mornings, a light breeze whipped the brightly coloured leaves around their ankles and some got very carried away and blew as high as their knees! They kicked their feet through the leaves, causing even more of a flurry.

The weather was not all that changed.

The school work became more complex and Mr Hornby took more of the English and Mathematics classes. Learning fractions with fractious Mr Hornby was a real challenge for Harper; in fact he dreaded the lessons. Mr Hornby rushed the stick of chalk over the blackboard as if the chalk were hot and he could not wait to be released of it. He handled the blackboard brush in the same manner, wiping away the calculations of the most odd configurations of numbers while Harper was still busily writing them down. Two-thirds plus seven-eighths, three quarters plus two fifths and such like had Harper in sixes and sevens but Mr Hornby ploughed on - writing and brushing; brushing and writing.

The children were also back in the long trousers.

The highlight of the school week for Harper was his additional English classes and so Harper also looked forward to the English lessons, as he could show off what he was learning with Mrs Wordsworth. She had declared his achievement to date 'superb' which was a significant improvement on her first evaluation!

Harper put his new and extensive vocabulary to *excellent* use. For example, he issued a written invitation to all of the pupils in his school year; all twenty-nine of them were to attend a bonfire party at number two Pear Tree Lane.

To add style to excellence, Harper used Great-Aunt's heavily embossed ivory writing paper and fountain pen. Ink took to it beautifully; well, the *very* expensive ink in Great-Aunt's ink-well did anyway! Inspired by the beautiful script he had seen in the scroll in Pinikerty's clutch, he wrote in a style that *could* have been beautiful had speed, not haste, driven his pen over each sheet!

The invitation, sent well in advance of the event, read:

Dear Parents

Your child is cordially invited to attend a bonfire party at number 2 Pear Tree Lane, Eldersham on the 14 October at 12:30pm to 3:30pm sharpish. I should be honoured if he would attend.

Do not be alarmed at the thought of a bonfire as it will be handled responsibly by someone who knows how. Please just wave your child off at the

gate of your own home; DO NOT bring him to the party (you do want your child to be independent don't you?).

He will be fine, I will look after him (and the others), at this small and peaceful party.

PS: If your child is a girl, and a pupil in your son's year at school, she is also invited. However, be warned that the number of girls will be limited for the good reason that you must already know – we don't have many of 'em at our school. It's tradition you see.

My most sincere and distinguished sentiments

A person living at number 2 Pear Tree Lane

With plenty of advanced notice, Harper expected a good turn-out. Ever organised, Great-Aunt had told Harper that she would be in Goldsbourne on bonfire day for some arts conference or other. She explained she would be leaving Eldersham at noon and arriving back home at three forty-five in the afternoon.

Harper's handwriting and writing style were clearly good enough to persuade the fifty eight parents that Great-Aunt herself was the author and, therefore, the exceedingly generous, brave or silly host of the bonfire party. They all sent their children to number two Pear Tree Lane at 12:30pm on the 14 of October. Neville Mortimer had insisted on bringing along his younger sister, Jemima, to Harper's disgust and horror.

By the time that the first guest arrived, Harper had everything in order.

The twelve sausages Great-Aunt had bought from Mr Buchanan were laid on the hearth in the dining-room. For a split second, he wondered how he would divide them if all thirty children wanted to taste them. He pushed the nasty fraction -*12/30* that appeared in his mind's eye out of sight and decided that it was going to be an 'each man for himself' sort of affair. Each 'man' would have to make do with a bite of a sausage. He remembered that there would be thirty-one of them altogether with Jemima but he again banished the 12/31 that reared its head.

The poker was nearby for him or the others to poke the sausages through for roasting in the fireplace and Great-Aunt's metal colander was on the hearth. Once all of the guests had arrived, a pair of them would be responsible for heaping a few handfuls of chestnuts into the colander. Agatha and Hugo would then, in turn, suspend it over the fire to roast them, using the cast-iron drapery rod.

He had diluted blackcurrant cordial, one bottle to a splash of water in Great-Aunt's wine decanter and glasses were at the ready, littered here and there, waiting to be stepped upon or kicked asunder by twenty-seven boys... and three girls.

Harper had also dragged the bag of chestnuts that he and Matthew had gathered over the past few weeks from the back garden, through the kitchen and into the dining room. He lay it beside the fireplace. The nut-cracker was resting itself beside the colander waiting to be of service.

Great-Aunt had done her part, although purely accidentally of course; a low fire was burning nicely in the fireplace. As the dining room was the heart of the house, both socially and geographically, it had the largest fire place of all. A low fire burned there from mid-September to the end of March every year.

Great-Aunt also left music playing whenever she left Harper alone (offering him company of sorts) and so music played in the background.

Soon all of the guests arrived - Jemima in tow with Neville. Happily, none of the parents took against the advice Harper had given - that the children arrive unaccompanied and he confidently brushed away the children's questions about Great-Aunt's whereabouts.

Once the wave of excitement that the house was free of adults passed, Harper delegated tasks to each of the children. He took responsibility for placing the sausages on the poker for roasting and throwing lumps of coal and wood on the fire to keep it going; Ivor was to take turns with William to hold the sausage-filled poker in the fire; Daniel and Edward were to take joint responsibility for loading the colander with chestnuts and Gregory and Jeremiah were to unload the colander of roasted chestnuts. Annabelle and Zaccheus were to crack the chestnuts open. Harper ruled that, in the event of a squabble about one or the other hogging the nutcracker, each was to have a turn with the nut-cracking until his or her palms hurt with the effort. Until then, the other was to wait a turn with patience. Molly was to crack the chestnuts open with her teeth if the two were too slow to keep up with demand. Archibald and Frederick were to let Harper know when the cordial ran out. (Cry baby) Humphrey was to taste the first offerings of cooking to ensure that they were edible and (Clever Clogs) Clive was to take responsibility for making sure that none of the drinking glasses broke. They were Great-Aunt's champagne flutes, wine glasses and goblets after all!

Jemima sprinkled her energetic charm about the room, entertaining Daniel, Edward, Frederick, Gregory, Hilary, Hugo and Ivor and so on and so forth with her wit, as they toiled. The Anvil's Chorus played in the background.

A while into the genteel soiree, Harper decided that he did not fancy the smell arising from the fireplace. He was not sure whether the chestnuts, sausages or colander were the culprit and he did not care. He declared all items unfit for consumption even before a whining Humphrey could.

As they had been cooped up in the house for about twenty minutes, the wild beast in them cried for the great outdoors. Harper led the troop out to the garden after instructing them to abandon food, glasses and tools on the hearth. Harper had the good sense to warn his guests to keep off the flower beds and they did. There was plenty of open space, nook, cranny and tree to suit every taste, without troubling the flowers and manicured shrubs.

A series of games and sport broke out at random, most of which only a small contingent of joy-thieves steered clear of, sitting about the garden with various expressions of alarm and disapproval. Jemima, though younger than all of them, threw herself into the heart of every game without fear or reservation and Harper #decided that she was perhaps not so bad a guest to have after all. However, the generous appraisal was withdrawn by the end of the day. One game went slightly wrong and the 'slight wrong' was not lightly brushed off by her mother!

Jemima had (with complete enthusiasm) agreed to be held by the limbs and hurled into the bushes which grew near the enemy camp. She was a rouse to distract a band of outlaws, while their prisoners escaped. The good folk were to escape while Jemima was discovered, questioned and tortured. One or two of the good folk were to return to her rescue, should circumstances such as her still being alive, require it. "After three," they had whispered with one voice. Then 'one' ... 'two' ... and on three, having swung Jemima twice to give both them and her momentum, they used all of their strength to hurl her into the bushes.

These good folk then dusted off their hands and dashed quickly behind the various shrubs and tree trunks of number two Pear Tree Lane, listening curiously to hear Jemima's fate from their places of hiding. Once the outlaws were evidently distracted as planned, the good folk would make their escape. They awaited the enemy's oppressive questioning:

"*Who are you? What are you doing here? How did you get here? You are not alone are you? Are you friend or foe? You are not part of the wicked-crew are you? For we swear to kill you and throw you to the dogs if you are.*" Then poor attempts at ferocious barking made by the boys.

Instead, their prickling ears were greeted by loud cries and high treachery, "Ouch, ouch, ouch; you've got to come out of hiding and help me. You've thrown me into the nettles!" Jemima cried.

Well, as if that was not enough, even when rescued from the nettles that had survived Great-Aunt's weeding, Jemima cried and cried. When she had cried through a damp dishcloth full of soap suds and continued to cry even *after* Harper had rubbed her face raw with a tea towel, he knew that he could not tolerate any more tears. He told Neville he would have to leave the party and take his nuisance-rat sister with him. Jemima wailed at the moniker. Harper nominated Agatha to escort the two home, as she looked the oldest of the bunch and would be best able to contrive something sensible to say to Jemima's parents.

Alas, Jemima's mother was unimpressed by the escort and the state of her precious daughter. Without being prodded and probed, Jemima spilled out Harper's secret to her mother; Great-Aunt was not at home. There were in fact *no* adults at number two Pear Tree Lane at all. Mrs Mortimer quickly got the picture; a multitude of children had quite literally been playing with fire!

Mrs Mortimer pulled on her coat and Wellington boots and dashed to number two Pear Tree Lane as fast as she could with the three children in tow. She expected to arrive at a pile of cinders and the charred bones of the village's children, save her own. Fortunately, or unfortunately, depending on which way one came at it, Mrs Mortimer's arrival came seconds after the Boy Scouts of the group had successfully lit the bonfire made largely of miscellany that Harper found in the garden shed.

Snatching her own children from danger by way of a forceful push of each abashed face, Mrs Mortimer followed her nose through to the side of house to the back garden and, seeing the boys about to fan the flames, shouted very dramatically, "Stop at once, or you'll all be *burned alive*. Step aside ... step aside immediately, step away from the *flames*!" The more daring of the boys laughed their heads off at the prospect of being burned alive by a few licking flames but Mrs Mortimer meant business. No boy would burn while she was around and so she dashed past them calling testily for Agatha's assistance. When Molly helpfully stepped into the breach, Mrs Mortimer pushed her back, "The lanky one, not *you*."

Poor Agatha was made to raid the cupboards for a bucket. She found a pot before a bucket and Mrs Mortimer grabbed it, filled it with water and ran into the garden with it. She approached the bonfire bravely and, with all her force, threw the contents of the pot onto it. (It was more routinely used to boil fruit to make jams but it served this new purpose very well.) It put out the fire and wet the boys that stood near to it. After the initial thrill of the cold, the boys laughed and ran about like giddy chickens, before heading into the kitchen themselves. Mrs Mortimer had inspired a new game which would not stop for another seven minutes. It was now three thirty-nine in the afternoon ...

Harper found a pan and, filling it with water, spilled a quarter of its contents onto the kitchen floor before running into the garden and tipping the contents on his peers nearest by. Hugo did the same, as did the other sheep, Daniel, Edward, Hilary and six others who found mugs, glasses and soup ladles as effective for their purpose as the pots and pans.

Mrs Mortimer's voice was long drowned out by the absolute din made by the children in the throes of play. In the end, all she could do was sit on the bench at the back of the garden, clasp her children to her and wait, both for her sopping wet hair and clothes to dry in the autumnal breeze, and for Harper's errant guardian to make an appearance. Neville tried to squirm from the embrace. It was simply not done - not in front of friends but Mrs Mortimer's grip was a firm one. She looked at the children soaked through from their watery game just once more to shout, "You'll catch your *death* of cold!" but, this time, her words were more a sincerely expressed wish than a warning.

Great-Aunt arrived home and was accosted by Mrs Mortimer who dashed down the path at the side of the house to meet her, while all the children but hers were in their play-filled oblivion. "There you are!" she accused and she led Great-Aunt by her own anxious steps back into the garden, as if by the wrist. On arrival at the gate, with a flourish of her arm, she invited Great-Aunt to survey what had become of her garden.

Great-Aunt saw a gaggle of children, a pile of her belongings - valued belongings charred in some places, sopping wet in others gathered in a heap on the lawn. Just as her mind tried to gather a grip of the story her eyes were taking in, Mrs Mortimer piped darkly, "It's worse inside." Again, as if the house were hers and not Great-Aunt's, Mrs Mortimer led the way to the kitchen. By this time, Harper was aware of Great- Aunt's arrival. All of the children suddenly stood stock still, aware for the first time that they had wreaked a kind of havoc that would not be tolerated in their own homes. One by cowardly one, they skulked out of the garden and made their way home. Soon - and certainly by the time Great-Aunt had seen the wreckage of the kitchen and dining room, all of the children except Neville and Jemima had fled. Even Harper was at the side gate when Great-Aunt summoned him back to the house for an explanation.

Harper could tell that she was furious. She was sipping some sort of spirit from a china cup and she was clenching the cup far too tightly. He remembered the liberal array of glassware - beautiful glassware, on and around the hearth in the dining room. Hopefully, none were broken or chipped if Clever Clogs Clive had done his job properly!

Mrs Mortimer had kept enough of a silence and now she made a hullabaloo about the whole affair. Great-Aunt listened with tight-lips nodding in agreement now and again as Mrs Mortimer said harsh things about the children and their behaviour. Then Mrs Mortimer narrowed in on Great-Aunt:

"Where did you take yourself off to anyway?"

Great-Aunt begged Mrs Mortimer's pardon.

"Often leave the boy with the fire *raging* do you? It's not right you know."

Great-Aunt was now bristling, "I do as a matter of fact but that has precious little to do with you."

"'*Don't bring them*'," you said.

"What?" Great-Aunt asked

"'*Do not be alarmed at the thought of a bonfire*'," Mrs Mortimer continued.

"What?" Great-Aunt asked again. Harper was now flushed with guilt and worry.

"'*It will be handled responsibly*'," Mrs Mortimer said, continuing to cite from the letter of invitation to the party.

"What?" Great-Aunt asked yet again - like a parrot Harper thought.

"'*They will be fine, I will look after them*'," Mrs Mortimer continued with rich sarcasm. "Well, fancy going a-gallivanting after making such promises."

"What promises?" Great-Aunt said.

"What I want to know is *why* you invited the children to your home when you *clearly* had no intention of being here?" Mrs Mortimer pulled a crumpled letter of invitation from her pocket and handed it to Great-Aunt. Great-Aunt read the letter - she was horrified! It was *her* paper and *her* ink but ...

At first, Great-Aunt was at pains to persuade Mrs Mortimer that she had had no part in sending out the invitations and that she knew nothing of the party until she had arrived home and found her cottage full of children! However, Mrs Mortimer seemed to gather an ill strength from Great-Aunt's feelings of guilt and confusion and so Great-Aunt changed course and rounded on her.

"So *this* is the invitation that you and the other doting and diligent parents responded to is it?"

"Yes," Mrs Mortimer said. An arm akimbo on her hip and a vicious frown on her forehead - well what could be seen of it under the fringe that clung to her forehead in damp clumps.

"And you have a young boy yourself?" Great-Aunt continued.

"Yes - and a little girl," Mrs Mortimer answered again.

"And there was nothing about the request that you '*do not* escort your children, just wave them off at the gate' that gave off the smell of a rat?" Great-Aunt continued.

"That horror of yours called my Myma a nuisance-*rat*!"

"He is *not* mine," Great-Aunt snapped. Then she continued referring to the letter, "... Ar, well, let's see! It's signed by '*A person who lives at* number two Pear Tree Lane'. '*A person who lives at* number two Pear Tree Lane'? Did *that* not alert you to the fact that the author was perhaps someone other than whom it purported to be – a child perhaps?"

"No," Mrs Mortimer replied.

"Well then, I must ask you to get off my property and I must ask you to do so immediately. This house and its inhabitants are hostile to the silly. Off, off, off, off, off!" Great-Aunt practically sang as she ushered Mrs Mortimer from the house and through the garden. Great-Aunt listened carefully though as Mrs Mortimer kept up her complaint, telling a *version* of what had happened to her poor dear Myma.

What hope did the girl have if her Mother insisted on calling her 'Myma' Great-Aunt wondered but what she said was, "Shame on you for sending not only one but two of your children here."

When Great-Aunt shut the gate against Mrs Mortimer and her children, she challenged Harper. She wanted an explanation for the whole sorry, soggy, saga; the invitations, the dangerous attempt at cooking in the fireplace, the sausages and chestnuts lying around the fireplace, treating Jemima like a sack of rotten potatoes, using her belongings for bonfire fuel and the near flood in the kitchen.

Harper did not apologise as such, he merely said that he would not attempt to cook indoors again. Great-Aunt said that she would take him to apologise to the Mortimers the following day but Harper politely refused. He pointed out that the error lay with the parents who had not only sent their daughter out to a party for *older* children knowing that danger and roughness were *guaranteed*, but they had sent her out in *shorts!* He said he was sincerely sorry that Jemima had parents who sent her where she wasn't invited and hoped the nettle-rash went away soon!

The day after the bonfire, Great-Aunt was approached by the most avid of the gossip-mongering villagers who had heard of the incident from Mrs Mortimer.

"Millicent dear, tell me it isn't true!"

"It's not true dear," Great-Aunt replied.

"Oh Millie, you don't know what I'm referring to yet!"

"Do tell me then," Great-Aunt said sweetly.

"This matter of your boy being left *quite* alone at a party you called for his friends. They'd have burned the house down had Mrs Mortimer not stopped their activities... for all the thanks she got. It's not true is it dear? 'Not the Millie I know,' is what *I* have been telling the gossips! Is it true dear?"

"Of course not dear. You know the *doting* parents concerned don't you? Do you *imagine* that any of *them* would fail to *speak* to the host before sending their darling children out to a *bonfire*?"

A clearing of the throat and violent blushing in reply.

"My dear?" Great-Aunt called as she walked away. "He is *not* my boy. Good day to you!"

Chapter Twenty-three

Harper Hepplesthwaite: 10/10 for a great birthday treat!

Another big change was afoot.

It was the 20th day of October and it was Harper's birthday. It had been uneventful the year before, on account of Mother being busy and then there was the Mowbray affair shortly afterwards which made the spartan celebration a very distant memory.

He rolled out of bed and noted that he did not feel a jot of difference - even though he was *a whole year older* than he had been the day before. A glance in the bathroom mirror also confirmed that nothing had really changed. He lifted his upper eyelid; all was present, correct and very much the same. He opened his mouth to its fullest extent and looked inside; all was present, correct and just as it was the night before. He looked into his nostrils, at his armpits and feet; again all was present, correct and unchanged. Great-Aunt made a mighty fuss of him, laying on his favourite breakfast of tiny jam and chocolate pastries with a glass of the creamiest milk.

Great-Aunt left Harper in suspense as to how he was to spend his birthday, until the evening before. She was taking him out on a trip to Knoxham in Laurie's open-topped motorcar to buy a present of his choice. Harper was delighted when he discovered that Laurie had been invited along.

They set out early as Great-Aunt wanted to be home just after lunchtime as she had a commission to complete. It had to be framed and ready for postage to meet the client's deadline. Great-Aunt drove. It was slightly chilly but dry and so they drove with the top open.

They chatted and laughed about everything and nothing all the way to Knoxham. Laurie asked Great-Aunt to point out the spot where PC Payne had stopped them."Don't encourage Harper," Great-Aunt said light-heartedly. Harper then shared with them all that Mrs Mainwaring had disclosed to him of *her* school days and they roared with laughter. Great-Aunt left it for another occasion to caution him to do as *she said* and not as Mrs Mainwaring *had done*.

By the time they arrived at Knoxham, Great-Aunt declared that it was time to stop for elevenses and so they stopped for some tea and a generous slice of chocolate cake.

Before they started the return journey home, Laurie took the driver's seat and drove them to an intriguing cave of a shop. The stonemasonry which was also exposed on the inside of the shop was a sight to behold. The merchandise was the most delightful handmade and mechanical toys and objects of interest. Wooden figurines with limbs that could be made to leap and jump at the pull of a string or two; wooden pianos whose keys jangled out a tune when a lever was slowly lowered. However, what captivated Harper and, therefore, became his birthday present, was a miniature village made of wood, complete with a belfry, railway station, coal freight trains and a level-crossing.

He thanked Laurie without a single prompt from Great-Aunt. Now he would not mind being left alone for the rest of the day half so much!

When they arrived home, Great-Aunt made a light meal and assured Harper that she would be back in time to make them a tea fit for a birthday celebration. Laurie and Harper took his present to the attic and Laurie persuaded him to set it up in a corner of the blue room near to the window. Harper felt it would be silly to protest, particularly as the other room was congested with other antiques.

"Happy birthday, Harper!" Laurie called as he made his way down the stairs, leaving Harper to explore and enjoy his present. Soon, Great-Aunt called to let Harper know that she was leaving the house and would be back shortly.

"Righto!" Harper shouted back to indicate that he had heard. The front door closed and Harper was alone.

He looked about the room warily, then he remembered that his two week spell of compulsory banishment to the room had passed without incident. There were no unwanted visitors from the chimneybreast - nothing had happened at all.

Harper suddenly felt very lonely; *very* lonely indeed. He wished that Mother and Daddy were with him, even if just for the day, just for his birthday.

Harper turned his attention back to the miniature village – his little empire. He wanted to take the whole thing apart to discover how it had all been put together but he quickly decided against it and rang the bell in the belfry instead. Then he pulled the lever that lowered the level crossing and was about to set a train in motion when he heard singing. Two voices, one baritone and the other alto emerged from the chimneybreast and stood on the hearth. Immediately following, were another two characters who descended the grate on either side of the hearth with a synchronised and musical clicking of their heels. They were carrying a blackboard.

They were tiny and loosely in the ilk of the Wighorns. However, there were some differences. These creatures looked perfectly formed, with glistening white teeth, perfectly coiffed hair and skin so smooth that it appeared polished.

With elegant steps and a tip-tapping of their musical shoes, they tap-danced to a tune that was unknown to Harper and all the time they beamed at him with their fabulous glistening teeth, "One over three, one-third;

two over five, two-fifths; three over four, three-quarters; one over eight, one-eighth....." They came to a standstill at the centre of the hearth, each tapping his right foot and clicking his fingers while continuing to beam at Harper.

Next, both whistled and elegantly extended their right arms towards the fire-place and, Harper's eyes rendered big with surprise, followed their direction. There, climbing down the grate, was another creature - bespectacled, bald and bearded. He was wearing a white coat resembling the laboratory coat worn by Mr Burnsom for his scientific experiments. In his left hand was a long length of white chalk. Having bowed to Harper, he walked to the blackboard held aloft by the burnished creatures and started to scribble some fractions on to the blackboard. With his back to Harper, Harper could see that the hair that had fled the top of his round head had found a place of refuge on his chin, for his beard was very long and very bushy.

He whisked the stick of chalk across the board with lightning speed, second only to the speed of his explanations. After each one, he would look at Harper over his shoulder with a smile, seeking a sign that Harper found his lesson illuminating. Harper clearly did not deliver, as the two happy souls broke into song and tap-danced, guiding the miniature Teacher thus, "Slow, slow, slow, slow, tis best if slow Mr Beardsby. Slow, slow, slow." So... Mr Beardsby did indeed *go slow*.

Mr Beardsby told Harper about denominators and numerators. He meant well but his explanation left Harper all at sea! He raised a knobbly finger, cautioning Harper against despair. This caused the two dancers to break into song, "Here come Sweetness-and-Delights-Galore and the Happy Helpers to share more, more, more."

Suddenly, the hearth teemed with Wighorns, each and every one dazzling and wonderful in its own way. All were elegantly dressed in yellows, reds, purples, blues, greens and every possible colour that gave a rainbow its character. Each bore in the right hand a platter and these platters were full of *all* delights that one can imagine (and some that one could *not possibly* imagine). There were jellies, hard boiled sweets in the shape of animals, soft sweets in tiny geometric shapes, chocolate cakes, cakes sprinkled with coloured slithers of iced sugar, a Victoria sandwich, ice-creams and brightly coloured, perfectly round fruit. As they showed Harper their offerings, they danced and sang. Harper was discouraged from eating any of the treats by a song. He obeyed!

Then Beardsby began his lesson again. He scribbled **3/8** on the blackboard and then he deftly sliced one of the cakes into eight pieces. With encouraging smiles and winks at Harper, he pointed from the eight slices of cake to the eight at the bottom of the fraction. When Harper gave a nervous nod back, Mr Beardsby then separated the three slices of the cake so that they stood separately on the platter and pointed to the **3** in the fraction that stood above the **8**.

Then Beardsby scribbled **2/8** on the blackboard and looked back to Harper. He nodded again, though less certainly this time. Beardsby persevered slowly, writing out a plus sign on the black board which now read: **3/8 + 2/8.** He then moved the two slices so that they rested alongside the three and above the eight. Beardsby tried to explain again: **3 = numerator, 2 = numerator, 8 = denominator.**

Looking over his shoulder to check that Harper was following and, only when he was sure that Harper was very much taking it all in with his eyes at least (even if his mind was cake-bound), Beardsby repeated his count of the eight slices of cake. He then counted those that he had separated out. Beardsby scribbled on the board: 3/8 + 2/8 = 5/8.

He looked over his shoulder to check the whereabouts of Harper's concentration and happily found it on the blackboard but Harper looked confused. Beardsby continued slowly with the patience of Job. He had been instructed to deliver the lesson until Harper understood, no ... *loved* fractions! Next appeared eight divided by eight equals one.

3 / 8 + 2 / 8 = 5 / 8

5 + 3 = 8 (5 / 8 + 3 / 8)

8 / 8 = 1

Harper wanted to eat cake; he stopped caring for the lesson. It was suddenly becoming too complicated. Beardsby and Sweetness-and-Delights-Galore and the Happy Helpers kept up the entertainment and teaching.

When they were content with their day's work, which coincided with Great-Aunt's return home, they left a selection of delights for Harper. Then, with waves, winks and smiles at Harper, they disappeared into the chimneybreast. Harper left the room the wiser for the unusual lesson.

He wished that this more pleasant variety of Wighorns had replaced the other but he knew it was highly unlikely!

Chapter Twenty-four

Harper Hepplesthwaite: As mischievous as a monkey

Harper was delighted when the clocks went back in the last week in October. 'An extra hour in bed' he had enthused as he helped Great-Aunt to change the many clocks in the house. He was less impressed the following morning when he woke up in darkness. "Are you sure you are meant to tamper with the clocks..." he asked Great-Aunt, "and are you *sure* that you turned time the *right way?*"

Great-Aunt answered a cordial 'yes' to both questions.

"Please don't serve porridge for breakfast, Great-Aunt. Porridge and darkness is a bit much for a boy to bear on a Monday morning. But porridge and darkness were exactly what Harper had to contend with that Monday morning. He met Hugo and Agatha on the way to school and they told each other ghoulish stories as the sun rose slowly on their journey. They all had a blast, recalling the highlights of Harper's bonfire party.

As if the Monday morning needed to be improved upon, Mr Hornby was to teach the English class that day as Miss Honeywhistle was unwell. A double dose of Hornby it was, as he also took the first lesson of the day which was Mathematics.

They were still learning about fractions. After his lesson with Beardsby and friends, Harper rather enjoyed fractions and played rival to Clever Clogs Clive all lesson through, putting his hand up to answer virtually all questions save for the first two which were too simple for him to bother with! Mr Hornby almost warmed to him... nearly but not quite. He told himself, that all in all, the Harper was an incorrigible wretch.

They put away their Maths books and parked all numbers and figures in the tidy compartments of the brain where they belonged. Now it was time for the English lesson. Mr Hornby explained:

"Miss Honeywhistle is sadly unwell. We do not know when she will be back but we wish her a speedy recovery so that she returns to us soon."

"Today, you are going to learn similes. *Sim-i-les*. What they are, their function and some examples. To *hopefully* get your *tiny* little brains going, I am going to give *you* some examples and then you are to follow suit and give *me* some examples which I will note on the blackboard."

Mr Hornby's method was as dry as the Sahara desert. He did not have the way about his teaching that Miss Honeywhistle and Miss Wordsworth had. He launched in:

"*1. As sweet as honey;*

2. As bold as a lion;

3. As white as snow. Now, let me have your examples of similes please".

Frederick put his hand up, "As dark as night, sir."

"Cor-rect Frederick, cor-rect," Mr Hornby said.

"Archibald?"

"As sly as a fox, sir," Archibald said.

Now there were three keen arms in the air as the boys warmed to similes. Harper was one of them and he strained his eyes, his arm, his back to get himself selected but Hornby chose Hilary, "Yes Hilary?"

"As slow as a snail, sir."

Many examples followed: as stiff as a board, as deaf as a bat and so on.

"Yes, good," Mr Hornby said. Then he turned to the board to write these down and turned back again. Harper was still straining to answer and Mr Hornby reluctantly gave him his attention.

"Harper?"

"As Hornby loves Clarissa," he said.

The chalk in Mr Hornby's hand snapped and his face turned a livid red almost immediately. Mr Hornby did not shout and Mr Hornby did not whisper. Mr Hornby did not move an inch or a limb - in fact, it is doubtful that Mr Hornby blinked; he was just about breathing. He was stunned – no, he was flabbergasted.

A whisper went clockwise about the room and its answer circulated contrariwise:

"Who is Clarissa?"

"Miss Honeywhistle."

"Ohh!"

Then the room was as silent as a grave!

Mr Hornby looked as if he were about to explode and Harper decided to leave the room before the explosion. He rose slowly from his chair and stood to his feet for a second or two. Then he stepped away from his desk and made his way to the door, his eyes on Mr Hornby all the time. Once outside of the room and in the corridor, Harper quickened his step.

The sound of the door closing softly seemed to bring Mr Hornby to, for with great big strides, Mr Hornby left the room walking like a penguin with military training. He looked left and right and there was Harper on the right, making his way down the long length of the 'L' shaped corridor. Harper looked over his shoulder and saw Mr Hornby bounding towards him. Yet Hornby still did not say a word.

Harper quickened his step and so did Mr Hornby.

Harper broke into a trot - and so did Mr Hornby.

Harper broke into a jog - and so did Mr Hornby.

With Mr Hornby having the longer legs of the two, Harper reasoned that Hornby could corner him in a few strides.

Panic set in and he looked from left to right for a means of rescue or escape. The corridor was full of classrooms and, therefore, teachers who would see him if they happened to look right, facing the glass panels in the classroom doors. If they saw him, they would surely turn him over to Mr Hornby. He, therefore, threw himself to the ground. Crawling on his hands and knees here, then crouching below the glass doorways there, he made his way steadily down the corridor and away from Mr Hornby. Mr Hornby pressed on with his two legs, without a word – his face still as red as a beetroot.

At last tired from his rolling, lounging and diving, Harper stood to his full height intending to break into a run but, looking left and then right, fortune smiled on him. On the wall to his right, Harper saw a small red box. Amongst other things, it contained the words of an instruction: "*In an emergency, break glass and press button*". For the first time in a long time, Harper followed an instruction!

Having Hornby in pursuit was an emergency from which he needed rescuing and so Harper broke the glass and pressed the button.

The din that ensued from what was the fire alarm nearly forced his heart into his mouth. Teachers and children teemed out of the classrooms. Mrs Pickering made her way from her room to the corridor.

On seeing Mrs Pickering, Mr Hornby stopped still and found his voice. He shouted, "*There is no fire! I'm afraid the horrid wretch is trying to get at me. He told the class I love Clarissa and he is trying to escape the consequences of his impudence... but in vain if I have anything to do with it!*" As he spoke, Mr Hornby tucked the piece of chalk still in his hand into the left hand breast-pocket of his blazer. Mrs Pickering could not hear over the din and, unfortunately, the little she did hear was, "*Here's a fire, I'm a wretch ... I love Clarissa, but in vain...!*"

Mrs Pickering called on Mr Hornby to pull himself together immediately and instructed him to be in her office after the fire drill if it proved a false alarm. He tried to protest that it was indeed a false alarm and that he knew the culprit but he just appeared all the more desperate in his love for Clarissa and so Mrs Pickering sent him outside with the children. He was not a fit Fire Safety Warden in his state.

It was a while before the register was taken to account for every single child and teacher in the school and the fire emergency staff arrived and declared the school safe to enter. It took equally long for all to settle into their lessons after the disturbance.

Mr Hornby made his way to Mrs Pickering's office and she met him sitting there.

He started to speak and she quieted him, not wanting to cause him further embarrassment.

"Have you been drinking Mr Hornby? Only you are as mad as a March hare today!"

"I'm as sober as a *Priest*," Mr Hornby replied.

He unfolded the facts for Mrs Pickering and, as surely as night follows day, Harper was summoned to Mrs Pickering's room. She gave him a sound telling off and told him how dangerous and irresponsible his actions were. All he could say in his defence was that he was desperately worried about what Mr Hornby would do to him, angry as a lion as he was! He concluded that he had not realised that he was doing anything wrong, having followed the instructions for help in an emergency!

Mrs Pickering deliberately focused on the fire alarm and steered clear of any reference to Mr Hornby and 'Clarissa'. She dismissed them both from her room and held her head in her hands for a few seconds - she wished she could knock their heads together.

Mr Hornby wished he could shake Harper by the neck but he could not *(damned rules)* and so he did not. He walked back to the classroom but abandoned similes. They took up comparative and superlative adjectives instead. Both were pleased when the school bell rang to mark the end of the day. Harper was handed a note from the School Secretary who instructed him, "See that your guardian gets this." Harper knew that it meant trouble and Great-Aunt gave him a stiff telling off - and a spartan supper without dessert. Before retiring to bed, he told her that he was as sorry as could be. He was fed up of being chastised at every turn, simply for being a normal human boy.

The week turned into a really long one and Harper could not wait for the weekend

but it soon came around.

Chapter Twenty-five

Harper Hepplesthwaite: Not a dainty dish to set before one's friends

It was Saturday morning and Harper woke with the hope of an adventure. He had not formulated a plan of action but he knew his hope would be rewarded if he left the cottage for the great outdoors at the earliest possible opportunity. Once breakfast and chores were over with, Great-Aunt disappeared into her art studio, where she would be for hours.

Harper decided that he would venture into the High Elms Wood and spend the day there. Yes, he would venture into High Elms Wood with Agatha, Hugo and some sausages...

Great-Aunt had been to Mr Buchanan's butchery to replenish her supply of sausages following the bonfire saga and so Harper took a string of them with him. He may have apologised for certain things but he had only renounced cooking *in the fireplace* - not cooking *per se*! The sausages swung about his chest and back like a heavy scarf, draped as they were around his neck for convenience sake. They would keep their lunch time hunger pangs at bay.

When he called on Hugo and Agatha, he removed the sausages from around his neck and tied them around his stomach so that they were inconspicuous to adult eyes.

When Harper laid open his plan to them, Hugo hesitated but Agatha was raring to go and the 2/3 majority won! Building a treehouse in the Wood it was then. It would provide a perfect and secret retreat from adults. Harper put the sausages back around his neck and they headed in the direction of the lavender fields. Smelly as it was, it offered a shorter route to High Elms Wood.

They crossed the lavender field and all three exaggerated wildly with feigned fits of vomiting and other displays of disgust at the prospect of smelling of the pungent lavender. Harper sniffed at the sausages to ensure that they were not contaminated by the smell. They skipped over the babbling brook, crossing in single file, using the stepping stones that either nature, or else some civic minded soul had placed there for the purpose.

They walked for another third of a mile and then they were at the neck of the Wood. Harper's were the first intrepid set of feet to step in.

The Wood was magnificent. Tall elm trees vied majestically to reach the very skies. Hawthorns, willows, sycamores and other trees were also part of the landscape but they decided that they would spread to the east and west rather than northward. The grounds were littered with golden brown leaves which the three trampled under their feet, enjoying the crisp sound they made. At various junctures, the elm trees inclined towards each other in a bow, forming a high arch above their heads as if sealing them in the Wood for as long as they wanted its cover. Here and there were old wrought iron gates that beckoned, or barred, depending on the courage and curiosity of the walker. The three charged through them, heading north easterly on one path and south westerly on the other. They heard the rustling of foliage as rabbits, hedgehogs and deer roused to see the two-legged creatures dashing about their home. The birds ignored them and went about their daily tasks, talking and singing to each other.

One gate directed them to a Church, one of the oldest in the village. The Churchyard was full of ancient gravestones which leaned this way and that like rows of chaotic teeth. Two gravestones in particular, both bearing sculptures, attracted the attention of the three. One was a cherub with a harp and the other an angel and trump. Harper, the avid leader, prepared to read from them, after giving a low and respectful bow.

"What are you bowing for?" Hugo asked in a whisper and with a frown.

"To show *respect*! *I'll* want respect when I pass on and passers-by want to stop and read my memory-stone. Won't *you*?" Harper answered loudly and rather argumentatively.

"I suppose so. I don't think it's a good idea to shout though," Hugo replied, still whispering.

Harper shrugged but took the advice. Perhaps whispering was the more respectful way of going about it.

Agatha and Hugo gathered closer to hear him read; and he did so theatrically:

"*Here lie the mortal remains of the body of Archibald Terence Montgomery, father, husband, scientist and author whose soul soared to glory on the 20th day of July 1875*".

"Where do you suppose '*glory*' is?" Agatha enquired in a whisper.

"Heaven," Hugo replied with confidence. "*Definitely*, heaven!"

"A *village* in heaven," Harper corrected sagely. "You see - *we* are in Eldersham in Enger-land() and Archibald Terence Montgomery is in '*Glory*' in Heaven."

"Mmmhhh," was Agatha's reply to these wisdoms.

The three lapsed into a silence and even the woods were silent. The birds had flown away or given up their chirping. As Harper shoved his hands into his pockets, the movement caused the sausages to swing and touch Hugo's arm. Hugo nearly jumped out of his skin. "What was that?" he yelled.

"What?" the other two asked in chorus.

"Something or some*one* touched my arm," Hugo answered, looking about him in alarm.

Agatha and Harper frowned at him.

"Did *you* feel anything?" Hugo asked.

"No," they answered.

"Maybe it's Mr Montgomery and all this talk of glory that's given me the creeps - can we go now?"

"We can move on somewhere else but we're not *going* - we haven't done what we're here for yet *and* it's lunch time," Harper said, pointing to the clammy sausages about his neck.

They walked up a slight incline and settled in a small clearing. Harper laid the coat he was carrying on the floor and settled the sausages on top of it.

He told the two that they would need to fetch wood and leaves to light a fire. Hugo said that they did not need the leaves but Harper insisted that they did. They settled the matter with an arm wrestling match and Harper won the best of eleven, with Agatha playing the bored and partial referee.

They scrambled to fetch pieces of bark and twigs. As they prepared to ignite them, Harper told the two exactly what had happened once he left the classroom with Mr Hornby on his heels. They, in turn, explained how worried they were for him when Mr Hornby left the classroom looking as angry as a bear with a sore head.

"How did you know Miss Honeywhistle's name is Clarissa?" Hugo wanted to know as he nurtured the promising beginnings of a flame.

"Oh, there are some things a boy just knows," Harper said, tapping the side of his nose with a forefinger.

"Oh get off!" Hugo exclaimed. "You must have overheard it."

"*Maybe*," Harper said mysteriously. "It's amazing what a boy gets to hear by keeping his ear to the ground," With that, he threw the sausages onto the fledgling fire.

While they waited for their feast to roast, they shared stories and laughed the rest of the afternoon by. Harper and Hugo persuaded Agatha to tell them stories about her cousin's haunted house. "I won't be able to *sleep* if I think about it," she protested at first but her resolve quickly collapsed.

Alas, another batch of sausages went to waste as a weak fire and a light drizzle put paid to a lunch of roast sausages.

Harper felt lighter without the sausages about his neck and perhaps because they had not eaten any lunch. It was no bad thing that the rain had destroyed their plans for lunch. Sausages charred on the outside and raw on the inside would have had them in the company of the late Mr Montgomery before the day was out!

The drizzle soon turned to more determined and big rain drops. Following a hasty and undemocratic vote carried by 1/3, they abandoned the idea of making a start on the treehouse and prepared to leave the woods.

They could not re-trace their footsteps at first and so went about the Wood a few times in an attempt to leave. Along one of the mistaken routes, they came across an old unused well. Seeing an opportunity for sport, the three forgot their empty tummies, shed their coats and gathered stones.

Leaning precariously over the edge, they each dropped their stones into the well one by one and listened for the sound of the watery landing.

"I wonder how deep it is," Harper said and he shouted a few words into the well, enjoying the distorted echo that resounded.

"Umm, I wonder," Hugo said

"I'm not so curious that I want to find out," Agatha said, alarmed at the depth suggested by the echo. She didn't trust the other two not to suggest they climb in to discover the answer, tying their coats and jumpers together to make a rope!

They eventually made their way out of the woods, crossed the brook and walked through the lavender fields. "There has got to be another shortcut," Harper said, his hunger making the pungency of the flowers a nasty cocktail on his stomach.

"Oh, there is," Hugo said. "Over the bridge at..."

"*Why* didn't you say?" Harper exclaimed and Agatha echoed him.

"Didn't think I suppose. It's quicker over the bridge...."

"Arrgghh!" the other two sighed.

They went their separate ways with the typical nonchalant grunts and Harper was soon at the front door of number two Pear Tree Lane. He knocked on the door and Great-Aunt looked surprised to see him.

"Ar! You've been out then, have you?" She asked.

Harper did not answer the enquiry, he rather looked about him as if to say, "Well, if I'm on *this* side of the door...what else can I tell you?" He stepped into the house and walked towards the kitchen. Great-Aunt followed him.

"Wash your hands ...thoroughly!"

"Is there any other way?" Harper rejoined.

Great-Aunt ignored it. "I'll fetch you a glass of milk and a biscuit. Read a book or something. I'll make a start on tea in another hour. Laurie and Matthew will be joining us. See you shortly." With that, she swept out of the room in a paint-splattered tabard.

Harper drank the milk and ate the biscuit and then he went to his bedroom. He actually did thumb through an encyclopedia and read about the different creatures that lived in the very different natural habitats of the world. He was particularly drawn to the polar bears and completely lost track of time flying by.

While Harper had his head, thoughts and imagination on the snow of the Arctic Circle, Great-Aunt left off her art to set about making tea. She started with preparation of a home-made apple sauce to accompany the sausages, potatoes and green beans.

Alas, Great-Aunt discovered when it was much too late that she did not, in fact, have any sausages - not for herself, Harper or her guests. Therefore, they had toast and boiled eggs with pear tart and custard for pudding. Harper was threatened with a raw egg for his tea but he was spared by Laurie's protests. For his tea, he had toast with pear tart and custard, together with a robust telling off. Great-Aunt told him that he had rendered her *completely speechless* and then proceeded to lecture him with many lengthy speeches. It ended at last, "...

and aren't I the *unlucky* one that you did *not* eat the sausages half raw!"

Harper was not allowed to join the small party for conversation in the drawing room after supper. Matthew smiled smugly, nestling into a chair with relish. Harper growled and thumbed his nose at him. Great-Aunt sent Harper to bed with a nasty prospect to anticipate the following morning. "Starting at 9:30am *prompt* tomorrow morning, you will read the *entire* ninth chapter of encyclopedia Volume two. In the *blue room* and you cannot leave the room until 10:30am – or else!"

"Or else *what?*" Harper asked... in the quiet recess of his own mind, because he *did* know when he was beaten.

Chapter Twenty-six

Harper Hepplesthwaite: If Whizzlegrump minus Judge = 'x' what is 'x'?

Surely enough, after breakfast, Great-Aunt sent Harper to the blue room to read and to consider his behaviour - what changes he might make to it, why and *how quickly* he might make them.

He stepped into the room and looked around. The miniature village looked alluring and so, after setting a freight train in motion, he faced his reading task square on.

After a minute or two, the only sound was that made by Harper's finger as he drew it along the page to keep pace with his eyes as he read. Chapter nine of encyclopedia volume two was about the human digestive system. '*Magnificent*' Harper mouthed quietly to himself as he tried to visualise the length of the large intestine.

His reverential reverie was rudely interrupted by whistling. It came from the fireplace of course. Yet again, Harper watched as the Wighorns ascended and descended the grate of the fireplace, bringing with them the chairs and tables which quickly took the now familiar shape - a court-room.

Crouchlow, Cyril and Pinikerty were the first to enter.

They were followed closely by Pryson and Domble-bluff.

Pryson stumbled clumsily because Crouchlow deliberately treaded on his shoe laces. Pryson had loudly and publicly mocked him for spelling his name Pr*i*son instead of Pryson and now Crouchlow was repaying the slight.

Domble-bluff patronised Pryson with sympathetic smiles and enquiries as to whether he was up to the day's task which was bound to be significantly more trying than tying one's own shoe laces. Pryson was very embarrassed and mumbled a rude reply but only Cyril caught the words by lip reading. He made a note of the remark in a separate record book. A book that he kept secret and for his own use in the event that a pompous lawyer wanted blackmailing! "*Observation number 1,077*" he recorded.

Unusually, Domble-bluff noticed Harper at this early stage but not so as to give him a word of encouragement, a comforting look, or information. Nay, he railed *against him* - but what was Harper's charge? "Why?" he wondered, clutching the heavy encyclopedia to his chest!

"Fool of a boy, you stand accused of beating a member of court staff - *what* are you doing with that enormous book? Do you aim to *dash* at our heads as we gather to *uphold the law*, to *defend* you - uumm? Or do you propose to defend *yourself* perhaps? Is it full of sundry laws that will help you out of the pickle you are in? I doubt it very much and so I suggest you put it down immediately, or I-will-per-son-all-y see-to- it- that Whizzle-grump and his counter-parts have you flogged to within an inch of your impudent life... At least you've had the good sense not to bring the poker along with you this time – tsk!" With that, Domble-bluff turned on his heel and his facial expression immediately changed from hostile to amiable. Harper set the book down unceremoniously, causing it to land on its open leaves. Great-Aunt was bound to notice the crumpled pages and punish him but he could only think about one judgment at a time!

The jurors then filed into the room, all looking serene and ready to do business. In due course, Judge entered and took his place, while all others stood to acknowledge his entrance - on Pinikerty's order of course.

One empty seat remained and Harper wondered what had become of the missing Wighorn. Judge did not seem concerned; perhaps he had not noticed as, yet again, he seemed to be asleep. The empty seat was to the left of Whizzle-grump and between Stonehard and Snappernash. Whizzle-grump rubbed his long crescent moon of a chin as if deep in thought; deep in thought about something that troubled him. Stonehard's right eye was out on its stalk and took in Whizzle-grump's anxiety. Snappernash had his head bent low, as if he were offering his head full of wild black hair for patting. This meant that he had already fallen asleep and so it was little use troubling him with an enquiry. Stonehard settled back into his seat; he would have to wait and see if the unfolding of the hearing revealed the problem that worried Whizzle-grump.

Just before Crouchlow shuffled forward to hand the scroll of charges to Pinikerty, the final juror, Bumble-snore, made an appearance. He was wearing a black, short jacket with gold buttons and red trousers. Had he reversed his dress so that his jacket was red and his trousers black, he would have trimmed the appearance of his huge bottom by at least ¼ but, alas... ! Harper watched him amble from the fireplace and onto the hearth, before taking a tumble just as he reached his seat.

A concerned 'aarrr' broke out around the table but for two very different reasons.

Whizzle-grump's anxiety was realised. By mischievous design or foolish error, Bumble-snore had been allocated seating with him, Snappernash and Stonehard. He would *not* tolerate a mercy-infected pollutant in the camp. He was about to raise a strong objection when, without wanting to or really meaning to, Harper called out; '*Humpty-Dumpty*'. He pointed at Bumble-snore as he called out, as if to clear up any possible doubt in any mind that Bumble-snore was the object of his remark and pointing finger.

"*Isn't-that-the-one-that-fell-off-the-wall-and-couldn't-be-mended-despite-all-efforts-made-to-put-him-together-again?*" Knapsley asked Whizzle-grump. Whizzle-grump sneered back to indicate his lack of interest in the question and its answer.

"Indeed, I think it *is*. I believe you are correct," Ponderton replied comradely. Knapsley thumbed his nose at Ponderton in reply. He did not care much for the reassurances of one of *them!*

The other camp, Ponderton, Weyall and Temperton were naturally concerned for Bumble-snore's welfare but did not lavish him with any more attention beyond the 'arr', to avoid causing any further embarrassment.

Judge was surely awake because he turned on Harper and fumed:

"***Fainting off***, *I will tolerate,* ***silence*** *I will tolerate but* ***impudence and insolence*** *I WILL NOT! Any more of this Domble-bluff and I will give an order that the boy be taken dooown; I will give an order that the boy be taken down if there is any more of this Domble-bluff!*"

If looks could kill, Harper would have expired on the spot under Domble-bluff's hard chastising eye. This was a bad start, a very bad start indeed. Even the mercy-merchants and grace-guerillas, Weyall and Temperton wore a grim expression.

Harper had no idea what being 'taken down' involved but he determined to be silent and orderly - he did not want to find out!

Then, as if there had been no interruption at all, Judge brought the proceedings underway calling on Pinikerty to take the scroll and read the charges.

Pinikerty obliged, or at least tried to:

In the case of The Right and The Good vs. Harper Hepplesthwaite Esquire

"We've not had him *esquired* before...," Whizzle-grump challenged. Pinikerty looked down his nose in Whizzle-grump's direction. They both waited in silence.

Biggles-Dream-Porter suddenly mused aloud, "I cannot see the armour bearer in the boy *at all*. Esquire? An *esquire* puts me in mind of battlefields darkened with songs of war, replete with swords and shields borne bravely by ...."

Judge broke the impasse and the dreamy visions of Biggles-Dream-Porter with a sleepy but firm, "*GET* on!"

Biggles-Dream-Porter settled back into his seat with a yawn as he nestled his neck and chin in the ruffles of soft blue fabric gathered there as part of the huge collar of his velveteen jacket. His long legs protruded to the other side of the table and he crossed them at the ankle. Harper took in his long yellow shoes which curled at the tip.

Pinikerty began to read the charges in his usual manner. He was determined to ward off the unseemly behaviour that had dogged the past hearings:

"Charge one: Harper Hepplesthwaite did host a party without the consent of his legal guardian and owner of the property, number two Pear Tree Lane;

Charge two: Harper Hepplesthwaite did hold himself out to be an adult, thus deceiving *many* parents."

When Pinikerty had read the second allegation, Pryson stood to remind the Court of the charge from the previous hearing: Charge six – the assault on Grotshaw.

Pinikerty stood to his feet again (having sat down for Pryson) and testily told both him (and the Court) that charge six was very much in mind but had fallen to the *bottom* of what was a *very* long list.

Judge said that the charge should be dealt with last and Pryson sat down, feeling as if he had, in fact, fallen over twice in one short day!

Pinikerty continued:

"Charge three: Harper Hepplesthwaite did nearly burn number two Pear Tree Lane to the ground, by the activities carried on at the said party'.

Charge four: Harper Hepplesthwaite hurled a child into thorny bushes *just* for sport. He also did imperil the lives of *many* children, by playing with literal and *pro-verb-ial* fire."

Weyall whispered to himself, "If *that* is not opaque in meaning I'll eat my ... !"

"Charge five: Harper Hepplesthwaite did take sausages from number two Pear Tree Lane, without consent. Expressed another way, *he stole*;

Charge six: ..."

"What about the boy's *recidivism*?" snapped Snappernash, his voice rasping all the more because he had just roused himself from what he would call a comfortable 'half-sleep'. Half-sleep, full-sleep, or no-sleep, his mind already conjured horrid imaginings as to a fitting punishment for Harper. "He's been at the smart glassware yet again hasn't he?"

"I'm arriving at it!" Pinikerty snapped.

"I hate to interrupt but I must," Weyall said, rubbing his huge fold-ridden forehead. "Recidivism?" We'll need to ensure that the boy *understands* the charges against him. "*Recidivism*" is too difficult..."

"*He-did-it-again. He keeps going back to his crimes*!" Whiz-zle-grump snapped sarcastically with a wild eyebrow raised as he looked to Pryson to confirm that all was clear and well understood by the *wise* people in the room.

Snappernash left off grinding his teeth and joined in, "That's what you get when you let them off. In fact, we've been remiss. Let's summon the court staff so that the boy can peruse them all and select the choicest two. *One* to peel his grapes, *the other* to clean and polish his toe nails until they *shine*."

When Domble-bluff and Temperton protested with "tsks" Snappernash replied, "What - is the offer too *mean*? Is that too small a number to tend to him? Shall we make it four... six? Six men to serve him?"

"Order in my Court," Judge said languidly and without lifting his eyes or his gavel to drive home his point.

All obeyed and Pinikerty continued.

"Charge six: Harper Hepplesthwaite did make use of the finest most delicate of Millicent's glassware in his party for local ruffians;

Charge seven: Harper Hepplesthwaite did put pupils and teachers in fear of being burned alive with their books, by raising a false fire alarm.

Charge eight: Harper Hepplesthwaite did embarrass Mr Hornby, a teacher tasked with the nasty job of educating him."

Temperton nudged Ponderton and whispered, "It's becoming increasingly hard to tell when he is reading the alleged charges *from the record* and when he is *substituting his own views*."

"Gross-bias, gross-bias," Ponderton whispered back with a shake of his head.

Pinikerty continued, seemingly oblivious to the nudging, whispering and shaking of heads:

"Charge nine: Harper Hepplesthwaite did fail to show any remorse whatsoever in connection with these acts referred to herein... set out above."

Suddenly and without any warning, Harper started to make his way to the bench -Judge's bench. There was shock and horror in the court room; Harper Hepplesthwaite, already charged with serious offences against The Right and The Good, was charging towards the bench unbidden!

Domble-bluff bellowed at him, Judge shouted at him to retreat several times but still he advanced. Pinikerty nearly man-handled him back to his rightful position, by tugging at his trousers. Crouchlow intervened with a painful act of sabotage. He stopped Pinikerty in his tracks by delivering a sound kick to the shins.

"I'm only trying to plead guilty M'Lud," Harper protested. "I did the whole lot. You've got me fair and square," he said, turning to a shocked Pryson.

Domble-bluff was breathless with rage. Half standing and half sitting he gasped, "An adjournment your Lordship - I *pray* a brief adjournment." At some point, he must have run a hasty hand through his hair as it now faced a whole host of directions - mainly northerly!

As a result of stringent and long established rules and laws, Domble-bluff was not able to kick or whack Harper into changing his guilty plea to one of not guilty. Neither soft nor brutish entreaties changed Harper's mind. Domble-bluff had one final source of persuasion but one look into Harper's determined eyes told him that he should not seek recourse to it. If he did, Harper would ensure that Domble-bluff was found out and banished from the Court, banished from Freeham Chambers and driven outright from a life in the law. So, he withdrew the hand from Harper's calf that was poised to deliver the most vicious pinch that fingers and nails could administer and gave him a clumsy pat on the knee instead, as if belatedly admiring his honesty.

Harper shouted again, "Guilty of the *lot* M'Lud and *that's that*!"

Judge asked Pryson and Domble-bluff if they wished to lead evidence to assist with sentencing.

Pinikerty cleared a dry throat, and Pryson stood to respectfully remind Judge of charge six from the last hearing. Judge said that Pryson's respect was noted but that he did not need reminding as it was at the forefront of his mind.

Pryson stood and asked Judge's permission to call the doctor. Judge gave permission.

Domble-bluff was not too troubled by this decision. He had been surprised by new evidence before and done a wonderful job of batting it away - in his opinion! He requested Judge's permission for a conference with his client and they withdrew for a few moments. Domble-bluff fixed Harper with a chilling stare before he said a word. When he did say a word, it was a further warning that made Harper gulp. Harper gave his account of what had actually happened as quickly as he could and Domble-bluff listened without any interruption. Their conference at an end, the hearing resumed.

Doctor then took the witness stand. Pinikerty's brow arched higher and higher in jealous indignation as doctor spoke in increasingly wordy and grand terms. Pryson asked doctor questions and then Domble-bluff asked doctor *his* questions. Judge had one or two questions for him too.

The long and short of the exercise was that Domble-bluff had an answer to every point that doctor made:

Doctor said that his examination of Grotshaw revealed definite signs of bruising. Having got doctor to establish, for a fact, that the alleged victim was Grotshaw and that the examination took place in the most narrow and dark section of the chimney breast, Dombley-bluff cast doubt on whether doctor was sure that it was Grotshaw that he had examined.

Where doctor was sure that it was Grotshaw, Domble-bluff cast doubt on whether, in the dim light of the chimney breast, doctor could be certain of what he believed he saw of the alleged injuries.

Where doctor was certain of the nature of the injuries Grotshaw sustained, Domble-bluff cast doubt on whether his limited medical equipment was adequate for the job of examining the injuries to see *what* caused them and *when* they had occurred.

Once Domble-bluff got doctor to confirm the description of exactly how Grotshaw had said the injuries had been caused and that he had examined Grotshaw's injuries that morning, he delivered the final death blow with a hammer of a fist in a velveteen glove:

"Can you, doctor, with any certainty, considering where Grotshaw lives and works, say that the alleged injuries were not caused by falling lumps of charcoal?"

"No."

"A tool or piece of equipment carried by a fellow worker or someone other than the accused?"

"No."

"The heavy blows of a fellow-workers fists, administered in response to Grotshaw's attitude and indolence?"

"No."

Domble-bluff said nothing for about 10 seconds. Then he continued, "What *day* is it today doctor?"

"Sunday, sir."

"And you are absolutely certain, are you, without *any* shadow of doubt in your mind given the dark conditions of the chimney breast, that the alleged injuries were not sustained on a Saturdy?"

"No."

"Or a Mondy?"

"No."

"Or a Tuesdy?"

"No."

"Or a Wednesdy?"

"Or a Thursdy?" And so on...

Doctor was forced to answer 'no' to all of Domble-bluff's questions and Domble-bluff took his seat, having no further questions to ask.

Doctor mouthed a pathetic '*sorry*' to Pryson as he retreated to the gallery. Pryson did not acknowledge him but Domble-bluff did with a brief nod and tight-lipped smile. Pinikerty's raised brow came to rest at last, content that doctor was back in his rightful place because Domble-bluff had wiped the proverbial floor with him.

Then Domble-bluff took the floor again. Pryson had had his chance, rubbing Harper's character in the mud, making him sound like an unruly, cruel jackal-hyena of a child. He had asked Harper if he had been brought up by wild wolves. When Harper shook his head vigorously, Pryson asked him if there was a material difference between his human parents and wolves. Odious man, Harper thought!

Domble-bluff came to his rescue: It was *the boy* that had been assaulted *not Grotshaw*! If Harper's account was accepted as the truth (and there was no reason why it should not be), *he* was the one who deserved a legal remedy. Harper's face had been *trodden upon*, his hair *pulled* and used as a ladder. There had been *no provocation* by Harper. Any injuries that may have occurred were quite possibly the result of Grotshaw's *own horseplay*, or the result of an unfortunate tripping accident.

Domble-bluff continued, stating that the doctor, though possessing big eyes, *did not* have all of the equipment necessary to work out exactly *how* the injuries had occurred, or *when* they occurred. Harper Hepplesthwaite was at risk of being *punished* for alleged scratches, marks and scrapes that *no one* in the court had seen and, even if they had been seen, could have occurred hours, days *or weeks* before the encounter with the boy.

In fact, the claim that Grotshaw was so badly injured that he was laid in bed from the day of the alleged attack was perhaps a convenient lie to mask Grotshaw's renowned indolence. Pryson bristled at the insinuation and Judge gave a low warning growl, "Tread with caution Domble-bluff; Domble-bluff tread with caution."

It was too late for Pryson, Harper Hepplesthwaite was found not guilty of the sixth charge.

Even Whizzle-grump, Snappernash and Stonehard could not argue with the force of the doubt cast on the doctor's evidence by Domble-bluff's points. Their point was that the boy Harper should have gone down anyway on account that only in exceptional circumstances do the truly innocent get brought to court at all. Therefore, he ought to have faced punishment, simply for coming to the attention of the law. There was also the issue of his recidivism! However, Whizzle-grump was hardened against Harper as Harper saw in the hastily scratched out inky black letters of his note to Snappernash and Stonehard: '*Next time, we take the matter into our own hands. We* ***finish*** *him orf, once and for all.*'

In connection with the allegations to which Harper pled guilty, after hearing from Pryson and Domble-bluff, Judge sentenced Harper to a thirty minute lesson of algebra (equations to be precise). The class was to be held in the blue room at four o'clock sharp the following day.

They all stood as Judge left the court and, after a few respectful minutes, they all shuffled out, ushered by the ever so humble Crouchlow.

So far, the number of times that Harper had escaped the intentions of the nasty jurors, was 2/2. He did not know how, but what he did know was that, without Judge's intervention, Whizzle-grump was murderous!

The following day, Harper had no idea how he managed to get himself home after school and in the blue room with thirty seconds to spare before the clock struck four o'clock.

At four o'clock precisely, tell-tale small pieces of debris fell from the fireplace. Three characters appeared. Two had military gait and shoes that clicked against the parquet flooring, bearing a blackboard between them. A third followed behind them. One of the two offered a long stick of chalk to the third and the other held a duster in his hand which hung rigidly by his side.

The third creature was dressed in a white coat as Beardsby had been but there was something very different about all three. On the basis of that difference, Harper had no expectation of Sweetness-and-delights-galore making an appearance! Where the others had smiled and winked and done everything possible to be pleasing, these three had their faces twisted into scowls and frowns and they did *everything* possible to appear strict.

Harper's attention was forced to the blackboard by the sounds of chalk being scratched against it. Harper had become comfortable with fractions but he was not prepared for the horrible collaboration of numbers, letters and brackets that Wildbrow (for that was his name), etched on the blackboard.

Wildbrow had eyebrows that were so long and bushy that they twisted upwards before disappearing into his wild furiously red hair. He had a small angry pair of vivid purple eyes that Harper only saw when they were turned on him to require an answer to the impossible conundrums he was scratching out on the blackboard.

The two helpers also looked as if they were extremely cross with Harper and they were ready with disapproving 'tsks' and shakings of the head when Harper failed to answer the questions, or failed to answer them correctly. They were nearly half way through the lesson before the atmosphere eased - and then only because Harper finally grasped that:

If a + a + 3 = 11; then a was 4; and

If 6 + 6 - b = 7; then b was 5; and

C was 8, if 7 + 9 – c = c.

Wildbrow somehow made Harper consider it all a game of intrigue and discovery and so, by the end of the lesson, he warmed to it. He declared '*a*' a four; '*b*' a five and '*c*' an eight. In the penultimate equation of the lesson, Harper made a mistake declaring an 'e' a four instead of a five in the equation: **11 - 5 -1 = e**, but that was more hasty exuberance than a lack of understanding.

At four thirty prompt, the lesson was brought to a close by the disappearance of the creatures.

Between the jurors and Wildbrow, Harper might just be able to scramble into Mr Hornby's good books by the skin of his teeth.

Chapter Twenty-seven

The grocer, the butcher, the kind sweet-maker – all went after a certain Hartley-Baker

Winter made its presence felt in Eldersham, stripping many of the trees of their leaves and decorating all with its frost and snow.

The villagers did not wait for the twelve days of Christmas before decorating the trees, shrubs, shops and Churchyards with tinsel and lights; the school children did not wait for the twelve days of Christmas before their excitement at the prospect of Christmas presents, holidays and fun in the snow began. The school teachers certainly did not wait for the twelfth day of Christmas before starting preparations for the school's Christmas play.

In one way or the other, everyone and everything in Eldersham was caught up in the happy and busy haze of the season and it all started on the very first day of December with a feverish pitch!

Great-Aunt had some wonderful news for Harper. She knew it would make him giddy with delight but the weight of disappointment would be awful if it did not come to fruition and that was sometimes the fate of even the best laid plans. She decided to keep the news under her hat until the *very last possible moment* and so she gave Harper a pair of Wellington boots instead. The snow promptly arrived shortly after the purchase.

And make good use of them he did, especially when the snow was at its deepest. He would take to the fields and build snowmen of various shapes and statures and the pantry was always the lighter when he made a complete family of four or five. Well, each one needed a carrot for a nose and raisins, sultanas or peas for buttons and eyes! After making two sets of families, he favoured stones and twigs to messy foods. Great-Aunt's various hats and scarves were also permanently lost to the well-dressed icy families.

On one particular day, Harper decided that he would go into the centre of the village to make a purchase of his own, from where else but Mr Pudimore's Sweets! He had Great-Aunt's happy consent. She had use of Laurie's car to drive into the village to buy a few groceries and so they arranged to meet at eleven o'clock prompt, outside of Pudimore's Sweets.

The snow was still crisp, clean and largely un-trodden. Harper took a scenic route and got to the centre of the village, approaching it from the hill and gully of a long and winding road which led to the grounds of what was called the old school. The street was largely deserted because the snow made the hill treacherous terrain to ascend or descend, except for those as brave of heart as Harper. He walked past Mrs Bridges' wool and haberdasher shop, past Mr Greening's grocery, the bakery and even the butcher's shop. Then he was under the awning of Pudimore's sweets and, although the doorway to sweet heaven was just a few delicious steps away, he paused outside to look through the shop window and feast his eyes from the aspect of his cold cupped hands. Mr Pudimore was busy weighing toffee humbugs, pouring them from large containers onto scales and from scales to smaller containers. 'He'll soon be measuring them into a small white paper bag for *me,*' Harper thought to himself. He marvelled that Mr Pudimore did not pop one into his mouth and that his cheeks were not bulging with sweets.

With his taste buds well exercised in anticipation, Harper barged into the shop, making a racket that made Mr Pudimore jump. Some of the humbugs fell onto the counter and rolled onto the floor. Mr Pudimore tutted and set his glasses aside as he bent to retrieve them.

"It's *your* bell sir," Harper said, as his greeting, apology and defence.

"I'm quite used to *that*, it's the door coming off the hinges that's new on my nerves," Mr Pudimore said good naturedly enough. "What can I tempt you with little man?" he said, clapping his chubby hands together.

"One of everything please sir," Harper replied without a trace of humour, because he did not intend any.

Mr Pudimore put his eye glasses back on and his eyes grew and resembled Robin's marbles.

Mr Pudimore chuckled and, taking his glasses off again, he walked the few steps to the customer side of the counter.

They both looked at the many shelves of delights and Mr Pudimore became quite animated as he talked to Harper about the different sweets. He told him how they were made, some of the ingredients, how the wonderful colours were created, how the top side of one sweet came to be pink, while its underside was white and so on. On the basis of this visual tour, each container seemed to promise better. There were red and yellow perfectly round sweets, round red and white sweets, yellow, red and green square sweets, pink sweets with a dusting of powdery sugar and red and blue sweets that resembled colourful string, to describe but a few. Most of the colourings were from vegetables and plants Mr Pudimore said but Harper was not disgusted.

When they passed the containers full to the brim with mint flavoured sweets, Harper woke from his sweet reverie to declare, "I *won't* have any of *those* if it's all the same to you sir." Mr Pudimore chuckled again - what a delightful little boy, he mused to himself, pleased that Harper indulged his tales of the intrigues of confectionery making and his former life as a glassmaker in Brislingham in the south-west of the country.

Then it was time for Harper to make his selection and Mr Pudimore helped him to choose well. Harper paid for a bag full of a colourful variety of sweets. Harper did not mind that Mr Pudimore's scales were uneven, because they were definitely tipped in his favour. Before he stepped out of the shop, he popped a hard boiled turquoise sweet into his mouth and bid Mr Pudimore goodbye. "Goodbye," Mr Pudimore said, "mind how you go now."

"I will do sir," Harper called over his shoulder, as he patted the bag of sweets. He stepped out into the cold and was busy wrestling the bulging bag of sweets into his pocket when his attention was caught by a sight.

Mrs Hartley-Baker, a villager from the west of Eldersham, was trotting at quite a pace down the slight incline in the road past the butcher, the baker and the haberdasher. Her shopping trolley followed hard on her heels and she occasionally raised a hand to secure a very fine looking hat which threatened to absent itself from the one-woman-race that she seemed to be taking part in.

At last she was brought to a rude stop as she stumbled and eventually fell to the ground – face first. The haberdasher, baker and butcher all left their respective businesses to come to the rescue. One shoe went this way, a head of cauliflower another, while a joint of lamb taking off down the road was stopped in its tracks only by Mr Buchanan's big left foot.

Mrs Hartley-Baker's hat tumbled away from her and the rest of her belongings. Harper went after the hat, clutching a hand to his pocket lest his sweets followed the same path as her belongings. The hat rolled and tumbled on and on as if it had legs of its own. Harper ran after it, huffing and puffing with the effort.

The butcher, baker and haberdasher set about getting Mrs Hartley-Baker sitting on her bottom. With a heave and a ho, the three of them managed to set her upright on the edge of the pavement with the reinforcement of Mr Buchanan's sturdy shins behind her and the haberdasher's hands pressing against her shoulders at her front. Mrs Hartley-Baker was in too much of a daze to sit upright on her own account.

Harper stepped forward and set the fine hat on Mrs Hartley-Baker's head. The rim obscured her eyes but it mattered little as her eyes were virtually closed - only the merest slither of the cornea could be seen if one peered closely as Harper did when the *'thank you'* he expected was not forthcoming.

Once they had all caught their breath, various discussions broke out over Mrs Hartley-Baker's head as she sat and they stood.

"Is that everything safely back in the trolley?" The baker enquired.

"Believe so," the haberdasher, Ms Woolsey, said, looking up and down the street. She could find a needle in a haystack and cauliflower was hardly small!

"A nasty tumble that was," Mr Buchanan commented, drawing nods and '*indeeds*' from the others.

"The snow looks very beautiful but isn't it an awful pest?" Mr Pudimore commented. He had left the heaven of his shop to join them on the pavement.

"Right Mrs H, let's get you on your feet and into the warmth," Mr Buchanan tried, keen to get back to his work.

"I'll put the kettle on," Mr Pudimore added helpfully but paused for a few moments before stepping away to do it.

Mrs Hartley-Baker was mute.

Harper noticed the three enquire silently with their eyes, whether she was alright or needed medical help. The ever observant Harper assisted, "She *must* be conscious, because she's pulled her skirt hem over her knee. It was up here a few moments ago." Harper helpfully pointed to his own thigh and then at Mrs Hartley-Baker's. This explanation drew a low whimper from Mrs Hartley-Baker but that was all.

They took Harper's word and sought to hoist her to her feet. Alas, Mrs Hartley-Baker could not, or would not, stand on her own two feet and so slumped against Mr Buchanan. Mr Buchanan locked his arms around her middle and, in a lifting and dragging motion, manoeuvred her into Mr Pudimore's shop where a chair and cup of sweet tea were soon waiting. "Here we go Mrs H, here we go," he soothed. Harper followed them in.

Her hat fell off once again. Harper did the honours - half-heartedly this time after his last thankless effort. It sat precariously once again - at the ready to fall off.

Well, it was 11:30am and Great-Aunt arrived to find that Harper was not outside Pudimore's Sweets. She, therefore, ventured inside and was soon fully acquainted with the morning's events but not directly from Mrs Hartley-Baker. No, she was still mute.

"Right!" Great-Aunt declared. "Let's get her into the car shall we? She appears to be in shock and needs to be warmed as quickly as possible - I will take her home with us."

Great-Aunt diagnosed that Mrs Hartley-Baker's pride had taken a tumble and so removing her from the concerned gazes would help her mend.

Mr Buchanan was called upon to abandon the trussing of joints, to hoist Mrs Hartley-Baker onto the back seat of Laurie's car. Once again, her hat went about its own business. Once she was settled on the back seat of the car, Harper (having caught the hat) clambered on to the back seat to restore it to its owner's head. This time Harper waged war with the bouncy curls of her hair. He stuffed the curls under the hat with both hands and, when all but the most rebellious of tufts and tendrils were safely pushed, pulled and packed away, Harper sent the hat down on Mrs Hartley-Baker's head with force. Now only the very tip of her nose and mouth could be seen from under the rim of the hat. "*That's* done it Miss," he said.

Mrs Hartley-Baker stayed mute. Harper dusted his hands of the business and climbed into the front of the car beside Great-Aunt. Once he had checked for the safety of his sweets, he turned around in his seat and watched his charge all the journey through with his face lodged between his seat and Great-Aunt's; there was no sign of life.

"Now we have the small matter of getting *into* the house." Great-Aunt said as they arrived at number two Pear Tree Lane with the silent Mrs Hartley-Baker. She did not respond to soft entreaties from Great-Aunt and so she struck her cheeks smartly instead. This worked and they made their way into the cottage, slowly but surely. Mrs Bradshaw from number four noticed and helped in the effort.

As Great-Aunt settled Mrs Hartley-Baker into a comfortable chair in the dining room, she asked for a stiff drink to be brought. For the first time since the fall, Mrs Hartley-Baker opened her eyes to their normal extent.

Mrs Bradshaw and Harper set about fetching a stiff drink. Harper left the room on the right for the kitchen and Mrs Bradshaw remained in the room and bore left for the drinks cabinet.

Harper poured half a packet of loose-leaf tea into a china cup and then added the same amount of honey. He added a little water from the kettle and tried to stir the stiff concoction with a teaspoon. "Well, that's *stiff,*" he said as he made his way back to the dining room.

He found Mrs Hartley-Baker quite awake with chubby hands eagerly clasping a tumbler of a honey brown and lethal smelling liquid! Harper chalked 'stiff drink' as another adult saying of the 'raining cats and dogs' variety!

Mrs Hartley-Baker remained mute, even when Mrs Bradshaw lifted her legs one at a time to examine the soles of her shoes and offered a monologue about the necessity of one wearing 'sen-si-ble' shoes in the snow. "It's the Podiatrist in me," Mrs Bradshaw explained. "One *never really* retires."

Mrs Hartley-Baker shut her eyes and Great-Aunt became alarmed. Perhaps she should have taken her to a hospital after all. Had her kind deed been misguided?

"Mrs Hartley-Baker?" Great-Aunt called, gently tapping on her lap.

"Mrs Hartley-Baker... can you *hear* me dear?" Great-Aunt asked with some desperation.

"In a crisis, a double-barreled name is as useful as toffee," Mrs Bradshaw mumbled.

"Baker?"

"Baker?"

"Are you alright *woman*?"

Mrs Hartley-Baker was indeed alright, although she bristled at her proud name being chopped about and then abandoned altogether all in the space of seconds. It was only after a second tumbler of a *stiff* drink and Laurie's arrival that Mrs Hartley-Baker showed signs of being very well indeed. She opened her eyes, stood to her feet with easy strength and announced her departure! "Good day to you all and thank you for your ... hospitality. *You'll* be taking me home won't you?" she told Laurie and that was that.

Chapter Twenty-eight

Harper Hepplesthwaite: The playing of the merry organ sweet singing in the choir...

Every Friday afternoon, the local choristers, led by a Mr Forsyth descended on number two Pear Tree Lane for carol practice. On occasions that they left cymbals and a trumpet behind, Harper and Matthew had such fun with them, playing many an unmelodious tune as they parading up and down the stairs and to and fro in the garden.

There was also the grand piano of course which Matthew played very well. Matthew created music to match the short and humorous limericks that Laurie taught him and he taught Harper how to play the chorus and refrains of some Christmas carols.

'O come All ye faithful', 'Come thou long expected Jesus' and 'Hark the herald angels sing' were favourites. Harper had no time at all for 'The Little Drummer Boy' because it sounded like a dirge and 'Greensleeves' was silly because *sleeves*, no matter their colour, had *nothing* to do with Christmas!

Harper was quite a diligent student all things considered but he was certainly not the most patient and, when Matthew played out the jaunty "c-c-c-d - c-c-g - a-g-a-b-c-c", the opening notes of 'Good King Wenceslas', Harper was all ears, and keen to master the tune. After a few false starts of: 'c-c-c-g - c-c-b' and so on, Matthew resumed control of the keys and played and sang the whole song through.

Harper was less impressed when he heard King Wenceslas' request to be '*brought flesh*' but the tune had him and so he was determined to play it. He simply drowned out the offending word with a loud request for *cake* instead of flesh.

Then Matthew taught Harper a few harmonising notes to add to the chorus and Harper played well. His attempts to play a complete verse were less successful because he wanted to master it all *immediately*. Between them both (and with *plenty* of persuasion from Matthew), they decided that there was only one thing for it. Producing a scout-knife from his pocket, Matthew suggested that Harper etched the notes 'a' to 'g' on to the keys of Great-Aunt's grand pianoforte. The very piano that had been in the family for generations. The letters were crudely etched onto the keys with vigour and haste and, before he left for his own home, Matthew had Harper playing Good King Wenceslas at a good and accurate pace, courtesy of the damaged keys!

Mr Forsyth made the discovery the following Friday.

"It really is a beautiful instrument, Millicent," Mr Forsyth said. "Extremely well preserved aside from the scratched keys - but little matter."

Great-Aunt stopped short. "What?"

"I said that it really is a beautiful instrument," Mr Forsyth said, projecting his voice over his shoulder. "Extremely well preserved aside from the scratched keys. It is well tuned and carries a tune perfectly...."

Great-Aunt looked perplexed and so Mr Forsyth started to repeat his sentiments yet again, "The piano..."

"I heard you Mr Forsyth," she said in a deathly quiet tone. She inspected the keys herself and felt the etching with the pads of her fingers. 'Harper' she thought - 'obstinate, tinkering, nuisance Harper'.

She summoned him from the garden and he traipsed into the room grasping a fistful of snow to demonstrate that he had been disturbed at a crucial point in his play. Great-Aunt watched a tiny puddle form on the parquet floor but it was a small matter compared to the damaged piano.

Great-Aunt wore a grim frown.

Harper wore a grim frown. He had a snowman with a misshapen head waiting for him.

Harper's frown melted the more quickly of the two.

Mr Forsyth's mouth was pursed into a concerned '0'.

Great-Aunt reprimanded Harper, threatened to send him home alone on the next possible train.

Mr Forsyth's mouth curved with concern into a broad 'n'.

Great-Aunt remembered that she had a small audience and frog-marched Harper out of the room.

Great-Aunt told him how many generations before him had enjoyed the piano. Harper told her how good it was that someone in the family had decided to make the task of playing the thing more simple – *at last*.

Great-Aunt rejected his argument and sent him to the blue room for the remainder of the evening.

Harper stood stock still. Images of Whizzle-grump, Snappernash, Stonehard and his ostensible shield and defence - Domble-bluff, filled his mind. His eyes grew wide and he gulped.

Harper decided not to take the blindest bit of notice of the instruction. After all, based on past events, he would either find himself in the blue room against his wishes, or face trial for his alleged misbehaviour at a later date. It was, therefore, pointless to hand himself over willingly; not when a snowman's head wanted shaping anyway. His rebellious mind made up, he ventured back into the garden, making bold imprints in the snow with his Wellington boots and singing: "*Mark my footsteps my good page, tread thou in them boldly, thou shalt find the winter's rage, freeze thy blood less coldly*". He soon forgot his punishment as he worked away at perfecting his snowman's head.

Chapter Twenty-nine

Harper Hepplesthwaite: 'Break a leg' Mr Hornby

Back at school, preparations for the nativity play were moving at quite a pace. The performance was set for the twelfth day of Christmas.

Miss Honeywhistle threw herself into the plans with her usual enthusiasm, rallying willing support from the friends and patrons of the school to make costumes and props. Mr Greening the grocer and Mr Buchanan the butcher were to provide the manger and hay and Mrs Woolsey the haberdasher was to provide wool for the sheep and head-scarves for the Wise Men.

Mr Hornby nominated himself production director and Miss Honeywhistle selected him as one of the Wise Men. He threw himself into both roles.

"It would be a shame to trot out the same old thing yet again Miss Honeywhistle."

"Well the '*same old thing' - the nativity -* is history and we cannot go about re-writing *history* now can we Mr Hornby?"

"Pe-rish-the-thought! Let's just bring the thing to life making use of our expansive school grounds." So, to take advantage of the school's terrain, they were to open the huge doors of the assembly hall that backed on to the school grounds and use both as stage for the performance to support the narrative as appropriate. "The lay of the grounds was *made* for the three Wise Men to *ascend* it, the shepherds *recline* on it, the babe lie in the manger at *rest* at the top of it." It was true. The school sat on a plateau at the top of a hill and the assembly hall opened on to the grounds.

At last the twentieth day of December arrived and it snowed for the whole day as if on cue. The likely sweltering heat of the first Christmas did nothing to cast a shadow on the imaginations of the thespians. The final rehearsal was held in the morning.

Harper was initially cast as part of the chorus of angels but Mr Hornby ruled the casting 'wholly inappropriate' and so Harper was re-cast as a Shepherd. By Harper's reckoning, this was a reasonable second best to the strong and commanding Angel Gabriel, especially when he learned that the Shepherds would have a crook.

He still felt an opportunity had been missed when he saw Angel Gabriel, resplendent with strength and majesty, suspended mid-air by a rope and some other clever and secret mechanism telling Mary and Shepherds the nature and future of the unborn babe.

Agatha played Joseph on account of her height and Hugo was roped into the chorus of angels.

At last, the performance opened.

A solitary large star made by Miss Honeywhistle's fine hands opened the performance, sparkling as it streaked slowly across an inky black sky before coming to rest in the East, the East also recognisable as the left hand side of the hallway doors that led on to the grounds.

Archibald had the privilege of making the first appearance on the impressive stage with a solo rendition.

"*I saw three ships come sailing in*

On Christmas day, on Christmas day
I saw three ships come sailing in
On Christmas day in the morning"

As his voice faded the two solitary figures of a man walking with a staff and another sitting on a donkey passed behind a curtain heading towards the east. Joseph, Mary and donkey were en route.

Humphrey was quite in character as he announced to the weary couple with smug cruelty that there was no room at the inn. They promptly came upon a benevolent inn-keeper and, no sooner were they admitted baby Jesus appeared wrapped in swaddling clothes and lying in a manger.

A curtain separated them from the spectators and the Shepherds filed onto the stage with their crooks in hand.

Angel Gabriel appeared to the shepherds in fabulous style, announcing the good news of the birth of Jesus Christ in Bethlehem and Humphrey appeared again, this time with a chorus singing the first two refrains of 'While Shepherds watched their flocks by night, all seated on the ground'.

As he sang, Harper the Shepherd looked far into the horizon with a hand shielding his eyes from the bright light of the Palestinian moon.

When Humphrey sang the second verse, Harper shook with all his might and distended his eyes to their fullest extent. Thus Harper portrayed the '*mighty dread*' that filled the troubled hearts of the Shepherds.

Then the Shepherds rose and headed east following 'yonder star' and Harper prodded a sheep with his crook.

The curtain closed on the scene and, when they opened, the Shepherds were sitting at the right hand side of Mary, Joseph and the babe. Harper had perched comfortably on an upturned milk crate, nodding and smiling his approval at the three.

Humphrey and chorus appeared again, singing: "O *come all ye faithful, joyful and triumphant o come ye, o come ye to Be-eth-le-hem; come and adore Him...*"

Harper did not need any prompting; he portrayed his faithful, joyful and triumphant adoration by fussing the cheeks of the baby Jesus!

Then attention was turned away from the assembly hall and to school grounds by the dimming of all lights except a floodlight shining on the eastern star. It was time for the three Wise Men to climb the hill of the school grounds to meet and worship Jesus Christ. The three Wise Men (otherwise known as Mr Hornby,

Mrs Pickering and Miss Wordsworth) wore elaborate, colourful and bejewelled head-dresses and robes of red, gold, purple, yellow and blue. Their faces were coloured with charcoal black eye brows, moustaches and beards.

Harper knelt precariously on a crate for a better view. When Miss Honeywhistle shot him an anxious glance, he patted the rump of the nearby donkey to assure her that all was well - he was merely in character and enjoying the performance!

Wise Man Hornby carried a lit lantern, so that a live flame brightened their way as they walked from the bottom of the hill to meet the babe Jesus Christ at the top of the hill. Wise Men Pickering and Wordsworth were on either side of him carrying small decorated boxes that declared their content as 'frankincense' and 'myrrh', in bold letters.

Those close to the stage saw the ascent of the three Wise Men. Those further away from it watched in keen anticipation. As the three approached the brow of the hill, Wise Man Hornby pointed to the guiding eastern star. The playing of the merry organ increased in volume and so did the voices of the three Wise Men with Mr Hornby in fantastic bass-baritone:

"We three kings of Orient aaarrrrrrrrgggggggggghhhhhh-hhhh..."

Alas, Harper and the crate slid down the hill and careered towards the sages. Wise Man Wordsworth leaped to the left and Wise Man Pickering to the right. Mrs Pickering's suggestion that they wear Wellington boots for the performance was prescient. They ignored 'yonder star' beckoning them to the East as they flew south and west to retrieve their headscarves and gifts. Harper and crate rushed into collision with Mr Hornby's shins sending him falling and flaying about in the snow. All three sustained an injury to their pride – only the Grand Old Duke of York and his ten thousand men fared worse.

When they stood to their feet, they were without beards and moustaches and there were only two eyebrows between the three of them.

Harper surfaced and beguiled his part in the debacle by prodding an imaginary sheep up the hill and back onto the stage in Bethlehem.

Muffled laughter spread through the assembly hall like the gospel and was just as happily received by the relieved Teachers - well most of them. Mr Hornby stopped in his tracks. He heard the laughter in the distance and became livid with rage. "I hear laughter. They are ridiculing us. We cannot go on - surely you can see that...?" He appealed to Mrs Pickering.

Without waiting for an answer, he marched ahead shouting, "Stop! Stop! Stop!" and, for good measure, he waved his arms to indicate that the performance was over.

Mrs Pickering charged forward to stop him, "The show *must* and *will* go on - laughter and children go hand in hand with the theme - "Joy to the World" etcetera." Mrs Wordsworth promised to have a word with Harper and Mr Hornby stopped in his tracks. Until then, the identity of the child on the crate had been unknown to him and he certainly had not assumed any deliberate intent. Of course - it was the sum of all his nightmares; Harper Hepplesthwaite!

"The perfidious ruffian! I might have known *he* was the culprit. *Monster* of a boy –I will *throttle* him. I will *box* his wicked ears. I will..." Mrs Pickering interrupted the tirade with a reprimand but Mr Hornby believed strongly in his cause and would not be corrected or quieted.

"I am the *director* of this production and I declare it at an *end*!" Mr Hornby said authoritatively.

"You are *not* the director. I *am* the Headteacher and I *repeat* that the show *must* go on," Mrs Pickering rejoined with factual calm.

Acknowledging himself as the weaker party to the dispute at last, Mr Hornby implored Mrs Pickering to keep Harper well away from him. They reached a compromise on those terms. The Three Wise Men continued their sojourn to worship the babe so that the play came to a natural end for the faithful audience.

By the time the Three Wise Men appeared in full view and knelt to worship the babe, Mr Hornby's headdress stood askance on his head and all had lost their sagacious bearing. Their gifts looked like mean carriers of bad news but gentle Mary seemed to receive them with humble gratitude. Harper gave an approving nod with the delivery of each gift and especially the gold, "Well - Isn't that kind?" he exclaimed patronisingly as Mary accepted it.

Miss Honeywhistle and choir joined in the singing of 'Hark the herald angels sing'. God and sinners may have been reconciled but Mr Hornby refused to be reconciled to the boy Harper.

On the 21st day of December, Harper spent quarter of an hour in Mrs Pickering's office receiving a dressing down and the School Secretary handed him a letter for Great-Aunt's attention.

"And what do you have to say for yourself young man?" Great-Aunt asked when she had read the letter.

Harper was silent.

"You caused absolute chaos – yet again!"

"It was an *accident* Great-Aunt. I slipped in the snow and I have apologized."

"Well I hope your apology was sincere *and* that this nonsense stops. The trick is to *think before* you engage in tomfoolery, not go about offering sincere apologies *after* the messy consequences."

Silent contemplation from both.

"You're excused – get out of my sight."

Harper left the room. As he made his way up the staircase to his bedroom he mouthed: "*Bring me cake and bring me wine...*" wishing he could command Great Aunt as Good King Wencelas did his servants.

Chapter Thirty

Harper Hepplesthwaite: Well here it is - Merry Christmas...

It was the 22nd day of December and Christmas was nearly upon Eldersham.

Number two Pear Tree Lane had brought all of the local traders to its doorstep in the final week before Christmas. Mr Buchanan had delivered the biggest turkey that Harper had seen in his life and more produce than he and Great-Aunt could hope to eat; even with the help of Laurie, Matthew *and Mrs Mainwaring!* Mr Greening had delivered *so* many carrots, parsnips, potatoes, Brussels sprouts and oranges and Laurie had brought load upon load of firewood from the cellar to the dining room.

Mr Pudimore had made a delivery too but his wares were hidden from view in pretty boxes; striped ones, spotted ones, round ones and square ones, all tied round and about with ribbons. Harper speculated that Great-Aunt was perhaps putting together generous hampers for the neighbours and for charitable gifts.

Harper spent most of the 23rd day of December at the home of Laurie and Matthew. While he was away, Great-Aunt had help preparing number two Pear Tree Lane for guests. Every room and every item of furniture was dusted and every floor scrubbed and polished. Not that Harper noticed when he returned, although he did find that his toys and books were *not* where he believed he had left them.

He was tasked with a fantastic job – adding a final touch to the decoration of the Christmas tree. He opened one of the boxes from Pudimore's sweets and found inside it tiny chocolates in the shape of disks in gold and silver wrapping. Each one had a fine gold thread at the top which he was to hang on the Christmas tree.

The plans for Christmas Eve were well-laid. Laurie and Harper were to visit Knoxham, starting the day at ten o'clock in the morning. Great-Aunt acquiesced without much apparent curiosity, or interest. In fact, she suggested that they stayed away until early evening.

At six o'clock in the morning on Christmas Eve, Harper sprang out of bed ready for his day out. He started to make his way down the staircase as gingerly as his excitement allowed but Great-Aunt heard him and promptly sent him back to bed. "Wait for the sun to rise for goodness sake or you'll be quite the cantankerous devil by eleven o'clock," she said.

Harper traipsed back up the stairs. Too excited to fall asleep, he mused about Christmas Day, the Wighorns and whether or not Great-Aunt knew of their existence - and the meaning of 'cantankerous'. He wondered whether Sweets-and-delights-galore and her merry helpers would make an appearance for Christmas. With such contemplations weighing on his young mind, Harper fell asleep and awoke two hours later.

Great-Aunt met him as he stumbled into the bathroom and again as he stumbled out - too quickly in her view. "Today of all days Harper I need to be confident that you are clean enough to face the world - clean enough to look as if *someone* in the world cares for you."

"I'm always clean Great-Aunt ...!" Harper replied calmly, hoping that his calm would distinguish him from a cantankerous devil.

"Well, only in so much that you never smell – but, today, I want you to be *so very clean* that you *squeak*. Now get back in there again please and *this time* be thorough."

Harper turned on his heel and stepped back into the bathroom.

"Don't just wet your hair, or run the tap to humour me. Actually, I'll run a bath for you."

"Oh what a hellish start to Christmas," said Harper.

"There is nothing 'hellish' about cleanliness my boy."

Harper looked at the cloud of bubbles made by the combination of the lurid blue liquid and water gushing from the tap. His attitude changed from one of nonchalance at the science unfolding before his eyes, to disgust when the sweet fragrance of the froth filled the air.

When he was satisfied that he was as polished and shiny as possible, Harper left the bathroom, got dressed and waited for Laurie who arrived just in time for breakfast.

After breakfast, Laurie helped Great-Aunt shift furniture about from one room to another. They did not explain why and Harper went about his own business in the garden. Mrs Mainwaring had descended as she was to spend Christmas with them. She had commandeered the kitchen and was busy baking cakes and biscuits – tasting as she went along, of course, at an approximate ratio of one to four.

At last, it was time for Harper and Laurie to set off. Great-Aunt insisted that Harper wore a hat, gloves and a scarf. Harper was, of course, willing to wear his Wellington boots but protested against the other items. Great-Aunt told him that wearing every single item was a precondition of his outing. Harper gave up his protest and stood patiently while he was wrapped, buttoned and zipped up. “Poor baby Jesus Christ in his swaddling clothes,” he mumbled. Great-Aunt did not say a word but she tied the knot in the scarf around his neck more tightly. Harper feigned choking which was also ignored.

He wove an unusual path to the gate to make his own fresh foot-prints in the snow.

"Now, where do we start?" Laurie asked once they arrived in Knoxham. “I say we start at Mr Aptinstall’s Antiques. We might just be fortunate enough to find some treasures there." Harper gave a nod of approval and they set off towards Aptinstall's Antiques.

On their way, they came across choristers and a band. They filled the air with Christmas cheer with trumpets, voice and a drum. Harper was caught up in the spell-binding atmosphere. He left Laurie's side and approached the gentleman with the drum. Keen to play himself, he offered some words of flattery before he made his request. The drummer was somewhat preoccupied but, spotting Harper close by his side and apparently talking to him, he inclined towards him as he played. The conductor strongly disapproved but his disapproval came too late to influence either Harper or the drummer.

"What an *extremely* smart jacket you have on sir, the gold buttons are *magnificent*." The drummer nodded and then resumed an upright position. Harper had not finished with him yet and so he took a position in front of the drummer, preventing him from moving forward. The drummer inclined towards Harper to hear his words. A ripple of confusion now troubled the band and the conductor's cheeks burned red but not because of the cold! "Can I beat the drum sir - just a couple of strokes?" The drummer shook his head, smiled to himself and continued to play - but Harper stood his ground.

When Harper looked at the drummer and noticed the indignation that was beginning to creep across his face, he knew he would not accede to his request. Harper therefore, decided to take matters into his own hands. He reached upwards and gave the drum two clumsy whacks. It was this disharmony in the band that identified Harper's whereabouts to Laurie. The drummer beat Harper's fingers with the drumsticks and Harper kicked his shins and fled to Laurie. After a few discordant notes, order was restored and the band made the short sojourn from the village hall to the village square. This was their second post. The final post would be the Churchyard but there were a good few more in between, as they were to perform all day and through to the early hours of the evening.

Laurie asked Harper what had happened and Harper told him everything. Laurie told Harper that he would forfeit his Christmas presents if he did anything as despicable again. After a few moments, he recited a limerick about a drummer and a boy in playful voice and a friendly atmosphere was restored between them.

Aptinstall's Antiques was all the more intriguing with the festive decoration. The experience was second only to Harper's first visit to Pudimore's sweets. There were miniature ships with sails that looked as if they were billowing in the high sea winds, there were miniature steam wagons, a Doble model E and other motor vehicles from the seventeenth, eighteenth and nineteenth centuries.

Laurie stopped to pore over a lamp and an old smoking pipe. He mumbled something about 'beautiful craftsmanship' and Harper rolled his eyes in reply. They left the shop with a ship, lamp and smoking pipe wrapped in brown paper that belied the beauty of the goods.

After a delicious lunch, they left Knoxham and drove back to explore the Christmas delights of Eldersham. There were plenty.

They visited the sculptor's shop and admired familiar and unfamiliar objects and creatures made from wood, bronze and glass. The shop was one of the oldest in the village, owned and run by the same family for generations. Laurie explained that the current owner, Mr Potter, was a friend.

There were elves, fairies and soldiers all appearing as visual riddles - asking the observer if there was life in them after all. Harper was particularly struck by the figure of a cobbler wearing black wire glasses hammering at a shoe with melodious taps of a tiny hammer. He longed to pick it up to examine its mechanism - but he resisted. In Harper's reckoning, this was a truly wonderful mystery.

At the same time, something truly wonderful was unfolding at number two Pear Tree Lane. Of all the intrigues and wonders that Harper had seen that day, better awaited him there. Mother and father had arrived in Eldersham.

Father insisted on leaving the cottage in search of his son. He left the house after obeying Mother's call to wrap up warmly but the reminder that he was no longer in warm foreign climes was unnecessary!

Harper's concentration was broken when he saw, from the vantage point of an ornate mirror, that a man was behaving suspiciously. Of all the intrigues in the shop, this man was unduly captivated by an insignificant, worn box that was *not* for sale. Harper noticed that the man was wearing a very smart coat and hat but carrying a rugged sack full of groceries. Harper could see potatoes, carrots and beans.

Suddenly, the man lifted a candlestick-holder from the shelf and lowered it into his sack of groceries before moving hastily on to the figurines. A fairy, elf, gnome and two soldiers followed the candlestick-holder into the sack. Harper was stunned and it took him a while to find his voice - but when he did, he made it heard ... to the far reaches of the neighbouring village. "Stop thief... *after* that man!" No one took up the call sufficiently promptly for Harper's liking. They rather turned to stare at him with a mixture of disapproval and curiosity and so, when the thief made his way from the shop at a steady but determined pace, Harper took after him, glad for his trusty Wellington boots.

It took a while for the adults to note anything untoward but, when they did, Laurie was the first out of the shop after Harper. He caught up with him with some effort. "What the *blazes* is going on?" He asked Harper.

Indignant at the prospect of being chided for being citizenly, Harper was shirty in his reply; "I'll tell you what the *blazes* is going on. Your friend, Potter has been robbed and it seems that I'm the only one who tried to stop it and now the robber has escaped from under all of your grown-up noses!"

"What on earth would you have me say to Millicent if you came to any harm. If the man is a thief as you say, he would not take kindly to you calling him one now would he?" Laurie explained.

"I don't care much for what the *thief* takes kindly to. Anyway he'll be well on his way now. He flew off on a bicycle while you adults polished your manners!"

Laurie sighed, "Never mind, young man, I'm sure the police will catch up with him some-day soon."

In the meantime, the oblivious choir sang out, "... tis the season to be jolly, tra lah lah lah lah, lah lah, lah,lah..."

The winter darkness was descending quickly. As a final stop, Harper and Laurie went to the Churchyard in the centre of the village square where mulled wine and mince pies were being served to those gathered to listen to the carols. Harper stood on the box of a trumpet to gain height and beguile the cheerful distributor of mulled wine, concerning his age. Alas, the distributor was a vigilant woman who gave him a stern "tutt" of disapproval. Harper seized a mince pie instead. Having eaten the mince pie, Harper looked around him for some prospect of fun.

As he perused the small crowd that had gathered, Harper thought he could see the thief lurking yet again, this time on the fringes of the crowd gathered around the carol singers. His identification became firm when he saw the thief's hand slip into the pocket of a gentleman's coat before he took off rather briskly. Harper shouted, "*Stop thief!*" and broke away from Laurie to run after him.

"We must get him this time!" he called over his shoulder to a stunned Laurie. Then to the crowd generally, he exhorted, "After him - don't let him get away. Stop the thief!"

With some distance between them, the thief had time to clamber onto a bicycle, carrying the bag awkwardly as he rode. Harper ran with all his might. Laurie ran behind him but his interest was not in apprehending the thief. He needed to catch the wayward Harper before he came to harm.

The thief pedalled like mad and Harper ran with all of his heart and energy. As the distance between Harper and Laurie grew, Laurie lost heart and energy. He just about managed to shout a cautionary note to Harper; "Stop immediately, you must stop!" but Laurie immediately regretted not conserving his breath to keep up with Harper, rather than shouting warnings he knew Harper would never heed.

Harper was quick in his reply, if not reassuring, "Don't you worry Laurie, he's a thief alright, but not of children!" Laurie did not argue or say more; he had no breath to spare even if he wished to.

The thief unwittingly slowed to get a better hold on the loot that was escaping his grasp and Harper closed the gap between them.

A small party had joined the chase, not wholly clear as to the object of the chase but Harper soon put that right when a second wind gave him just enough to call once again – "Stop thief!" Harper's youth gave him the advantage and the town planning assisted him as he headed downhill. He ran with all of his might and managed to get ahead of the bicycle, blocking his path. The thief, who was no gentleman at all, raced towards Harper with no intention of stopping or swerving. In the nick of time, Laurie could just make out the image of a stranger snatching Harper from certain injury as the thief pedalled on. What a sharp and brave chap Laurie thought to himself, gratefully and then with sudden alarm, he wondered if the individual was the rogue's accomplice!

"Harper!" the stranger called, lifting him into the air and pulling him towards him. Laurie watched with growing alarm, by now breathless.

"Get off me Mister - put me down right now!" Harper shouted. "How do you know my name? What an audacity, picking up a boy!" Harper pummelled the chest of his captor and Laurie prayed for strength to reach Harper in safety so as to rescue him.

"Harper ... it's me!"

"Daddy?"

"Yes, yes Harper it's me."

"Daddy it's you - it's you..."

"My dear boy, it is me, yes it is. How are you? I've missed you!"

"Daddy."

"Yes, dear boy - it's me. Now, let me have a look at you," he said but he could not let his son go.

"Laurie, Mr Beauchamp - it's Daddy! It's my Daddy... it's my Daddy! He has left the other children to come home to me!" With that, Harper burst into tears and his father held him to his chest.

Laurie stood back and left them to the precious moment. When the first rush of joy and surprise had subsided, he stepped forward and introduced himself. Mr

Hepplesthwaite was cordial and thanked him for taking care of his son - or trying to.

The thief was now well out of sight and virtually out of mind. The small crowd had turned into happy spectators of the sanguine scene and they broke into a light applause as they watched the story unfold and explained to each other what they believed had occurred. A few dabbed away the odd tear and Laurie was one of them.

The trio drove home, talking as if they would never stop. Harper held Daddy's hand instinctively and as an assurance that he was not dreaming. When they arrived home and Mother stood in the doorway to receive them, Harper's heart gave way and he cried and cried and cried as he never had before. It was going to be the most wonderful Christmas of his young life.

When he collected himself, he told the adoring adults gathered that he could do with a stiff drink. Mother and Daddy shot stern and concerned looks at Great-Aunt before dissolving into laughter.

The fireplace blazed warmly and rich smells of cinnamon, nutmeg and oranges filled the house. There was laughter and conversation as each took their turn to regale the happy group with their own tales. Harper looked from face to face, speechless for a while with a joy that he could not articulate - even with all of the wonderful words Mrs Wordsworth had put to his disposal. Great-Aunt was so happy for him and all doubts concerning the wisdom of her decision to give him the Wellington boots instead of advanced notice of this happy news melted away.

After a few hours, Harper fell asleep and Mother took him from the drawing room to bed. Mother, Daddy and Mrs Mainwaring took sleeping quarters in the attic. The rooms, including the blue room of course, had been transformed so that they looked less like the playgrounds that they had become to Harper.

With the additional guests, all of the fireplaces in the house roared and licked with lively orange and yellow flames.

The happy inhabitants of number two Pear Tree Lane woke to a crisp and bright Christmas day. Harper woke before everyone else and wondered if it had all been a dream. He considered that, if it was; he was content with it but he soon threw off the bedclothes and ran about the house from room to room seeking his parents. He was too excited and nervous to call just in case there was no answer because it had all been a dream.

He found Laurie on the third floor and he ran to the attic, first running into the room at the front of the house and saw Mrs Mainwaring wearing the most bizarre and huge head-dress. Fat toes protruded from the blanket that covered her. She was still deep in sleep as her loud snoring gave testimony.

Harper dashed into the blue room and found his darling parents there. He also saw a sight that filled him with horror: a fire blazed in the fireplace, the tall flames licking at the grate and stretching up into the chimneybreast. What would become of the Wighorns if the chimney-breast *was* their actual home!

Later that day, when the embers died and turned grey with cold, Harper would kneel on the hearth and bend to look as far as he could into the chimneybreast. He would wish that Grotshaw, or Skulkins, would step out and onto his nose.

He would sit quietly in the room for a while, without a sound of any activity in the fire-place. No sign of Crouchlow, Seeral Hearall, or Pinikerty. Neither Pryson nor Domble-bluff would make an appearance. He would wonder if Snappernash, Whizzle-grump, Stonehard and Knapsley were but a dream. Temperton, Weyall, Ponderton, Biggles-Dream-Porter, Wellersay and company, a mere puff of smoke; Judge, a figment of his imagination.

However, in those first few moments of his Christmas morning, Harper settled down to enjoy his parents' company. Sitting on the pillow between them, he woke them by lifting father's left eye-lid and Mother's right. *If* (but only if) all was well with the Wighorns, Pinikerty would surely list *that* in the scroll of charges which as always would read: **The Right and the Good vs. Harper Hepplesthwaite ...**